ON THE LOST COLONY WORLD OF PETRARCH, HUMANITY EXPERIENCES A SECOND RENAISSANCE AND A SECOND VENICE . . .

Gianni looked up at his home city of Pirogia, which was luminescent in the morning mist, suddenly seeing it through the eyes of strangers, suddenly seeing it as magical and fantastic. Bridges were everywhere, spanning canals, arcing over waterways, swooping between the taller buildings—buildings that seemed like giant cakes, their walls painted in smooth pastels and adorned with festoons of ornamentation in bright colors. Where the rivers were too wide for bridges (and even where they weren't), long, slender boats glided, in the design Gianni's ancestors had copied from the barbarians of the North, for the people of Pirogia were always eager for new goods, new artifacts, new ideas, and copied and modified with delight, shrugging off their mistakes and embracing their successes.

Pride in his home swelled Gianni's breast. "It really is a score and more of islands," he told his friends, "but my people have done wonderfully in welding them all together, haven't they?"

TOR BOOKS BY CHRISTOPHER STASHEFF

A Wizard in Bedlam
A Wizard in Mind
A Wizard in War

A WIZARD IN MIND

Christopher Stasheff

A TOM DOHERTY ASSOCIATES BOOK
NEW YORK

A WIZARD IN MIND

Cover art by Darrell K. Sweet

A Tor Book
Published by Tom Doherty Associates, Inc.
175 Fifth Avenue
New York, NY 10010

Tor Books on the World-Wide Web:
http://www.tor.com

Tor® is a registered trademark of Tom Doherty Associates, Inc.

ISBN: 0-812-53648-7

First edition: March 1995
First mass market edition: January 1996

Printed in the United States of America

0 9 8 7 6 5 4 3 2 1

To the girl who inspired it all—
you know who you are

PROLOGUE

A spy can't quit and stay healthy—everybody knows that. In fact, a spy can't quit and stay *alive*—but Magnus d'Armand was still living, even though he had resigned from the Society for the Conversion of Extraterrestrial Nascent Totalitarianisms more than six months before—still alive, and not really terribly worried about it.

Of course, SCENT wasn't a secret service with missions of mayhem—it was (officially) a private organization dedicated to subverting dictatorships before they started, by converting planets to democracy before they developed out of their Middle Ages. So Magnus wasn't really a spy, though he *was* a secret agent. He was also a secret wizard. That helped, sometimes. A lot.

At the moment, he was sitting in the control room

of his spaceship, talking with its robot brain. "Well, Herkimer, which planet shall we subvert next?"

"There is a wide choice." Herkimer supplied the sound of index cards flipping behind his rather theatrical sigh. "I do not suppose I could persuade you to consider a planet for which democracy is obviously the ideal form of government?"

"You could persuade me to try the planet, but not the democracy—at least, not without a massive amount of proof. After all, that's why I quit SCENT—because I wasn't willing to impose democracy on a society it wasn't right for."

"And because you disapproved of some of SCENT's methods—yes, I know." Herkimer didn't mention the other reason for Magnus's reluctance to "impose" democracy—the young man's father, Rod Gallowglass, who was one of SCENT's most famous agents (though Rod himself didn't know about it), and had spend most of his life laying the foundations of democratic government on Magnus's home planet, Gramarye. The young man's need to separate himself from his father, and to establish his own reputation, no doubt had a great deal to do with both his quitting SCENT and his reluctance to establish democracies.

"I can't accept sacrificing good people just to give an edge to your favorite form of government," Magnus told him. "Societies come in a great number of different forms, Herkimer, so it only makes sense that they need different forms of government. If I find a planet that requires a dictatorship, I'll work to establish a dictatorship!"

"Certainly, Magnus—if you do find such a society." Herkimer had already scanned his complete SCENT database, along with the d'Armand family archives that he had down-loaded from Fess, the family robot. With that knowledge in his data banks, Herkimer could easily see that although dictatorship might be good for a society, it wasn't good for the people, unless there were some way of guaranteeing their civil rights—in which case, it wasn't a complete dictatorship anymore, but was on the way to becoming something else. "The planet Kanark might be the sort you are considering." He put a picture on the screen.

Magnus frowned, studying the peasants in their felt caps and faded blue tunics as they waded through a yellow field with scythes, singing in time to the sweep and lift of the blades. "The planet is eight percent greater in diameter than Terra," Herkimer informed him, "but with ninety-eight percent of Terra's gravity, presumably indicating fewer heavy metals in the planetary core. Its rotation is twenty-two hours, forty minutes, Terran standard. The axial tilt is nine degrees; distance from the sun is one-point-oh-five AU."

"So it's slightly colder that Terra?"

"Yes, and the ice caps are greater, as is the landmass. Still, there is no shortage of free water, and maize, millet, barley, and wheat grow well."

"Presumably brought in by the early colonists."

"The records of the pioneers indicate that, yes," Herkimer confirmed. "The economy is still agricultural, though with an increasing industrial base."

"So the majority of people are farmers?"

"Yes—yeomen. Eighty percent of them own their own hectare or two. The remaining twenty percent are approximately evenly split between merchants and agricultural laborers employed by the largest landowners."

"Who are, of course, the government."

"Yes. The government is pyramidal, with small landowners governed by larger. The wealthiest dozen men in each sovereign state constitute the highest authority. They agree on legislation, but each acts as both judiciary and executive over his own estates. Land ownership and rank are hereditary."

"An aristocracy, and a rather authoritarian one." Magnus frowned. "Let's see how these noblemen live."

The picture of the field workers was replaced by an interior picture of a large, circular room, paneled in wood but with the roof beams showing. Tapestries adorned the walls, large windows let in sunlight, and a fire burned in a huge fireplace. Half a dozen people were moving about. Magnus frowned. "They're all dressed decently, but not richly. Where are the rulers?"

"The duke stands near the hearth. The others are his family."

Magnus stared. "I would scarcely say they were dressed sumptuously—and the room is certainly not richly furnished! In fact, I'd call it rather Spartan. Let me see a yeoman's house."

The picture dissolved into a view of a similar dwelling, except that the roof was only a foot or two above the heads of the eight people. Three were obviously teenagers, two middle-aged, and the other three, children. The windows were smaller than in the duke's house, and the walls were decorated with arrangements of evergreen branches instead of tapestries.

Magnus frowned. "It would seem that wealth is fairly evenly distributed. Is there evidence of oppression?"

"Only in the punishment of criminals—which includes political dissenters. It is not a wealthy planet."

"But most of the people are content." Magnus shook his head. "There isn't much I can do there to make them richer, and they seem happy enough in any case; I might make their lives worse. Let me see people who toil under a more oppressive regime."

The screen cleared, and Herkimer put up the sound of cards flipping again, to indicate that he was searching his data banks. Magnus waited, feeling oddly troubled. The aristocrats were no doubt acting in their own interest first and foremost—but they seemed to be aware that their own prosperity depended on that of their people, and that their power was based on the yeomen's contentment with life. Magnus really had no reason to interfere. He didn't doubt that government of the people should be for the people—he just wasn't all that sure who should be doing the governing. In this case, the aristocrats seemed to be doing well enough for everybody— which seemed wrong.

"Andoria," Herkimer said, and the screen lit with a picture of a row of people wearing only loincloths, bent over to cut grain with sickles.

"Spare me the geophysical data." Magnus leaned forward, feeling his heart lift. This looked like a more promising setting for oppression—though now that he looked more closely, he could see that each of the peasants was well fed. They, too, sang as they worked, and the song was cheerful. "Begin with the government!" Magnus was already feeling impatient.

"The government is an absolute monarchy," Herkimer said, "with overtones of theocracy, for the monarch is a god-king."

"God-king?" Magnus frowned. "Is this Neolithic?"

"Bronze Age, but with some surprisingly sophisticated notions, no doubt supplied by original colonists whose Terran-style culture fell apart without a high technology to preserve the infrastructure. All land is the king's, and is administered by his stewards, each of whom supervises a hundred or so bailiffs."

"How are they chosen?"

"Candidates are selected by examination, but the final selection is the king's."

"A civil service!"

"Yes, but one that is largely hereditary. The king tends to appoint the sons of the same families, generation after generation, century after century. New blood enters the civil service only when one of the families fails to produce a male heir, or the scion of the line chooses another profession—for example, the priesthood, or the army."

"There's a standing army, then?"

"Yes, but it's the king's, and only the king's. The officers tend to come from the old families, but may be promoted from the ranks. In both civil service and army, new appointees constitute approximately twelve percent of the personnel."

"So there's *some* vertical mobility." Magnus pursed his lips. "I gather, from the fact that the king feels it necessary to maintain an army, that his civil service's main purpose is to assure abundant income for himself and his household."

"No, though that purpose certainly seems to be well served." Herkimer replaced the picture of the field with the interior of a stone palace, lush with decoration, a marble floor polished mirror-smooth, and a double file of bare-chested soldiers with spears leading to a golden throne on a high dais, on which sat a tall man wearing a robe richly ornamented with golden beadwork interspersed with gems. "The god-king charges his stewards with seeing to the welfare of his people. They gather every bit of surplus grain into royal granaries, yes—but the people are fed from those granaries, and clothed from the cotton and linen produced by the corps of king's weavers."

"So every facet of life is governed and everything is taken from the people, but everything is given to them, too—at least, everything they need," Magnus mused.

"It is. In sum, only fifteen percent of the wealth goes to support the luxury of the king and his administrators."

"Scarcely excessive," Magnus said in exasperation. "I can hardly call that oppressive. Don't you have anything more promising?"

"Searching," Herkimer told him, and the card ruffle sounded again as the screen filled with dancing points of light. Magnus sat back, feeling nervous and edgy, then wondered why he should be so dismayed to find two societies that didn't need his help.

But he didn't have any other purpose in life—his family could take care of themselves and their home planet, Gramarye, quite nicely without him—and he had already given up on falling in love and devoting his life to a wife and children. He was only twenty-one, but had already had some bad experiences with women and romance—some very bad, and none very good. What else was a rich young man supposed to do with his time? Well, not rich, exactly—but he had a spaceship (a guilt offering from the really rich relatives) and could make as much money as he needed whenever he needed—make it literally, being a wizard. Well, not a real wizard, of course—he couldn't work real magic—but he was tremendously gifted in telepathy, telekinesis, and other powers of extrasensory perception. Of course, he could have devoted his life to building up as great a fortune as his relatives had—but that seemed pointless, somehow, without anyone else to spend it on, and a rather unfair use of his gifts. His brief experience with SCENT, and his rebellion against it, had given him a solid feeling of satisfaction at helping an oppressed serf class who really needed liberating. He had been looking forward to that feeling of elation again—perhaps even looking forward to the strife and suffering that produced it. He wondered if, somewhere deep, he secretly believed he deserved punishing.

"This would be considerably easier," said Herkimer, "if you would also allow me to investigate planets that currently have SCENT projects under way."

Magnus shook his head. "Why waste time and effort when someone else is already working to free them?" Besides, he found himself unwilling to oppose his father's organization. On the last planet, when he had seen for himself that what the SCENT agents were doing was wrong—or rather, that they were doing wrong things in order to accomplish something right—it had been another matter; he had felt the need to step forward and take a stand to protect good people whom the SCENT agents were willing to abandon. But deliberately landing on a SCENT planet with the intent to upset what they were doing was another matter entirely. "No, there is no need to duplicate effort."

"As you wish," Herkimer said, with a tone of resignation that made Magnus long for the good old days when robots were unable to mimic emotions. "Your next possibility is the planet Petrarch." A pastoral scene appeared on the screen, a broad and sunny plain with the walls of a medieval city rising from it. Carts rolled along the road that ran from the bottom of the frame to the city's gates.

Magnus frowned, not seeing anyone being oppressed. "This is a retrograde colony, I assume." *Aren't they all?*

Not quite, he answered himself. A handful of Terran colonies had been so well planned, and so fortunate, that they had been able to establish industrial bases before Terra cut them off, in the great retrenchment of the Proletarian Eclectic State of Terra. Most, however, had fallen apart as soon as the support of Terran commerce and new Terran equipment was withdrawn, some even reverting to barbarism and Stone Age technology. Most, though, had regressed no further than the Middle Ages and, without electronic communications to hold together continent-wide governments, had fallen into feudalism of one sort or another. Petrarch, at least, seemed to have pulled itself together a bit.

"Petrarch orbits a G-type sun at a distance of one and one-third astronomical units," Herkimer began, but Magnus cut in to abort the lecture before it started.

"Once again, spare me the geophysical data until we're sure whether or not there's any political problem worth our interference."

"I assume you mean 'intervention,' " Herkimer said primly.

Magnus had the fleeting thought that perhaps he should change the robot's voice encoder to give it a crisp, maiden-aunt quality. "Is there reason for it?"

"Abundant reason," Herkimer assured him. "When Terra withdrew its support, the culture virtually crashed. The infrastructure could not be maintained without electronic technology, and on every continent, the result was anarchy. People banded together in villages and fought one another for the little food and fuel that remained. As one village conquered its neighbors, warlords arose, and battled one another for sheer power."

Magnus turned pale; he knew what that meant in terms of the sufferings of the individual, ordinary people. "But that was five hundred years ago! Certainly they have progressed past that!"

"Not on two of the five continents," Herkimer said regretfully. "They remain carved up into a dozen or more petty kingdoms, continually warring upon one another."

And when petty kingdoms warred, peasants did the fighting and dying—or were caught between two armies if they weren't quick enough about running and hiding. "What of the other three?"

"There, barbarism is the order of the day. There are hunting and gathering societies, herding societies with primitive agriculture, and nomads who follow the great herds. Here and there, small kingdoms have risen ruled by despots, but there are no empires."

"Let's hope nobody invents them." Fleeting visions of torture chambers, armed tax collectors, and starving peasants flitted through Magnus's mind. "Yes, this sounds as though there might be work worth our doing. Now tell me the history."

"Petrarch was originally colonized during the twenty-third century," Herkimer told him as the screen filled with the towering plasticrete towers of a Terran colony. Women in full-length gowns of brocade and velvet passed before them, with men dressed in doublets and hose. Here and there, one wore a rapier, though it had a rather solid look, as though scabbard and hilt had been cast in one piece.

"Yes," Magnus mused, "that was the century that was famous for the Renaissance revival fad of its last decade, wasn't it? I remember Fess teaching us children that it was a prime example of mass silliness."

"That was indeed the century, the decade, and the fad, though the silliness passed quickly enough everywhere else in the Terran Sphere. On Petrarch, though, it became permanent."

The picture changed, though the dress styles remained. The background, though, was that of the low plasticrete buildings typical of any early Terran colony, with here and there the timber-and-stucco houses of the first phase of building from native materials. Magnus saw the occasional costume with wildly exaggerated shoulders, two-foot-high hats with crown upon crown, or veils that fluttered behind a lady for several yards of fluorescent color. "They seem to have made some very flamboyant developments."

"They did indeed, but only within the Renaissance context. On Talipon, an inland in the center of an inland sea, dress styles fossilized—and so did architecture, painting, and all aspects of its culture."

"An odd occurrence." Magnus frowned. "Was there a cause, or was it merely a mass aberration?"

"The cause was the Proletarian Eclectic State of Terra's coup d'etat. When PEST became the government of the Terran Sphere, it cut off contact and support for the outlying planets, and Petrarch was virtually frozen at its current cultural level."

"It was fortunate that the colony had developed an economy and technology that could sustain that culture." Magnus frowned. "I'm surprised that constant war didn't force them back to the Stone Age, as it did on so much of the rest of the planet."

"They seem to have formed alliances between

resource-rich states and manufacturing states," Herkimer explained.

"Alliances, or conquests?"

"Some of the one, some of the other. The more remote districts did regress, some even becoming rather primitive."

"So there are three barbarian continents, two feudal continents, and an island of modern culture?"

"Definitely not modern—perhaps late medieval, even Renaissance."

"How large is this island?"

"Approximately four hundred ninety kilometers by one hundred thirty-five. It contains a group of independent city-states, constantly feuding with one another—but their wars are limited, they share a common language, and there is a constant interchange of people moving from one city to another."

Magnus smiled sourly. "It almost sounds like one nation with a great number of rival sporting teams."

"A good analogy," Herkimer said with approval. "Some of the sports are rather lethal, of course, and the different cities are adamant in not submitting to anyone's law but their own—but they do indeed constitute one nation."

"With no national government?"

"None at all. In fact, each city-state governs itself as it sees fit. There are monarchies, aristocracies, oligarchies—even a fledgling republic of more or less democratic tendencies."

"It could be used as a center for enlightenment about the rights of humanity, then," Magnus said thoughtfully. "I take it the city-states are agricultural?"

"Several are early industrial, and a dozen coastal cities are mercantile. Two have risen to prominence, establishing virtual trading empires—Venoga and Pirogia."

"Ideal for spreading advanced ideas! Yes, I think Talipon will do nicely as a base of operations. Are there any obstacles to my efforts?" Magnus remembered the futurian anarchists and totalitarians who continually tried to defeat his father's efforts to develop democracy.

"None except AEGIS," Herkimer said helpfully.

Magnus sagged. "No obstacle but an off-planet do-gooder society trying some uplifting of its own! Only an unofficial branch of Terra's interstellar government! Should I really bother?"

"Oh, yes," Herkimer said softly. "AEGIS is not a prime example of good organization."

That, Magnus reflected, was an understatement. AEGIS, the Association for the Elevation of Governmental Institutions and Systems, was a private, nongovernmental organization that nonetheless received hefty donations from the Decentralized Democratic Tribunal, the central government of the Terran Sphere, because its activities helped bring retrograde colony-planets back into contact with the civilized worlds, and prepared them for membership in the DDT. AEGIS was dedicated to raising the cultural level of the planets with which it worked. In order to do this, it tried to minimize war, improve the economy, and inject the fundamental ideas of civil and individual rights into the culture—it considered human rights to be prerequisite to education and development in the arts. Its members approached their work with an almost missionary fervor, but frequently didn't realize what the results would be. Their efforts usually did tend to produce some sort of predemocratic government, though. Usually. AEGIS had been known to come up with a monarchy or two. They didn't care, as long as it promoted the development of the human soul.

"Amateurs," Magnus said scornfully. "They're incapable of seeing the results of their own actions. Bumbling, clumsy . . ."

"But well-meaning," Herkimer reminded him.

"Well, yes, but we all know which path is paved with good intentions. Is AEGIS working throughout the whole planet, or only on Talipon?"

"Primarily on Talipon, but with the idea that the island's influence will spread to the rest of the world, through its energetic merchants and merchant marine."

"Well, they had one idea right, at least—the most obvious. I think I'll see if I can augment their work in some unofficial manner. At least, if AEGIS is working there, I can't do much more harm than they will."

"There is that," Herkimer agreed. "How do you intend to proceed?"

Magnus took on a contemplative look. "Given the incessant feuding, I would probably be most effective if I fell back on my former disguise—a mercenary soldier."

"You will certainly have entrée to any city you wish to visit."

"I'd rather not wind up as an entrée . . ."

Herkimer ignored the remark. "Will you use your previous pseudonym, too?"

"Gar Pike? Yes, I think I shall." Magnus pursed his lips. "It would be a little too obvious if I simply showed up in the middle of Talipon, though. I had better land in one of the less developed kingdoms on the mainland, and work my way to the island more or less naturally."

"That should disguise you from AEGIS's scrutiny," Herkimer agreed. "After all, you will rather stand out among the Taliponese."

"Really?" Magnus frowned. "Why? You will give me a crash course in their language, won't you?"

"Of course—but the average Taliponese man is five and a half feet tall."

Magnus was nearly seven.

CHAPTER 1

Old Antonio pointed ahead and shouted. Young Gianni Braccalese looked up, saw the plume of black smoke ahead, and felt his heart sink.

Only minutes before, Gianni had run a finger around the collar of his doublet, wishing he could take off the cumbersome, padded, *hot* garment. The sun had heated the fields to baking by midday, and now, in midafternoon, the breeze had died down, so the only thing moving was the sweat from Gianni's brow. If only they hadn't been so close to Accera! It wasn't much of a town, of course, but its two merchants were important sources of the grain and cotton that would fetch so high a price at home in Pirogia, and of the orzans that would make so beautiful a necklace for any lady who caught Gianni's eye—so he knew he must not shame his father by appearing bare-chested, no matter how hot it might be. He scolded himself for not having thought to take off his doublet in midmorning, when the day began to grow hot—but it was the first time he had led a goods train in summer, and only the fourth time he had led a goods train at all. He had turned twenty after All Saints' Day, so it was only a matter of months since his father had promoted him from his duties as a clerk, to actual trading. He was very anxious to make a good showing—but now this!

He stared at the black plume, feeling his stomach hollow with dread. Only one thing could explain so large a fire—a burning town. "Speed!" he called to Antonio. "We may be in time to save a life!"

Old Antonio gave him a sour look, but dutifully shouted to the drivers to whip up their mules. Gianni felt a burst of gratitude toward the older man—he knew, almost as well as though he had been told, that his father had bidden old Antonio to watch over him and teach him trading. The drivers and the guards were all very polite about it, but there was no question as to who was really managing the train—though with every trip, Gianni had needed to ask fewer questions, had been more sure in his directions and in his bargaining. He had even acquitted himself well in two minor skirmishes with bandits.

This, though—this was something of an entirely different order. Bandits who could attack a goods train were one thing—bandits who could sack a whole town were another! Admittedly, Accera was not much of a town, so far from the coast and with only a small river to water it—but it had had a wall, and its men had known how to handle their crossbows as well as most!

Why was he thinking of them as though they were gone?

He cantered along on his horse, with anxious looks back at the mules who bore his father's wealth. The drivers had whipped up the beasts with gentle calls, not wanting to make any more noise than they had to, and Gianni went cold inside as he realized the reason. Whatever bandits had lit that fire might still be nearby—might even be in Accera itself! Gianni loosened his rapier in its scabbard as he rode, then swung the crossbow from its hook on his saddle. He might be a novice at trading and leading, but he was an expert with weapons. Every merchant was, in a land in which the distinction between trader and soldier was less a matter of vocation than of emphasis and of the way in which he had made his fortune.

The wall of Accera grew from a line across the fields to a solid structure—and there was the breach! It looked as though a giant had taken a bite out of the wall—a giant with no taste for flesh, for dead men lay all around that hole and some lay half in, half out of it, their pikes still resting against nerveless fingers. Gianni slowed, holding up a hand to caution his men, and the entire train slowed with him. This was no work of starving peasants gone to banditry to find food—this had been done professionally. The condotierri had struck.

Mules began to bray protest, scenting blood and trying to turn away, but the drivers coaxed them onward with the skill of experts. They rode through the breach with great care, Gianni glancing down at the bodies of the men of Accera, then looking quickly away, feeling his gorge rise. He had seen dead men only once before, when Pirogia had fought a skirmish with the nearby city of Lubella, over their count's fancy that his daughter had been seduced by one of the merchants' sons. They had fought only long enough to satisfy the requirements of the count's honor—and to leave half a dozen men dead, all to provide a high-bred wanton with an excuse for her pregnancy. Gianni still wondered whom she had been shielding.

Now that they had slowed, the traders went cautiously down the main street of the town, between rows of cream-colored, mud-brick buildings with red tile roofs, glancing everywhere about them, crossbows at the ready. The sound of weeping came from one of the shadowed windows, and Gianni felt the protector's urge to seek and comfort, but knew he dared not—not when enemy soldiers might be hiding anywhere. Then he saw the dead woman with her skirt thrown up about her waist and her bodice ripped open, saw the blood above and below, and lost all desire to try to comfort—he knew he could never know what to say.

On they rode, jumping at every shadow. Gianni saw broken doors and shutters, but no sign of fire. He began to suspect where he would find it, and felt dread rise within him.

Something stirred in the shadows, and half a dozen crossbows swiveled toward it—but it was only an old man who hobbled out into the sunlight, an old man with a crutch and a face filled with contempt, saying, "You need not fear, merchants. The rough bad men have left."

Gianni frowned, stifling the urge to snap at the old man. The blood running from his brow showed that he had suffered enough, and the huge bruise on the left side of his face showed that, crippled or not, he had fought bravely to defend his family—as long as he could.

Old Antonio asked, "Condotierri?"

The old man nodded. "The Stiletto Company, by their insignia." He pointed farther down the road. "There lie the ones with whom you have come to trade—if they have anything *left* to trade."

Antonio nodded, turning his face toward the plume of smoke. "I thank you, valiant vieillard. We shall come back to help where we can."

"I will thank you then," the old man said with irony. "In the meantime, I know—you must see to your own."

Gianni frowned, biting back the urge to say that Signor Ludovico and his old clerk Anselmo were only business associates, not relatives—but he knew what the old man meant. Accera was a farming town—they had brought trade goods to exchange for produce, after all—and to the farmers, the merchants were a tribe apart.

They turned a corner from the single broad street to see the stream flowing in under the water gate to their left, and the burning ruin of the warehouse to their right.

"The western end still stands!" Gianni shouted. "Quickly! They may yet live!" He dashed forward, all caution banished by the old man's assurance that the condotierri had ridden away. Antonio, more experienced, barked to the drivers, and crossbows lifted as men scanned their surroundings.

To say the western end of the warehouse still stood was a considerable exaggeration—the roof had fallen in, and the main beam had taken the top half of the wall with it. But the fire had not yet reached the shattered doorway where a body lay, nor the corner where another body slouched, half-sitting against the remains of the wall. Even as he dismounted and ran up to them, Gianni was seized with the ridiculous realization that neither wore a doublet or robe, but only loose linen shirts and hose—shirts that were very bloody now. He knelt by the man in the door, saw the dripping gash in his neck and the pool of blood, then turned away toward the other body to cover his struggle to hold down his rebellious stomach. He stepped over to the corner, none too steadily, and knelt by the man who lay there, knelt staring at the rip in his shirt, at the huge bloodstain over his chest—and saw that chest rise ever so slightly. He looked up and saw the gray lips twitch, trying to move, trying to form words . . .

"It is Ludovico." Antonio knelt by him, holding a flask of brandy to the man's lips. He poured, only a little, and the man coughed and spluttered, then opened his eyes, staring from one to the other wildly . . .

"It is Antonio," the older man said, quickly and

firmly. "Signor Ludovico, I am Antonio—you know me, you have traded with me often!"

Ludovico stared up at Antonio, his lips twitching more and more until they formed an almost-silent word: "An-Anton . . . ?"

"Yes, Antonio. Good signor, what happened here?"

Why was the old fool asking, when they already knew? Then Gianni realized it was only a way of calming Signor Ludovico, of reassuring him."

"C-condotierri!" Ludovico gasped. "Sti—Stilettos! Too . . . too many to fight off . . . but . . ."

"But fight you did." Antonio nodded, understanding. "They drove away your workmen, and . . . beat you."

"Workmen . . . fled!" Ludovico gasped. "Clerks . . . home!"

"Ran home to try to defend their wives and children?" Antonio nodded, frowning. "Yes, of course. After all, the goods in this warehouse were not theirs."

"Fought!" Ludovico protested. "Crossbows . . . there . . ." He gestured at the wreckage of a crossbow, broken in both stock and bow, and Gianni shuddered at the thought of the savagery with which the condotierri had punished the older man for daring to fight them.

"Thought me . . . dead!" Ludovico wheezed. "Heard . . . talk . . ."

"Enough, enough," Antonio soothed. "You must lie down, lie still and rest." He gave Gianni a meaningful glance, and the younger man, understanding, whipped off his cloak and bundled it up for a pillow.

"Not . . . rest!" Ludovico protested, lifting a feeble hand. "Tell! Conte! They . . . spoke of . . . a lord's pay . . ."

"Yes, yes, I understand," Antonio assured him. "You heard the condotierri talk about being in the pay of a nobleman. Now rest—we can reason out the remainder of it well enough. Water, Gianni!"

Gianni had the flash ready and unstoppered. Antonio poured a small amount between Ludovico's lips. The merchant coughed as he tried to speak a few more words, then gave over the effort and drank. The taste of clear water seemed to take all the starch out of him; he sagged against Antonio's arm.

"The wound?" Gianni asked.

"It must be cleaned," Antonio said regretfully. "Pull the cloth away as gently as you can, Gianni."

This, at least, Gianni understood from experience. Delicately, he lifted the cloth away from the wound; it pulled at the dried blood, but Ludovico didn't seem to notice. Gianni probed with a finger, very gently, managing to keep his stomach under control—here, at least, there was a chance something could be done. "It's wide, but low."

"A sword, and the soldier twisted it." Antonio nodded. "It pierced the lung, but not the heart. He may yet live. Still, it must be cleaned. Dribble a little brandy on it, Gianni." Then, to Ludovico: "Brace yourself, for there will be pain—there must be."

Gianni waited a few seconds to be sure the man had heard, but not long enough for him to protest, then tilted the brandy bottle as Antonio had said. Ludovico cried out, once, sharply, then clamped his jaw shut. When he saw Gianni stopper the bottle again, he sagged with relief.

"Clean the space around him," Antonio told Gianni. "It would be best if we do not move him."

Gianni frowned. "The bandits . . . ?"

"They have been and gone. They would need sharp sentries indeed, to learn that new goods have come into the town—and why should they post watchers where they have already been? We are as safe here as behind a stockade, Gianni. Set the men to putting out the fire, as much as they can; these walls will still afford us some shelter."

Gianni did more—he set the men to clearing a wide swath of everything burnable. When night closed in, the fire was contained and burning itself out. Tent canvas shaded poor old Ludovico, and the mules were picketed inside what remained of the walls, chewing grain; their packs lay nearby, and the men sat around a campfire, cooking dinner.

Antonio came out from beneath the canvas to join Gianni by the fire.

"Does he sleep?"

Antonio nodded. "It will be the Great Sleep before long, I fear. The wound by itself will not kill him, but he has bled too freely—and much of the blood is in his lungs. He breathes with difficulty."

"At least he still breathes." Gianni turned back to the steaming kettle and gave it a stir. "Do you really think a nobleman sent the Stilettos to do this work?"

"No," Antonio said. "I think he heard the soldiers discussing their next battle, and whose pay they would take."

Gianni nodded. "The Stiletto Company last fought for the Raginaldi—but they've come a long way from Tumanola."

Antonio shrugged. "When there's no work for them, mercenary soldiers turn to looting whoever has any kind of wealth at all. They needed food, so they came and took it from Ludovico's granary, and while they were at it, they took the wool and cotton from his warehouse—and, of course, the orzans."

"Must we bargain with them for it?" Gianni asked indignantly.

"You don't bargain with condotierri unless you have a high, thick city wall between their spears and your hide," Antonio reminded him. "Talk to them now, and they will take all your father's goods—as well as our lives, if the whim takes them." He turned and spat into the darkness. "I could wish the Raginaldi had not made a truce with the Botezzi. Then their hired dogs would still be camped outside the walls of Renova, not here reiving honest men."

"It's an uneasy truce, from all I hear," Gianni reminded him, "and wearing thin, if the soldiers see new employment coming."

"A fate to be wished," Antonio agreed. "Soldiers in the field are bad enough, but at least a man can find out where they're battling, and stay away."

"Renova and Tumanola are the strongest powers in this eastern edge of Talipon," Gianni said. "Their battlefield could be anywhere."

"True, but at least their troops would stay there, putting up a show of fighting and taking their pay, not going about robbing poor peasants and honest merchants," Antonio replied. "Idle soldiers make the whole of the island a devil's playground."

He did not quite say the soldiers were devils, but Gianni took his meaning. "Is it possible that some noblemen sent them to loot Accera as a punishment for some imagined insult?"

Antonio shrugged. "Who can tell with noblemen? They're apt to take offense at anything and order their men to any action."

"And who can say, with mercenary soldiers?" Gianni returned. "When they're being paid, they're an army; when they aren't, they're condotierri, worse than any mere rabble of bandits."

"Far worse," Antonio agreed. "I only wonder that it has not yet occurred to them to steal a whole city."

Gianni shuddered, taking Antonio's meaning. If the Stiletto Company ever did decide to conquer a city to rule for themselves, it could not be one ruled by a noble family, for if they did, all the noblemen of Talipon would descend on them en masse, with every free lance they could hire to fight for them. No, the mercenaries would seek easier game, some city of merchants who ruled themselves—Gianni's home, Pirogia.

"These condotierri may be working for themselves, or for one of the noble houses—it's impossible to tell," Antonio summarized. "But Accera lies within the lands claimed by Pirogia, before our grandfathers overthrew the conte and chased his family out. The attack may be only that of a hungry army needing practice, but it's not a good sign."

"Rumor says that the merchants of Tumanola grow

restive, seeing how well we govern Pirogia," Gianni said, "and that they have begun to petition their prince for some voice in the conduct of the affairs of the city."

"The same is said of Renova." Antonio scowled, shaking his head. "Me, I can only wonder how long it will be till both great houses march against our Pirogia, to put an end to the upstarts who're giving their merchants such troublesome ideas."

One of the drivers cried out from his station by the remains of the wall. "Who goes there?"

"A friend," answered a deep voice, "or one who would be."

Antonio was on his feet almost as quickly as Gianni. Both turned toward the voice—and saw the giant step out of the shadows.

The stranger towered over the sentry. He looked to be seven feet tall and was broad-shouldered in proportion and, though his loose shirt and leather jerkin hid his arms and chest, his hose revealed legs that fairly bulged with muscle. Gianni could have sworn the rapier at his hip was as long as the guard was tall.

Rapier, leather doublet, high riding boots—there was no doubt about his calling. The man was a mercenary. A giant, and a mercenary.

He was black-haired and black-browed, with dark deep-set eyes, a straight nose, a wide mouth, and a lantern jaw. His nose was no beak, but there was something of the hawk about him—perhaps the keenness with which he scanned the merchants—though no cruelty; rather, he seemed quietly amused. "I greet you, merchants."

He spoke with a strong accent, one Gianni did not recognize. So, then—a giant, a mercenary, and a foreigner! Not surprising, of course—most of the mercenaries were foreigners from the mainland. He did not ask how the giant knew they were merchants—with their mules and packs, it was obvious. "Have you been watching us all afternoon?" he asked.

"Only since I found the town at sunset. I had a scuffle with some bandits back there"—the giant nodded at the hills outside the town—"three of them. They won't fight for a long while. No, no, they still live—but my horse does not. I saw you, and thought you might have an extra horse to sell."

They did have spare mounts, but Gianni said anyway, "It was not one of our men who died."

"I had thought not—your men talked too much while they dug the grave."

"These bandits who beset you—did they wear dagger-badges on their jerkins?" Antonio asked, stepping up beside Gianni.

The stranger nodded. "Long, slender daggers—stilettos, I think you call them."

Antonio turned to Gianni. "He isn't one of them."

"If he tells the truth." But Gianni could not think of a single reason why the Stiletto Company would send a man to spy them out, instead of falling upon them in a body—and he might need a professional fighting man before he saw Pirogia again. He held up a hand, palm open. "I'm Gianni Braccalese."

"Well met, Gianni." The giant, too, held up an open palm, the sign of friendship—or, at least, that they weren't enemies. "I am Gar."

Yes, the accent was very heavy—he made Gianni's name sound like "Jonny," missing the first *i* completely. "No family name?"

Gar shrugged. "I come from a poor country, too poor for second names. May I share your fire?"

"We will be honored to have you as a guest." Gianni bowed him toward the campfire. Gar came and sat near the flames, opening the pouch that hung from a strap over his shoulder, across his chest, and down to his hip. He took out a waxed ball. "I have a cheese to share."

"It's welcome." Gianni took a loaf from their journey bag and cut a slice with his dagger, then handed it to Gar. "The stew has yet a while to simmer."

"I thank you." Gar laid a slice of cheese on the bread, cut it down the middle, and gave half to Gianni. Antonio was content to sit near, watching the two young men perform the simple ceremony with approval.

"You're a mercenary soldier, then?" Gianni asked before he took a bite of bread.

Gar swallowed and nodded. "A free lance, no member of a company. These bandits I fought were?"

"The Stiletto Company, yes—unemployed, for the moment. There's no work for you there."

Gar grinned. "I wouldn't hire out to those who have attacked me."

Gianni felt the thrill of bargaining begun. "But you are for hire?"

The giant nodded, chewing.

"Have you letters of reference?" Antonio asked. He knew the man probably did not, most likely could not write, but it was a good ploy for lowering his price.

The giant surprised them both, though; he swallowed and nodded. "Here." He took two folded parchments from his pouch and gave them to Gianni.

The young merchant opened them; Antonio came to read over his shoulder, keenly interested in discovering a mercenary who had actual letters. The first was in a foreign language, but Gianni had learned the tongue of Airebi, for his father's captains dealt with them frequently. It was from a merchant captain, who testified that he had hired Gar in Donelac, a land far to the north, and that the giant had done excellent service both as a sailor and a fighter. The other was in Taliponese, stating that Gar had been excellently loyal in transporting cargo from Venoga to Renova, and was very effective in fighting off bandits. That was especially interesting because Venoga was Pirogia's main commercial rival, only a little behind them in volume of trade, but considerably behind in wealth; Gianni suspected that was because the merchants there had not yet succeeded in ousting their conte, who took entirely too much of their profits, thereby limiting their ability to reinvest, and capped it by strictly limiting the luxuries they could buy or possess. He had not quite signed his own death warrant yet, Gianni reflected grimly, but the blank parchment was before the nobleman, just waiting for him to write.

The merchant ended with regrets that he could not employ Gar any longer, but would have no new trading ventures for several months. He recommended the mercenary to any merchant who had need of his services—and even to those who did not, just in case. Gianni nodded and refolded the letters, handing them back. "Those are good, very good." It occurred to him to wonder if there had been employers who had been dissatisfied and had therefore not given letters, but he dismissed the notion as unworthy. "Will you take our ducat to guard us against the Stiletto Company?"

"Or anyone else who might attack us on the way home," Antonio added quickly.

"Gladly," Gar said gravely.

With a feeling of triumph, Gianni took a ducat from his purse and held it out to Gar. The giant took it, saying, "I charge one of these for every seven nights I fight for you."

"That will be enough," Gianni assured him. "We have to go back to Pirogia—and go back empty-handed, since the Stilettos have stolen the grain, cotton, wool, and orzans we came to trade for."

The mercenary frowned. "What are orzans?"

Gianni stared, then remembered that Gar seemed to be fairly new to Talipon. "An orzan is a flame-colored gem—not very rare, in fact only semiprecious, but lovely to behold." He gestured at the burned-out shell about them. "Signor Ludovico wrote that he had gathered a bag of them to trade with us, but it's gone now—of course. Semiprecious or not, a whole sack of them would be worth a good sum."

"So." Gar smiled as he slipped the coin into his pouch. "We both have reasons to wish the Stilettos ill. Tell me of this Pirogia of yours. Is it true the merchants rule the town?"

Gianni nodded, and Antonio said, "We would sooner say 'govern' than 'rule.' "

"It is the fact that matters, not the word," the mercenary replied. "How did you manage to gain such power?"

Gianni smiled; he had learned an excellent way to fend off nosy questions. To the very first question, give a far longer answer than anybody could want—but with as little information as possible. He launched into a brief history of Pirogia.

CHAPTER 2

W e didn't exactly throw out our conte," Gianni explained, "any of them. It was more a matter of our great-grandfathers having become impatient with the restrictions of the princes and the doges—and with their taxing us as highly as they could while still leaving us any capital at all to work with."

Antonio said nothing, only glancing at his young charge with bright eyes every now and then. *Well,* Gianni thought, *at least, if I'm being tested, I'm passing.*

The stranger nodded with an intent frown. That would change, Gianni reflected wryly. He was very surprised when it didn't. "So merchants from six cities, who knew each other from trading, banded together and built warehouses on islands in a lagoon on the eastern tip of Talipon. The land was technically within the demesne of Prince Raginaldi of Tumanola, but it was a wilderness and a swamp, so he paid no attention."

"And where the merchants had their warehouses, of course," Gar said, "it was only natural that they build their dwellings."

Gianni nodded, surprised that the man cared enough to reason that out. "Within a few years, all of them were living there."

"And their clerks and workmen, of course."

"Of course." Gianni was beginning to wonder if perhaps this stranger was a bit too quick for comfort. "They built bridges between the islands, those that were close enough, and traveled to the bigger ones in small boats."

Gar smiled. "Even as a merchant in Renova might ride a horse to work, or haul his goods in wagons."

"A merchant in Renova wouldn't be allowed to own a horse," Antonio said. "He could own a wagon, of course."

"That was true for the merchants in Tumanola, too," Gianni pointed out, "but no law said they couldn't own boats."

"I begin to see the advantage of living far away from the prince's eye," Gar said. "How long was it before he began to realize they had built their own city?"

"When ships began to dock at the larger islands, and fewer docked at his own harbor. Then he levied a tax on all goods imported to Pirogia, but the merchants refused to pay it."

Gar smiled. "How many times did he demand before he sent his army?"

"Only twice—but when the army came, they discovered the other advantage of a city built on islands."

"What?" Gar asked. "The ability to see the enemy coming a long way away?"

"No," said Gianni, "the difficulty of marching on water."

Gar's smile widened. "Of course! A natural moat."

"A moat a quarter of a mile wide and a hundred feet deep."

"Didn't the prince send his navy?"

"Of course." Gianni smiled. "That was when the noblemen discovered what excellent sailors we merchants had become."

"Surely they fired cannon at your walls!"

"Pirogia has no walls," Gianni said. "What need would we have of them? Our lagoon is wall enough—that, and our fleet."

"Had your grandfathers had the foresight to build warships, then?"

"A few. Besides, there were pirates, so every merchantman carried cannon, and all our sailors knew how to fight a ship as well as how to sail one—still do, in fact, though pirates are rare now. The prince's captains came against us in galleys, but we met them in ships with lateen sails and tacked against the wind until we could turn and sail down upon them with the wind at our backs!" Gianni's eyes glittered with fierce pride; he spoke as though he had been there himself. "We shot off their oars; the balls ripped the sides of the galleys, and a hundred small boats harried them from all sides—small boats that pulled the enemy sailors out of the water, and we held the prince's captains to ransom."

"Surely he couldn't accept such a defeat!"

"Indeed he couldn't, and sent to the noblemen of other seacoast cities to bring an armada against Pirogia. Our great-grandfathers were ready, but they quailed inside—what could all their merchantmen do against so huge a fleet of galleys?"

"Outsail them?" Gar guessed.

"Indeed." Gianni grinned. "Their huge galleys couldn't move or turn as swiftly as our caravels—but even so, they might have won by sheer numbers had it not been for the tempest that blew their fleet apart. Our captains fell upon them piecemeal, in twos and threes. Most never came in sight of Pirogia, but limped back to land to mend their hulls and sails."

Gar nodded, gaze never leaving Gianni's face. "Was the prince content with that?"

"He tried to force the other cities to build a stronger navy and attack us again," said Antonio, "but Renova began to fight with Slamia over a boundary—a river had shifted its course—and Gramona thought it a good opportunity to seize some of Slamia's territory, while the conte of Marpa saw a chance to swallow some of Renova's mainland trading bases—but Borella took alarm at the idea of Gramona growing any stronger, so it attacked in defense of Slamia, and Tumanola itself had no wish to see Marpa gain more of the trade which the prince's merchant counselors were advising him to seize for himself, so Tumanola attacked Marpa, and . . ."

"I know the way of it." Gar nodded with a grim smile. "Soon they were all fighting one another, and forgot their concern about Pirogia in the stir. Had your grandfathers sent agents to foment trouble in Renova?"

"What—could building a mere dam in the hills change the course of a river?" Antonio said airly. "Or even a dozen of them?"

"And Tumanola's prince has never threatened again?"

"Well," said Gianni, "he has not moved against us, neither he nor any of his descendants. But they constantly make threats, they harry our ships when they can—and they have never left off demanding a share of our profits." He looked up at a thought. "Do you suppose it might be the prince himself who has hired the Stilettos?"

"We shall find out before we see our lagoon again," Antonio said grimly.

"What of the sailors your great-grandfathers captured?" Gar asked.

Gianni couldn't believe it. The man was deliberately asking for more history! "Most of them decided to stay in Pirogia and look for work—they knew a good thing when they saw one. Our grandfathers would only allow five of them to a crew, of course, and had them watched closely, in case they proved to be spies—but none did."

"And the rest?"

"When the battle was done, we let them go home. We ferried them to land, where we struck off their chains and let them wander where they chose. Some lurked about as a bandit tribe, but our city guard put an end to that quickly enough—after all, they only had such weapons as they could make from wood and stone. The others went home, so far as we know; in any event, they never came to Pirogia again."

Gar leaned back, hands on his knees, "A brave battle, signori, and worthy forefathers you had! No doubt you have built well on their foundation."

"Pirogia is a mighty city now," Antonio assured him, "though we still have no wall—and the stew is done."

Gianni ladled out servings into wooden bowls and gave them to Antonio and Gar. All about them, the drivers were eating and talking in low voices, except for the half-dozen on sentry duty. Gianni sat down again, dipping his spoon into his bowl. "What of yourself?" he asked. "Were you raised to sailing ships?"

Antonio looked up, alarmed—it was rude to ask a mercenary where he came from or why he had become a soldier. Rude, and sometimes dangerous—but Gar only smiled and said, "In my homeland, most people fished or farmed."

Gianni ignored Antonio's frantic signals. "What *is* your homeland?"

"A land called Gramarye," Gar answered and, anticipating his next question, "It's a very big island very far away, out in the middle of an ocean."

In his interest Antonio forgot his manners. "Gramarye? I have never heard of it."

"It's *very* far away."

"The name means 'magic,' doesn't it?"

Gar smiled. "I see you know some languages other than your own—but yes, 'Gramarye' means 'magic,' or a book of magic, and a magical land it is, full of mystery and intrigue."

"It sounds like the kind of place that would draw a man," Gianni said, then bit his tongue in consternation, realizing just how thoroughly he had forgotten his manners.

"It does," Gar said, "but it's home, and a village begins to seem a prison as a youth comes to manhood. I became restless and went exploring in my father's ship with an old and trusted servant. Then, when I found employment, the servant took the ship home. One job led to another, until I signed on aboard the ship of the merchant who brought me to Talipon, then was kind enough to write a letter recommending me when I wished to stay and discover more about your island. I enjoy seeing something of the world, though the danger and the hardship are unpleasant."

There was a cry from the corner of the wall. "Master Gianni, come quickly!"

Gianni was up almost before the call was done, running over to the corner with Antonio right behind him. Gar followed more slowly.

Old Ludovico lay, his face pale, his eyes staring at the sky. "He stopped breathing," the driver said.

Gianni leaned closer and held a palm over the old man's mouth and nose. He waited a few minutes, then reached up to close the merchant's eyes.

* * *

By morning, the villagers, those who survived, had begun to peer out of their houses. A priest newly arrived from a nearby monastery stared in horror at what he saw, then began the mournful business of conducting funerals. Gianni and his men stood about Ludovico's grave with bared, bowed heads, listening to the monk's Latin, then singing the "Dies Irae" in slow and solemn tones. Oddly, it made them all feel a bit better, and they began to chat with one another as they loaded their mules. They even set out on the road to Pirogia with a few jests and laughs.

"Your men cure their spirits quickly," Gar noted.

"Ludovico wasn't one of us," Gianni replied, "only a trading acquaintance."

Gar nodded. "Close enough for his death to shake you, not close enough to cause true grief. Still, your men have spirit."

"Meaning that they march in the shadow of condotierri and manage to smile?" Gianni suited his own words. "So many mules can't move in silence—so why not laugh while you stay vigilant? After all, would a whole mercenary company post sentries along the roadside to watch for fat travelers?"

"Yes, Gar said instantly. "At least, if I were the captain of such a band, I would set a few men to watch for every chance of plunder."

Gianni looked up, shaken. "Would you turn bandit, then?"

"Definitely not," Gar said, just as quickly. "But when you wish to guard against an enemy, you must think ahead, to what he will most likely do—and the best way to do that is to put yourself in his place and try to think as he does. So, although I would never allow men of mine to loot or plunder or attack civilians, I imagine how I would think if I *were* such a captain." He looked directly into Gianni's eyes. "Can you understand that?"

"Yes," Gianni said, somewhat shaken, "and it speaks of great talent or long training. You aren't so new to soldiering as you seem, are you?" He was very much aware that he still didn't know enough about Gar to be sure he was trustworthy, and wasn't about to miss a chance to gain a little more information.

Nor was Gar about to give it. "I was raised to war, as are most barbarians."

Gianni nodded. "Still, you're young to be a captain."

"And you're young to be a merchant," Gar returned.

Gianni smiled. "As you said—I was raised to it. Still, the goods aren't mine, but my father's, and I don't take the profit myself—I only receive a share."

"A share?" Gar raised his eyebrows. "Not a wage?"

"No—Papa says I will work harder if the amount of my pay depends on the size of the profit."

Gar nodded slowly. "There is sense in that."

Antonio only listened to the two young men chat, smiling with pleasure.

"But your father sends ships out to trade," Gar said. "Why does he bother sending men inland?"

"Because we must have something to send on those ships," Gianni explained. "If we sent only gold, we would soon have no gold left—and barbarians like you, and the nomads of the southern shore of the Middle Sea, have little use for precious metals. They have need of iron ingots, though, and of the cotton and linen cloth that our weavers make. The rustic lords of the northern shore love our tapestries and woolens and cottons and linens. Besides, gold is compact, taking up very little room in a hold. Why have a ship sail almost empty when it could carry a full cargo that won't drain our reserves?"

He was rather surprised that Gar seemed to understand every word. "There is sense to that," he said, "but couldn't your ships carry timber and grain from those trading voyages?"

"Why, when they are much more cheaply had here, near home?" Gianni countered. "The cost of bearing them to Pirogia is so much less. No, from the barbarian shores, we bring amber and furs and all manner of stuffs that are luxuries to the people of Talipon, and from the old cities to the east and the warlords of the south, we bring spices and silk and rare woods. Those are the cargoes that we can sell at a profit in Talipon, my friend—not the goods that they already have."

"There is sense in that," Gar admitted. "Who decides to trade in this fashion? The merchant princes of your Pirogia?"

Gianni laughed. "I would scarcely call them princes—solid city men, prosperous, perhaps, but they certainly don't live like princes. And no, my friend, the Council doesn't decide what to ship and what to import—my father does that, as does every other merchant. Each decides for himself."

"Then what does your Council do?"

Gianni took a breath. "They decide the things that affect all the merchants, and all the city—how much money to invest in ships of war, how much in soldiers, whether to hire mercenaries or train our own . . ."

"Your own," Gar said firmly. "Always your own."

Gianni blinked, surprised that the man would preach against his own trade. Then he went on. "They decide whether or not to build bridges, or new public buildings, or to shore up the banks of the rivers and canals—all manner of things affecting the public good."

"Say rather, the good of the merchants," Gar pointed out. "Who guards the interests of the craftsmen and working men?"

"The craftsmen have their guilds, whose syndics may argue in the Council if they care strongly about an issue that's being discussed." It occurred to Gianni that he could have taken offense at that question, but he was too busy explaining. "As to the laborers, I'll admit we haven't yet discovered how to include them in the deliberations, other than to charge each councillor with speaking about the issues to all the folk in his warehouses and ships."

Gar nodded. "How are these oligarchs—your pardon, the councillors—chosen?"

Gianni frowned, not liking the word "oligarch," especially since he didn't understand its meaning—but he decided it must be a word in Gar's native language and let it pass. "The merchants of Pirogia meet in assembly and elect the councillors by casting pebbles into bowls that bear the name of each merchant who's willing to serve that year—green pebbles for those they want to serve, red for those they *don't* want. There are always at least twice as many willing as there are positions on the Council."

"How many is that?"

"A dozen." Gianni wondered how his attempt to learn more about Gar had turned into a lecture on the government of Pirogia, and might have asked exactly that, had the condotierri not fallen upon them.

They came riding across the fields, shouting for the merchants to stop. "Ride!" Gianni called. "Do they think us fools?" He kicked his horse into a canter, and Gar matched his pace on one side, Antonio on the other. The drivers whipped their mules into their fastest pace, which the beasts were frightened enough to do—but the train could go no faster than a laden mule, and the condotierri came on at the gallop.

"They know we aren't fools—but neither are they!" Gar called to him. "They're frightening us into riding headlong because they have an ambush planned!"

"Ambush?" Antonio cried, incredulous. "From where?"

"There!" Gar pointed ahead at a cluster of peasant huts that had just come into view. "Scare us enough, and we'll think we're safe when we come to shelter, any shelter!"

Even as he said it, more condotierri burst out of the huts, galloping straight toward them. Gianni gave a frantic look back, but saw another group following hard on their trail.

"We're lost!" one of the drivers cried, and slewed his mule to a halt, throwing up his hands.

"Circle!" Gianni shouted. "Do you want to be slaves in the lords' galleys the rest of your lives? Form the circle and fight!"

The drivers pulled their animals around to form an impromptu fortress.

"They're soldiers!" the lone driver wailed. "We can't win! They'll slay us if we fight back!"

"Better dead and free than alive and in bondage!" Antonio shouted.

"Any man who wishes to live as a slave, leave now!" Gianni called. "Perhaps you can escape while the rest of us fight!"

That one driver bolted—out of the circle, down off the road, and over the fields. The others all held steady, staring at the mercenaries thundering down upon them.

"Slay the horses first!" Gar called. "A man afoot is less of a threat!"

A cry of terror made them all look toward the deserter, just in time to see a condotierre strike him down with a club. He fell amidst the grain, unconscious and waiting to be harvested when the battle was done.

"*That* is the reward of surrender!" Antonio called. "Better to die fighting!"

"Better still to fight and live!" Gar shouted. "But if you must die, take as many of them with you as you can!"

The drivers answered him with a shout.

"Fire!" Gianni cried, and a volley of crossbow bolts slammed into horses. The poor beasts threw up their heads and died with a scream; the next rank of soldiers stumbled and fell over the crumpled bodies of the first. But the third rank had time to swerve around their fallen comrades, and the drivers dropped their crossbows, realizing they wouldn't have time to reload.

Then the condotierri fell upon them.

It was hot, hard fighting, and it seemed to last hours, as Gianni caught blades on his dagger and thrust and slashed. Gar stood just behind him, back to back, roaring and slashing at rider after rider. In minutes, they were both bleeding; as their men fell, swords slashed them, skewered them, but they shouted with rage and didn't feel the pain as anything but a distant annoyance. The condotierri bellowed with anger as drivers thrust swords into their horses' chests, and the mounts buckled beneath the soldiers. Screams of anguish and agony filled the air, but more from the condotierri than the drivers—for the Stilettos were striking with clubs, trying to capture men for the slave markets, but the drivers struck back with swords and lances and axes. Finally the condotierri gave up hope of profit and drew their swords in rage. Gianni shouted in pain when he saw his men falling, blood pumping from chest and throat, then cried with anguish as old Antonio fell with his jerkin stained crimson.

Then a roundhouse swing struck his sword up and slammed the blade back into his forehead. He spun about, and as he fell, saw Gar already lying in a crumpled heap below him—before the horse's hoof struck his head, and the world stopped.

CHAPTER 3

The world went away; there was nothing but darkness, nothing but consciousness—consciousness of a spot of light, small or distant.

Distant; it grew larger, seeming to come nearer, until Gianni could see it was a swirl of whiteness. Closer then it came and closer, until Gianni realized, with a shock, that its center was a face, an old man's face, and the swirling about him was his long white beard and longer white hair. Hair blurred into beard as it moved about and about, as though it floated in water.

Beware, beware! His flashing eyes, his floating hair!

The words sprang unbidden to Gianni's mind, words he was certain he had never heard before—and surely not the type of thing he would have thought of himself. But those eyes *were* flashing, looking directly into his, and the lips parted, parted and spoke, in a voice that seemed to reverberate all about Gianni, so low in pitch that it seemed to be the rumble of the earth, issuing words he could barely understand because they throbbed in his bones as much as in his ears:

Your time has not yet come. Live!

And Gianni was astonished to find that he didn't want to, that the warm enwrapping darkness was so comforting that he had no wish to leave it.

This is not your place, the face said. *You have no right to be here—you have not earned it.*

But I can do no good in the world, Gianni protested. *I have seen that! I can't protect my men. I can't protect my father's goods—I'm not half the man my father is!*

Nor was he, when he was your age. The face spoke sternly. *Go! Or would you deprive him not only of his goods, but also of his son, who is more dear to him than anything he owns? Would you leave him to weep his grief in your mother's arms, and she in his?*

A pang of guilt stabbed Gianni, and he sighed, gathering his energies. *Very well, if you say it. I shall go.* His attention suddenly sharpened. *Yet tell me first, who are you?*

But the face was receding, and the voice was commanding, *Go! Go back to the world! To your mother, your father! Go! Go, and come not back until . . .*

His voice seemed to blur as he shrank to only a circle of whiteness, and Gianni asked, *Until? Until what?*

Come not! Come not! Come . . . Come . . . But the face had dwindled to a circle of light again, shrinking, growing smaller and smaller until it winked out, leaving a last word lingering behind: *Come . . .*

"Come back, Gianni! Come back!" a voice was saying, was urging gently. "Come back to the world! Wake up, arise!"

Gianni frowned, finding himself somewhat irritated. He forced his eyes open—only a little, then wider, for there was very little light. He saw the giant bending over him, his rough-hewn face even more craggy in the stark whites and sudden blacks of moonlight.

"He looks!" Gar marveled. "He opens his eyes! He lives!"

"Yes, I live," Gianni groaned, "though I would far rather not." He tried to push himself up, but his arm was too weak. Gar caught him and hauled him upright. Gianni gasped at the lance of pain in his head, then choked down the nausea that followed. "What . . . how . . ."

"It was a blow to your head," Gar said, "only that, but a very bad blow."

"I remember . . . a horse's hoof . . ."

"Yes, that would be enough to addle your brains for a while," Gar allowed.

Gianni blinked about him, trying to make out dim shapes through his haze of pain. "What . . . happened to . . . the day?"

"We lay like the dead, I'm sure," Gar told him, "and the condotierri had no use for corpses, so they let us lie—after looting our bodies, of course. My sword is gone, and my purse and boots."

Gianni looked down and saw his sword and scabbard gone, his feet bare, and his belt shorn. "Well, at least I have life," he grunted.

"And a miracle it is! I woke in midafternoon and forced myself up enough to crawl to water. I upset a considerable number of ravens and vultures, and came back to find them eyeing you."

"Thank you for upsetting them again."

"I labored long trying to revive you. For a time, I thought you were dead, but laid my cheek near your face and felt a ghost of breath from your nose. I've stretched all my meager store of soldier's healing lore, but you've revived."

"And am not happy about it, I assure you." Gianni clutched a pain-fried head.

"Here." Gar held out two small white disks in his palm. "Swallow them, and drink!"

Gianni gave the little disks a jaundiced look. "What are they?"

"Soldiers' medicine, for a blow to the head. Drink!" Gar thrust a wineskin at him, and Gianni reluctantly took the two small pills, put them in his mouth, then took a swallow of water. He almost gagged on them, then looked up gasping. "What now?"

"We rest until your head no longer drums, then go back to Pirogia."

Back to Pirogia! Gianni's stomach sank at the thought of confronting his father with the report that he had lost not only his father's goods, but also his mules and even his drivers—that he had lost the whole caravan. Stalling, he gestured vaguely about him. "Should we not . . . the bodies . . ." Then he blinked, amazed to see a long, low mound of fresh earth beside the road and no bodies about him, only a deal of churned mud. He realized what liquid must have softened the road, and almost lost his stomach again.

"I had to do something while I waited for you to waken," Gar explained. "There's nothing more to keep us here, and every reason to find a priest to bring back, so he can say prayers over them. Come, Gianni. It's far more my disgrace than your own, for you hired me to prevent this very thing—but I must confess my failure, and accept the consequences."

"I, too." Inside, Gianni shied from the thought of his father's face swollen in anger, but knew he must do even as Gar had said—report his failure and take his punishment. "Well, then, back to Pirogia." He started to struggle to his feet, but Gar held him back. "No, no, not yet! When your head has ceased to pound, I said! Give the medicine a chance to do its work! Wait half an hour more, Gianni, at least that!"

It was an hour, at a guess from the decline of the moon, but Gar did manage to pull Gianni to his feet and start down the road, though they held themselves up only by leaning against one another as much as they walked.

They tottered through the night, and Gianni would have said "Enough!" and lain down to rest a dozen times over, but Gar insisted that they keep on trudging through the dust. Even after the moon had set, he kept urging, "Only a little farther, Gianni!" or "Only another half hour, Gianni—we're bound to find a barn or a woodlot in that time!" and at last, "Only till dawn, Gianni. Let us at least be able to see if enemies come!" Gianni protested and protested with increasing weariness, until at last it seemed that Gar was holding him up. Over that blank and featureless plain they plodded, through a darkness that showed them only a lighter blackness where sky met land, with the occasional huddle of cottages in the distance, the occasional granary or byre. Gianni would have wondered why Gar thought it so important to keep him walking through the night, if fatigue hadn't addled his wits to the point where only one thought could take root, and that thought was: sleep!

Finally, the sky lightened with the coming day, and Gar ground to a stop, lowering his employer gently to the grass by the roadside. "Here, at least, we can see."

"I told you there were no barns, no woodlots, between here and Pirogia," Gianni said thickly.

"In fact, you did," Gar agreed. "Go ahead now, sleep. I'll wake you up if anyone comes to disturb us."

But Gianni didn't hear the end of the sentence. He fell asleep just as Gar was promising to wake him.

And wake him he did, shaking his shoulder and saying, with a note of urgency, "Gianni! Wake up! Trouble comes!"

Gianni was up on one elbow before his eyes had finished opening. "Trouble? What kind?"

"Horsemen," Gar said. "Can they be anything *but* trouble?"

"Only if they're another train of merchants." Gianni stumbled to his feet, looking down the road to where Gar was pointing, amazed to realize that it was midafternoon. Had the mercenary kept watch all that time, and not slept?

But he saw the cloud of dust already a little way past the horizon, heard the faint drum of hoofbeats, saw the glitter of sunlight off steel, and said, "That's not a troop of merchants."

"No," Gar agreed, "it's a troop of cavalry. You know this land better than I do, Gianni. Where can we hide?"

Gianni looked about him, feeling the first faint tendrils of panic reaching out about his mind. "Nowhere! This is table land—there's only the ditch beside the road!"

"And they'll see us if we try to run for the shelter of a granary—if we can find one." Gar was tense, alert, his eyes luminous, but seemed quite poised, quite cool-headed. The mere sight of him calmed Gianni a bit. "There *is* the ditch," the mercenary went on, "but they're sure to glance down and see us crouching in the mud . . . Hold! The mud!"

Gianni stared. "What about it?"

"Off with your doublet—quickly!" Gar yanked open his jerkin and leaped across the ditch, dropping the garment into the tall grass at the edge of the field of green shoots. "Off with your shirt, too! Quickly, before they can see us clearly!"

Gianni stared. Had the man gone mad?

Then he remembered that he was supposedly paying Gar to defend them both, and decided not to waste his father's money that he wasn't paying. He leaped across the ditch to join Gar in a race to strip to bare flesh, leaving only his hose, which were badly ripped from the fighting and the fleeing anyway.

Gar knelt to yank up fistfuls of straw and throw them over the heap of clothing. "Quickly, hide them!"

Gianni bent to help him cover the clothing, and in a minute, only a heap of dried grass lay there at the edge of the field.

"Now, get down! And dirty!" Gar leaped down into the ditch, scooped up some mud, and began to daub it over his chest and shoulders.

"I already am," Gianni protested, but he overcame distaste and slid down beside Gar, rubbing himself with dirt. "What are we doing, making ourselves look like complete vagabonds?"

"Exactly!" Gar told him. "You can't rob a wandering beggar, can you? Paint my back!" He turned about, daubing mud on his face. Gianni rubbed mud over his back, then turned for Gar to do the same to him. "More than vagabonds—brain-sick fools! Pretend you are mad, though harmless."

Gianni felt a surge of hope. It might work. "And you?"

"I'm a half-wit, a simpleton! You're my brother, guiding me and caring for me in spite of your madness!"

"The mad leading the feebleminded?" That had too much of the ring of truth to it for Gianni's liking—

but he remembered the lunatic beggar who sat at the foot of the Bridge of Hope at home, and found himself imitating the man's loose-lipped smile. "What if they ask for our names?"

"Don't give your true one, whatever you do—one of them might think you could fetch a fat ransom, or that I might be of use in the ranks! No, we give false names. Yours is Giorgio and mine is Lenni!"

Gianni stared. "How did you think of them so quickly?"

The thunder of approaching hooves prevented Gar's answer. He clapped a hand on Gianni's shoulder. "They come! Stay down—no one would think it odd for wayfarers to hide from condotierri, even if they were mad! Remember, you have so little mind that no one could care about you!"

"What does a madman say?" Gianni asked, feeling panic reach out for him again.

"Uhhhh . . . Giorgio, look! Horsies!" Gar crouched down and pointed up.

Gianni turned to him in exasperation—and saw the troop approach out of the corner of his eye. "Yes, G—Lenni! But those horsies are carrying nasty men! Down!" He found himself talking as he would to a baby. How would the beggar of the Bridge of Hope talk? He crouched beside Gar, hoping the horsemen would pass by without looking at them, hoping they would emerge unscathed . . .

Not to be. The captain rode by, talking in restless tones with his lieutenants about the Raginaldi and their displeasure that the Stilettoes had not punished those presumptuous merchants of Pirogia yet—but one of the troopers, bored, looked down, saw them, and his face lit in anticipation of fun. "Captain! See what we've found!"

The troop slowed; a lieutenant barked, "Halt!" and they stopped.

The captain rode back, looked down, and wrinkled his nose. "What are *these*?"

"Horsie." Gar beamed up at the cavalrymen with a loose-lipped grin.

"A simpleton," his lieutenant said with disgust, "and a beggar, from the look of him."

Gianni plucked up his courage and took his cue. He held up cupped hands, crying, "Alms, rich captain! Alms for the poor!"

"Alms? I should more likely give you arms," the captain said in disgust, "*force* of arms! Why do you not work, like an honest fellow?"

"Honest," Gar repeated sagely.

Gianni elbowed him in the ribs, snapping, "Hush, you great booby! I can't say why for the life of me, Captain! They'll give me work, yes, and I'm a hard and willing worker, but they never keep me long." He remembered what the beggar at the Bridge of Hope would have done, and looked up, startled, above the captain's head.

The captain frowned, glanced up, saw nothing, and scowled down at Gianni. "Why do they send you away?"

"I can't say, for the life of me," Gianni said, still gazing above the man's head. "I do as I'm bid, and scare the thieves away from the master's goods, or the farmer's . . ." He broke off, waving angrily and crying, "Away! Get away from the captain, you leather-winged nuisance! Leave him be!"

The captain and half the troopers looked up in alarm—"leather-winged" could only refer to two kinds of beings—but there was nothing in sight. The captain turned back to Gianni with the beginnings of suspicion in his eyes. "What thieves do you speak of?"

"Why, the leathern ones, such as I have just now afrighted, and the slimy crawling ones, and the little big-eyed . . . Ho! Away from his boots, small one!" Gianni lunged at the captain's feet, clapping his hands, then rocked back, nodding with satisfaction. "Oh, you know when someone's watching, don't you?"

"Brownie?" Gar asked. "Goblin?"

"Goblin," Gianni confirmed.

A whisper of superstitious fear went through the ranks: "He can see the spirits!"

"Spirits that aren't there!" The captain realized these beggars could be bad for morale. "He's mad!"

The men stared, appalled, and the nearest ones backed their mounts away.

Gianni spun, stabbing a finger at the air behind him. "Sneaking up on me, are you? Get hence, beaky-face! Lenni, knock him away for me!"

Gar obediently swung a backhanded blow at empty space, but said, "Can't see him, Giorgio."

"No need," Gianni said, with satisfaction. "You scared him away."

"Mad indeed!" the captain said quickly and loudly, before the troopers could start muttering again. "No wonder no man will keep you! Where are you bound, beggars? How do you think you shall live?"

"Oh, by honest labor, Captain!" Gianni swung back to the leader, all wide-eyed sincerity. "All we seek is an acre to farm, where we may raise doves and hares."

A hard finger tapped his shoulder, and in a dreamy voice, Gar said, "Tell me about the rabbits, Giorgio."

Gianni shrugged him off in irritation. Didn't the big clown know not to interrupt when he was trying to pretend? "Now, good Captain, if you had an acre of ground to spare . . ."

"An acre of ground?" the captain snorted. "Fool! We're mercenary soldiers! None of us expects to own land here!"

"Wherever your home is, then," Gianni pleaded. "Only a half-acre, good signor!"

"Giorgio," Gar pleaded, "tell me about the rabbits."

"Hares, Lenni!" Gianni snapped. "I keep telling you—hares, not rabbits!"

"Rabbits," Gar said, with absolute certainty. "Little, fuzzy, cuddly bunnies. *You* raise hares. Tell me about the *rabbits*, Giorgio."

"He plagues me with his demands for hare-raising stories," Gianni said, exasperated. "Please, your worship! If I can't give him land to farm, who knows what he'll do! Only half an acre, signor!"

"The only land I shall give you is six feet long and three wide!" the captain said with contempt, and to his lieutenants, "They're fools indeed. Spurn them and ride on."

"Shall we not have some fun with them first?" One of the troopers gave Gianni a leering grin that fairly froze his blood.

"Oh, very well!" the captain said impatiently. "But only a minute or two, mind! I can't linger here all day."

The troopers whooped and fell on the two unfortunates. A huge fist slammed into Gianni's belly and he folded in agony. Hard boots kicked his side, his hip, his chest, his belly again. He heard Gar roar, had a glimpse of the huge man shaking off troopers as though they were leeches, laying about him with fist and foot in blundering, clumsy movements that nonetheless laid condotierri about him like chaff on a threshing floor. Then a boot toe cracked into the side of Gianni's head, and he saw only darkness again.

Get up, get up! the white-bearded face was commanding. *You cannot tarry here!*

I can and shall, Gianni snarled. *I listened to you last time, and look what happened!*

Are you so afraid of a little pain, then?

Gianni winced at the thought of enduring more, but said, *Of course not, if there's a good reason. But I accomplish nothing by my suffering—I fail wherever I try!*

Who could succeed, against an army of bandits? But you can warn Pirogia of the mercenaries who seek to destroy it!

Destroy? Gianni's blood quickened; his attention suddenly focused on the swirling face. *Who said to destroy them?*

That captain! The lord who had hired him was an-

gry because they had not punished the insolent merchants! What sort of punishment do you think he expected?

Why—I thought that was only—the ambushing of our . . . Gianni stopped, thinking. *No—they had done that, hadn't they? And burned Signor Ludovico's storehouse.*

Even so. It's Pirogia they seek to punish—Pirogia, and your mother, your father!

I must warn them! Gianni struggled to sit up. *But who are you?*

CHAPTER 4

"Only me," the face said, but it was pulling in on itself, the hair calming in its swirl, the beard fading, the lines vanishing, nose shrinking, eyes growing larger. The hair turned brown, light brown, held by an enameled band, blowing in the breeze; the eyes were brown, too, but the face was young, and very, very feminine, with high cheekbones and a wide mouth with full, red lips that moved and said, "It is only Medallia, only a Gypsy woman going in advance of her tribe."

Gianni stared up at this vision of loveliness, unable to believe so bright a sight in the midst of the darkness his life had suddenly become. "What . . . where . . ."

"Lie still," she advised, "but let me lift your head

into my lap; I must bandage that ugly wound in your scalp."

So that was why his head ached so abominably. Gianni let her lift his head (though it sent a lance of pain from temple to temple), then lower it against the softness of her skirt. With his head up, he could see Gar, blinking at the woman—Medallia, had she called herself? Gar had apparently already had the benefit of her nursing, for he wore one bandage across his chest and another wrapped about his brow, like a headband.

Then pain stabbed again, and Gianni squeezed his eyes shut. As the spasm passed, he could feel soft hands winding a bandage around his head, and savored the sensation of the gentle caress, so calming, so soothing . . . He shook off the mood; he must remain vigilant. Opening his eyes again, he asked, "How did you find us?"

"I was following the road," Medallia explained, still working, "and I saw you lying in the ditch. I knew the soldiers had passed, so I feared they had robbed and beaten you."

"Well, there was another band who robbed us first," Gianni said, "but you're right—this band beat us even worse."

"How did you know there were soldiers ahead?" Gar asked, his tone so gentle that Gianni knew it must be false. What did he suspect?

"Soldiers are dangerous, for a woman alone," Medallia replied. "When I heard them coming behind me, I drove off the road and waited till they had passed—waited long, you may be sure."

"Wise," Gianni said, but between the gentleness of her touch and the beauty of her eyes, he was beginning to feel that he would have praised anything she said. Would he have felt this way if he had not met her binding his wounds?

Gar certainly didn't feel that way. All he said was, "Drove?" and looked about, then stared. Gianni frowned, turning his head very carefully, to see what Gar saw—but not carefully enough; pain stabbed again. He saw only what he had expected—a yellow Gypsy caravan, a high-wheeled wagon with a pair of donkeys to pull it, curve-roofed and with two windows on each side, a high chimney rising from the back with wires to hold it against swaying on bumpy roads. It was unusual for a Gypsy woman to travel alone, but surely the *caravan* wasn't surprising. Why did Gar stare so? "Have you never seen a Gypsy's home?" he asked.

"The Gypsies of my homeland have nothing of this sort," Gar answered slowly.

Medallia looked up in surprise. Then she frowned in thought, but looked away just before Gar turned back to gaze at her. She tied Gianni's bandage, saying, "You're merchants, then?"

"We were," Gianni said bitterly, "until we were robbed. Now we're beggars—and my friend thought it wise to pretend to be madmen."

"It *almost* worked," Gar said, aggrieved.

"It worked quite well," Medallia corrected. "You're still alive."

Gar looked at her in pleased surprise. "I thank you—again."

Gianni assumed he must already have thanked her for his bandages. "It's good of you, very good of you, to stop to help us. Few travelers would be so kind."

"We who live on the open road become accustomed to the notion that we must help one another," Medallia told him. "You're welcome to what aid I can give—and you're cold. I must find you clothing."

"Oh, but we have our own." Gianni turned to the mound of clothing—then stopped, staring in horror.

"Ah," Gar said, following his gaze. "Yes, when they came to beat us, they rode their horses everywhere, didn't they?"

"Is there anything left?"

Medallia went over to rummage through the sprawl of torn garments. "Rags to wash windows with—nothing more."

Gianni felt empty.

"I'll bring clothes."

Gianni started to protest, but Medallia had already turned away to go back to her caravan.

"A rare woman," Gar said, following the swaying form with his eyes.

"Most rare indeed." Gianni wondered what her figure was like, but her skirts were full, and she wore a shawl draped around her shoulders and down to her hips. He was sure she was beautiful in every way, though, for if she weren't, how could she move so sensuously? Especially when she didn't intend to. Gianni watched her climb up onto the driver's seat, then heard a door open and shut, heard her footsteps inside . . .

"How could she know it wouldn't be dangerous to revive us?"

Gianni jolted out of his reverie, staring at Gar, appalled. "You can't mean to molest her!"

"Never," Gar said, with all the resolution of profound morality and beyond. "But she couldn't have known that."

"No—that's true." A dark, slow anger began to course through Gianni, at any man who would take advantage of a ministering angel—but he knew enough of the world to believe such men existed, and suspected Gar knew it even better than he.

A door in the back of the caravan opened, and a set of steps fell down. Medallia descended, her arms full of clothing, and came back to the men. She knelt beside Gianni and held a shirt up. "Will this fit you?"

Gianni raised his arms—halfway. There he grimaced with the pain of a bruise, but started to force his arms higher.

"Don't." Her voice was gentle. "The bone may be bruised as well as the muscle. Here." She settled the fabric over his head and pulled it down. He did have to force his arms through the sleeves, then ran a hand down the front of the shirt, amazed at its texture. At first he thought it to be silk, then realized it was only a very finely spun cotton—but how had she polished it to such a sheen?

It didn't occur to him to wonder why she carried men's clothing.

Medallia looked him up and down, then nodded. "Perhaps a little too large, but no one will notice. Try the trousers, while I take the rest to your friend." She rose and moved away.

Tactful, Gianni thought—it could have been rather embarrassing to have her help him pull on his pants. He managed to bend stiff legs well enough to push them down the tubes of black cloth, then looked down, intrigued by the looseness of their fit. They felt so much more comfortable than his hose—but of course, they didn't show off the legs that he had exercised so hard to perfect.

He looked up and saw that Medallia was having a bit more trouble with Gar. The shirt fitted very tightly indeed, making the man's chest muscles appear even more huge than they were—and his upper arms strained the seams. The sleeves were far too short, but she disguised that by rolling them back a little, as though they had been shortened by intention, for hard work. The shirt didn't meet the belt, but she solved that by winding a wide sash twice around his midriff (though Gianni wasn't sure he liked the way her hands caressed the fabric over Gar's belly muscles). The trousers were far too short, but she said, "We'll have to find you some high horseman's boots."

She went back, then returned with the boots. "Those, at least, I have." Gar pulled them on, and Medallia stood back, eyeing them critically, then nodding. "They will be high enough, yes. You'll pass if the condotierri don't look too closely, and it will do to bring you home—but until then, you'd do well to stay where no one can see you. I think you would do better to ride than to walk for a while, in any case. Will the two of you come into my caravan?"

Would he! The blood pounded in Gianni's head at the mere thought, though he realized the invitation was quite impersonal. He reined in his rampant emotions and said, "You're most kind indeed! Yes, by all means, we'll be glad to ride with you!"

"Come, then." Medallia helped him up, and had to steady him as he found his feet. Gianni groaned with the pain as a dozen bruises screamed at him for the folly of moving. He felt his knees buckle, but Medallia's shoulder was a bulwark against unconsciousness, and he began to hobble with her toward the caravan. "Slowly, slowly," she crooned. "We'll be there soon enough." And there the yellow boards were, right in front of him. She tucked his fingers over the dashboard, saying, "Hold tight, now, till I bring your friend, for I think six weak hands will do better than two strong, in hoisting you up." She went back for Gar.

But the big man had already pushed himself to his feet and stood swaying, propping himself up with a pole that had a ragged end. With a shock, Gianni realized that the man must have broken a pike, and that its owner had taken the head with him, for steel was valuable. Medallia took Gar's hand and placed it on her shoulder (Gianni was surprised at the sudden jealousy he felt). Gar nodded gravely and followed, but Gianni could see that he wasn't leaning on the woman, only held her shoulder as a guide. She anchored him to the back of the wagon, then returned to lead Gianni there, too, then on up and into the caravan, where she lowered him onto a padded bench, then went back for Gar.

Gianni looked about him in amazement. He had never been inside a Gypsy caravan before, but had not expected it to be so neat, so bright and cheerful. The walls were painted ivory, with a pattern of flowers stenciled on; beneath each of the front windows was a padded bench covered in the beige-and-white striped cloth woven in his own city. The front windows were made from the bottoms of bottles melted together, coloring the light yellow and green and brown; the rearmost windows were clear and curtained, the glass divided into many small panes that could easily be cut from scraps. Two chairs faced one another to either side of the left-hand window—they looked to be nailed down, as was everything in this wagon that didn't hang from the ceiling—and between them, a tabletop was folded down against the wall. At the back, four feet from the door, stood a stove of enameled tile, almost as though it were guarding the entryway. Framed pictures hung on the walls—a scene of a city, a picture of a cottage in a wood, and a tableau of an old peasant couple sitting by their hearth. Could it be, Gianni wondered, that this young Gypsy woman wanted to live in a house as badly as most other young folk wanted to wander?

Gar was able to stoop through the doorway without toppling over, but it took some careful maneuvering for him to sidle around the stove without knocking down the chimney. That done, he collapsed on the bench opposite Gianni, closing his eyes, breathing heavily. Gianni was surprised to see that there was a limit to the giant's strength.

"Rest," Medallia advised, and laid a waterskin near

Gianni's hand. "Your benches have arms; hold to them, for the caravan sways a bit." Then she was gone with a rustle of brightly colored cloth through the little door at the front, to call to her donkeys. The caravan lurched into motion, and Gianni found that the arms of the bench were indeed useful. "Where is she taking us?"

"Where does the road lead?" Gar countered.

"To Pirogia, if she doesn't turn off to go to another city."

"Then she'll most likely take us to your home," Gar said. "I told her you were from Pirogia as she bandaged me—told her that I had promised to see you safely home, and was bound to do it however I had to."

"I thank you for that," Gianni said slowly, "and it seems that you shall indeed, though perhaps not in the manner you intended." He glanced out the window, then said, "She is very kind."

"Very," Gar agreed, "but she doesn't look very much like a Gypsy."

Gianni looked up in surprise. "How do Gypsies look? Surely she wears a kerchief and bright clothing, like any Gypsy woman I have ever seen—yes, and with brass earrings, too!"

Gar just gazed at him a moment, then said, "Well, if clothes are all it takes to make a Gypsy, then she must look like one indeed."

"Why—what do *you* think Gypsies look like?"

"Those of my homeland generally have dark complexions and black hair—and large noses."

Gianni shook his head. "I have never seen a Gypsy who looked like that."

"So," Gar said, more to himself than to Gianni, "the Romany didn't truly come to this plan ... to Petrarch."

Gianni frowned. "What plan did you speak of? And who are the Romany?"

Gar looked up, stared a moment, then smiled. "They're the folk who invented carts like this one, but the arrangement inside is quite different."

"A plan of decoration?"

"Yes, quite so—of management, you might say. 'Medallia' is a pretty name, isn't it?"

"Very," Gianni agreed, but he could have cursed Gar for having aroused his suspicions. Even he had to admit that "Medallia" didn't sound much like the names of the Gypsies he had known.

Gar distracted him from that line of thought. "I'm sorry I couldn't guard you well enough."

"Who could, against an army?" Gianni realized he was echoing the words of the face he had seen in his vision. He tried to ignore that and said, "I saw the amount of roadside that the bandits' hooves tore up. You fought enough of them, my friend."

Gar shrugged. "I had to make it look convincing. Who'd believe that so large a simpleton could be so easily overcome? Unless he was a total coward, which Lenni isn't."

Gianni felt a prickle of eeriness at the way that the big man referred to the simpleton he had pretended to be—but there were more important matters at hand. "We must warn Pirogia."

"Ah." Gar nodded, eyes glinting. "So. You noticed that conversation too, eh?"

"I wish there had been more of it! But what other merchants could they not yet have punished? They've certainly burned out Ludovico, and slaughtered us—at least, so far as they know."

"Yes, that's the one factor in our favor," Gar agreed, "that they think we're dead. But I noticed that the bandits who beat us this second time were Stilettos too, and when they trade stories with their friends who attacked our caravan, they may both mention a rather large man."

"You're hard to miss," Gianni agreed. "Still, the way you fought this time didn't exactly speak of training."

Gar grinned. "I *have* done my share of brawling. I know the amateur's style."

"So do I," Gianni said ruefully. "I seem to have practiced it."

Gar shook his head. "You fought as a trained fighter."

"But an amateur merchant," Gianni said bitterly.

"Not at all," Gar said, with a sardonic smile. "You're still striving."

"Well, we can scarcely lie down and die." Gianni said it with a twinge of guilt, remembering his dream. "We'll have to be more cautious in our progress back home."

"Thanks to Medallia, all we need to do is stay inside—though if she's attacked, I think we may both find we have the strength to overcome the pain of our bruises."

Anger surged at the mere idea, and Gianni said softly, "Oh, yes. We surely may."

It was a brave resolution. Fortunately, they had no need to put it to the test.

When they stopped for the night, Medallia brewed a rich soup from dried meat and legumes, fed them, then made pallets for them underneath the wagon. Her attitude and stance were firm, and neither man questioned her unspoken decision nor objected in the slightest, though they did groan a little as they climbed down the steps. Medallia pulled the stairs in, said, "I shall see you in the morning, goodmen," and closed her door. Gianni stared at it for a moment, letting his imagination picture what she was doing inside, but found that his body was too worn to work up any enthusiasm, and turned away with a sigh of regret.

His muscles screamed protest as he slowly, painfully, lowered himself to his knees, with one hand on the side of the wagon and Gar holding the other arm. Then Gar braced himself on Gianni's shoulder as he creaked down and bowed Gianni ahead. Gianni lay down, very carefully, and rolled under the wagon, across the nearest pallet, then onto the farther one. Gar came rolling after him, grunting with pain, then lay on his pallet staring up at the bottom of the wagon, gasping in quick shallow breaths.

"More than bruises?" Gianni asked with concern.

"A cracked rib, I think," Gar answered. "It will mend."

"Walk carefully," Gianni warned.

Gar nodded. "Be sure, I've had ribs cracked before—yes, and broken, too. But thank you for worrying, Gianni."

"Thank you for a scheme that saved us," Gianni replied. "Good night, Gar." He thought he heard the big man answer, but that might have been a small dream as he fell into sleep.

Sleep was black, until a small, swirling form began to appear. *Not again!* Gianni thought, and struggled to wake himself—but before he could, the object grew, and he realized that he wasn't seeing hair and beard swirling around a face, but veils floating around a supple body. Closer she came and closer, turning and undulating in a languid dance. Was that music that accompanied her movements, or was she music embodied? If it was sound, it was so barely audible that he thought he felt it, not saw it—as he also seemed to feel every turn, every gesture. Light grew about her, but somehow left her face in shadow. He longed to discern her form, but the multitude of veils only hinted at a lush and voluptuous figure, and certainly didn't reveal it.

Gianni. Her voice spoke inside his head—but of course, he realized; this was a dream, so it was *all* inside his head. *Gianni, hearken to my words!*

To every syllable, he breathed, then frowned at a thought. *Do you have a father?*

A father? Her tone was surprised. *Yes, but he is far away. Why do you ask?* Clearly, she had not been expecting that.

Because I have seen an old man who comes and

goes as you do. Perhaps her father wasn't so far away as she thought.

Does he indeed! Her tone was ominous. *Let us hope we never meet!*

Oh, but I am so glad we have! Gianni reached out, but found that whatever dream presence he was had no body.

No—not you. Her tone softened amazingly, then became inviting, seductive, as she said, *I, too, rejoice in meeting you, brave and handsome man of Pirogia! But know that contact between the dream realm and the real is forbidden, save to those living souls who have learned the art of the waking dream. I would not violate that rule if I did not have words of import for you.*

Whatever it is, I'll treasure the cause! What word have you for me? Gianni found himself hoping ardently.

Love, she said, and Gianni's hopes soared—then crashed as she said, *You must avoid it. Turn aside, turn away—do not fall in love with the Gypsy Medallia! Do not!*

Small chance of that! Gianni declared, with all the ardor of a newly besotted soul, *for I have fallen in love with you!*

The dancer stilled and stood awhile frozen, and Gianni gloated, thinking she had not suspected this! Could he take her by surprise, then?

But the dancer began to move again, the veils rising and falling as she turned, then turned again. *Do not,* she counseled, *for I am faithless and fickle, as likely to turn to another man in a minute as I am to return to you. No, in all likelihood, you shall never see me again.*

You couldn't be so cruel! Gianni protested.

She threw back her head and laughed in the tone of silver bells. *Oh, in affairs of the heart, I can be cruel indeed, Gianni! I am truly a woman without mercy! Nay, you are a fool if you fall in love with Medallia, but a greater fool if you fall in love with me!*

Then I am a fool no matter how I turn, Gianni said, with conviction. He found he didn't really mind the idea.

Not at all—you need not fall in love with either! the vision snapped, then turned away, with a gesture of finality—and Gianni woke.

He found himself staring at the bottom of the wagon above his head, startled to find himself back in the real world. Was he to spend his life lost in dreams, then?

If such divine creatures inhabited the dream world—yes. He was growing remarkably repulsed by reality anyway. He lay awake awhile, marveling at how faithless and feckless he was. And he had always believed himself to be constant and virtuous!

But then, he had never fallen in love before—or at least, never so deeply as this.

CHAPTER 5

They came into Pirogia through the land gate, Gar and Gianni sitting up on the driver's seat with Medallia, one on each side of her. The sentries didn't recognize Gianni at first and tried to bar them entrance, but when he protested, "I'm Gianni Braccalese," they stared in surprise, then threw their heads back and guffawed, staggering to brace themselves against the wall. Gianni reddened with embarrassment. "It isn't so funny as all that!"

"To see a merchant of Pirogia dressed up like a Gypsy?" one sentry gasped, wiping his eyes. "Oh, it's a tale to be savored and retold many times—not that I would, mind you."

Gianni took the hint. He sighed and said, "I don't have any money with me, or I'd invite you for a bite and a drink while I told you how I came by these clothes. Shall I meet you at Lobini's coffeehouse to tell you the tale?"

"Aye, and gladly! We're off duty at three."

"At Lobini's, then." The other sentry stepped aside and waved them through the gate.

Medallia clucked to her donkeys and drove in, Gar saying out of the corner of his mouth, "A bribe well and discreetly offered."

"Let's hope they'll be discreet in turn," Gianni sighed. "Yes, I've had some experience at the craft."

"Are you so ashamed to be seen with me as that?" Medallia challenged them.

"Never!" Gianni protested, and was about to explain at length, when he saw the twinkle in her eye and relaxed.

They rode across the causeway, and Gianni explained to Gar that there were charges of gunpowder every dozen yards or so, in case an army tried to charge across the causeway to attack the city. The big man nodded. "Wise." But his eyes were on the panorama spread out before him, and his lips quirked in a smile. "I thought you said this city was built on scores of little islands."

Gianni looked up at his home, luminescent in the morning mist, suddenly seeing it through the eyes of strangers, suddenly seeing it as magical and fantastic. Bridges were everywhere, spanning canals, arcing over waterways, swooping between the taller buildings—buildings that seemed like giant cakes, their walls painted in smooth pastels and adorned with festoons of ornamentation in bright colors. Where the rivers were too wide for bridges (and even where they weren't), long, slender boats glided, in the design Gianni's ancestors had copied from the barbarians of the North, for the people of Pirogia were always eager for new goods, new artifacts, new ideas, and copied and modified with delight, shrugging off their mistakes and embracing their successes. Their critics called them shameless imitators, devoid of originality; their enthusiasts called them brilliant synthesists. The Pirogians called themselves successes.

Pride in his home swelled Gianni's breast. "It really is a score and more of islands," he assured Gar, "but my people have done wonderfully in welding them all together, haven't they?"

"Most wonderfully indeed," Medallia said, and Gianni glanced at her, saw her shining eyes, and felt his hopes soar. On the road, he had been just one more unfortunate; here, he was a rich merchant's son. Surely she would now see him as more than something to be pitied, would see him as someone to be admired, perhaps even coveted . . . ?

The sentries at the inner gate frowned, slamming their halberds together to bar the way. "I'm Gianni Braccalese," he informed them, and they stared in surprise. Before they could start laughing, he said, "I'll meet you at Lobini's, if you want, to tell you why I'm dressed as a Gypsy and glad to be. For now, though, I need to see my home as quickly as possible."

They took the hint of the bribe and swallowed their mirth. "We'll meet you there the instant we're relieved," Mario promised. They had known one another from childhood, and Gianni was relieved by the implied promise that they would tell no one until they'd had their chance to rib him unmercifully and see how much hush money he offered them. Gianni didn't resent the minor extortion—every Pirogian expected every other Pirogian to make every penny he could in every way he could, as long as it wasn't blatantly immoral, or completely criminal—and bribery had never been outlawed in Pirogia.

Medallia drove her cart down broad streets and over bridges according to Gianni's directions, until finally they drew up in front of a wide two-story building that backed against the River Melorin, a building of pale blue stucco with the red tile roof that was so much the standard in Pirogia, a dozen windows above and below, and wide double doors for driving in wagons. They stood open now, and Gianni felt a sudden knot tie itself in his belly before he said, "You may drive in, if you will. My father and mother will more than welcome the fair lady who has saved their son."

"I'm no lady, but only a poor Gypsy maiden," Medallia said gently.

A lady was a woman born to the nobility, or at least as the daughter of a knight. Gianni knew that, but he said gallantly, "You're a lady by your deeds and your behavior, if not by birth. Indeed, I have heard of ladies born who lived with less nobility than fishwives."

Gar nodded. "It's true; I've know some of them."

Medallia gave Gianni one of her rare smiles, and he stared, feeling as though the sun had come out from behind a cloud to bathe him in its rays. Finally, he remembered to smile back—but Medallia had already turned away and clucked to her donkeys, shaking the reins. They ambled through the portal.

A heavily built, middle-aged man in gray work clothes was heaving crates from a stack by the wall up to the bed of a wagon, barking orders at the men who were helping him. Gianni stared, then leaped down to run and seize the last and lowest crate just as the older man was reaching for it. "No, Papa! You know the doctor said you shouldn't lift anything heavy!"

The older man stared, then whooped with delight and flung his arms around Gianni, bawling, "Lucia! Someone call Lucia! It's our son Gianni, come back from the dead!"

Then Gianni realized why his father had been wearing such somber clothing. He hugged back—time enough to take his medicine later.

Gar climbed down off the wagon and moved toward Gianni and his father, face set and grim—but before he could interrupt, a matron came running across the courtyard and fairly wrenched Gianni from his father's arms, weeping for joy.

"Mamma, Mamma!" Gianni lamented. "That I could have caused you such grief!"

"Not you," she sobbed, "but the blackguards who waylaid you! Oh, praise God! Praise God, and Our Lady!"

"There is no blame for him," Gar rumbled, "only for me."

Mamma Braccalese broke away from her son in

astonishment, and Papa turned to the giant with a frown, then stared up, taken aback.

"Papa," Gianni said quickly, "this is Gar, a mercenary solder I hired after I found . . ." He paused; he hadn't had time to prepare his father for the bad news. ". . . after I found the burned warehouse. Mamma, this woman is Medallia, who picked us up from the roadside and bandaged our wounds."

"Roadside! Wounds!" Mamma Braccalese turned to him in horror, yanking the scarf off his head and discovering the clean white cloth. "Oh, my son! What villains have done this?" Without waiting for an answer, she turned to hurry to the caravan. "My dear, I cannot thank you enough! Come, you must be weary from your travels! Come down, come down so that I may serve you some refreshment in my house! Giuseppi! See to the donkeys!" She ushered a slightly dazed Medallia up the steps and into the house, asking, "Have you come far? I know, I know, your people live on the road—still, it must be wearying! Oh, thank you so much, so very much, for rescuing my son! Come in, come in that you may sit in a soft chair and drink sweet tea! Tell me, how . . ."

The door closed behind them, leaving Papa Braccalese to scowl up at Gar and demand, "What do you mean? How have you hurt my son?"

"He hired me to protect him and your goods," Gar said simply. "I failed."

"Failed?" Papa stared, then reached up to clap him on the shoulder. "Not a bit, not a bit! You brought him home alive, didn't you? And not too badly wounded, if he could think to lift a crate so that I wouldn't!"

"But . . ." Gar stared, amazed to be praised. "Your goods are lost, stolen by condotierri!"

"Goods! What are goods?" Papa Braccalese brushed off the objection. "The cost of doing business, nothing more. My son, however, could not be replaced! The men lost, that's another matter, but not one you could have prevented. No, don't tell me now—come in to rest, and let us give you some drink that should restore a man!" He turned away, clasping Gar's arm and moving with such energy that even the giant was almost yanked off his feet and had to catch up in order to keep from falling. "Not a word, until you have a glass in your hand!" Papa Braccalese commanded. "Then you shall tell me all about it— but until then, not a word!"

However, when they did have glasses in their hands, he did indeed insist on hearing *all* about it, but from Gianni first. He sat mute, only listening, frowning, and occasionally nodding his head, until Gianni was done with his account and sat, waiting for the axe to fall—but Papa only turned and asked Gar what he had seen and done, then listened in silence while the giant told him. When he finished, though, it was Papa's turn, and he subjected both of them to a barrage of questions that would have sunk a galley. At last, satisfied that he had learned everything they knew, Papa Braccalese sat back, nodding, and said, "So. The Raginaldi have loosed the Stilettos on us merchants—not that they wish to slay us, of course, only to tame us, to yoke us and make us work for them, instead of for ourselves."

"That *may* be the case," Gar cautioned. "Gianni and I have only a few spoken words to judge by. It could just as easily be that the Stiletto Company is unemployed, and seeking their living in their usual manner."

"Well, if that's so, and we prepare for war but they don't attack, then we have lost nothing, have we? Except some time and effort, but the effort will have kept us healthy, and the time would have been idled away otherwise. There is cost, it's true, cost in hiring soldiers and training men and forging weapons and armor, but that's the cost of doing business, isn't it?"

"A rather high cost," Gar said, frowning.

"So? And what will be the cost if we do *not* arm, and the Stilettos *do* attack, eh? No, all in all, I think it will be cheaper to arm."

"Well ..." Gar looked rather befuddled. "When you put it *that* way, of *course* it's wiser to prepare for war."

Papa Braccalese nodded. "Let's hope the Council sees it that way."

"Some of them are skinflints," Gianni whispered to Gar as they entered the long wide room. "They would rather believe anything false than have to pay an extra florin out of their profit."

"You have watched their meetings before, then?"

"No, never," Gianni said. "I only know what rumor says—and what Papa curses when he comes home from a Council meeting. I wouldn't be here now, if they didn't need to hear my story from my own lips."

"And mine." Gar nodded. "There's much less question of accuracy, when they hear it from the survivors."

The Maestro came into the hall, and the merchants stopped gossiping in their small groups of two and three and turned to look to their elected leader for the year. Oldo Bolgonolo was a heavyset man in his late middle age, his hair grizzled, his face lined—but his eye still sharp and questing.

"Masters," he said, giving them their Guild title (for no journeyman and certainly no apprentice could hold office here), "we are met to hear disturbing news from Paolo Braccalese and his son Gianni. I know rumor has already borne it to all your ears, so let us begin by hearing it stripped of all the fat that grows as the story goes from mouth to mouth. Gianni Braccalese, speak!"

The master merchants had by now all taken their seats, and Gianni felt the weight of fifty pairs of piercing eyes upon him. He tried to calm his stomach as he stood, leaning on the table in case his knees turned to jelly, and began, "Masters . . ." Then he cleared his throat to rid it of the squeak in his voice—but his father's colleagues were understanding of human frailty, and made no comment. Gianni began again. "Masters, I was conducting a goods train to Accera, to trade with old Ludovico for grain and timber and orzans . . ."

He told them the story, his voice as dry and matter-of-fact as he could make it, showing emotion only when he had to speak of Antonio's death. The merchants stirred restlessly at that, muttering angrily to one another. Gianni waited for them to be done, then took up his tale again. They seemed impressed by Gar's improvisation to impersonate the weak-minded and showed surprise at Gianni's rescue by a Gypsy. But he saved the worst for last, ending by telling them about the remarks he had overheard, about a lord paying the Stilettos to discipline some unruly merchants, whereupon they erupted into a furious clamor of denunciation and calls for vengeance, countered by shouted arguments for caution. The Maestro let them work out the worst of their anger, and Gianni sat down, shaken but exhilarated.

Gar was staring at the shouting merchants. "These are your cool-headed men of business?"

Gianni shrugged. "We're human, and as apt to anger as the next man."

"I don't think I want to be next to that man," Gar replied.

The Maestro picked up a stick and struck a cymbal suspended near him. Some of the merchants looked up and stopped their debate, but others went on arguing furiously. The Maestro had to strike his cymbal again, then again and again, before they all subsided, muttering, and took their seats once more.

"I think you have all worked out the basic positions now," the Maestro commented dryly. "May we hear them stated clearly? No, Paolo Braccalese—this meeting comes at your demand, and it is your son who was attacked, your goods that were lost; I scarcely think you can see the situation clearly. You, Giuseppi Di Silva! What say you to this news?"

"Why, if it's so, we must arm as quickly as possible!" A tall merchant leaped to his feet. "Arm, and recall the fleet to guard our shores!"

"Nay, more!" shouted a shorter merchant with long yellow hair. He stood, thumping the table with his fist. "They've slain two drivers and a caravan master, and enslaved the rest! They've burned the warehouse of a merchant we deal with, and slain him! They've stolen the goods of a merchant of Pirogia and wounded his son! Are we to suffer these affronts with no revenge? Surely not—for if we do, we give them leave to do it all over again, to each and any of us!"

Angry shouts agreed with him. Equally angry shouts denounced them. The Maestro struck the cymbal again, and they quieted. "Clearly spoken," he said. "We have two positions set forth now—one that we defend our city, another that we seek revenge, which I assume means that we should send out an expedition to attack the Stilettos. May we have the opposite position stated so clearly as these? No, not you, Pietro San Duse—you would cloud your statement with so much insult and so much emotion that I would have to parse your words to find your meaning. Carlo Grepotti, you have spoken little, and that quite calmly—will you grace us with your words?"

An elderly merchant arose, a man with a face like a hawk and the ferocious eye of an eagle. "Grace? I fear there will be little of that in what I say, Maestro—but of good sense, I can promise you abundance! What I see in the hot words of my respected colleagues is waste, atrocious waste pure and simple! They would have us take hundreds of florins from the treasury—nay, thousands!—to train our young men as soldiers and sailors, to build more war galleys and buy cannon and swords, to feed and clothe and pay this force, and where is this money to come from? For surely the depleted treasury must be refilled! Have no mistake, my brother merchants—these thousands of ducats will surely come, directly or indirectly, from your profits! How will you tell your wife, when she asks for a new gown, that you must pay the soldiers first? How will you tell her, when the roof leaks, that you must buy a barracks for the soldiers before you can have that leak stopped? Be sure that, once begun, it will not end, for having spent the money, we must justify it if no enemy comes! How shall we do that? Why, by marching out and declaring war where there is none, just as my colleague Angelo has suggested even now! Then it's *we* who shall be taking away others' freedom, even as we fear they shall do to us!"

"And if the enemy does come?" the tall Di Silva demanded. "If they *do* come, and we beat them off?"

"Why, they you shall cry that we must always keep the army standing and the navy afloat, for fear others may come!" Grepotti retorted. "Then if they do not, you shall call for a war to conquer Tumanola and expel the Raginaldi, or some such, and overlook the fact that we have become conquerors! Thus we shall impoverish ourselves to turn Pirogia into a bully among cities—and all for what? The word of a boy who brings us no proof and no other witnesses!

Surely, my colleagues, we must have better grounds than this!"

"But we do have another witness," Di Silva retorted. "Let us hear from him."

"From a mercenary who will admit, I'm sure, that he failed in his duty? Surely he will seek to excuse himself, to justify himself!"

Gar's face turned to flint, and Gianni said instantly, in a low voice, "He speaks only to support his argument, Gar. He means no harm—and he wasn't there."

But the Maestro had noticed. "What do you say to that, young Braccalese?"

Gianni stood, anger overcoming nervousness. "That it was one mercenary against fifty, that we stood back to back with twenty-five against each of us, and could not possibly have won! Gar has done his job well, for I have come back to you alive!"

"Aye, and come back with two sentences overheard, nothing more!" Carlo Grepotti retorted. "You cannot even tell us surely who was the 'lord' this captain spoke of, nor who the merchants!"

Now Papa Braccalese rose. "Maestro?"

"Yes, Paolo," Oldo the Maestro sighed. "Have your say."

"My lord, hurt to any merchant is hurt to all! Even if my goods train had come home intact, I would have wasted the drivers' pay, the stevedores' pay, the mules' time, my son's time! I have no profit from that trip, and will have no more profit from that town, for old Ludovico is dead, and surely none will dare build where he has fallen! It isn't his misfortune only, but all of ours!"

Carlo Grepotti looked up with fire in his eyes, but Oldo said, "You have spoken well, Carlo Grepotti, and I thank you—but you have asked for the mercenary's word, and we shall hear it!" He turned to Gar. "Will you tell us your tale?"

"I shall." Gar unfolded himself to his full height, squaring his shoulders, and instantly commanded the hall. Everyone had seen him come in, but all now felt they had never seen him before. There was some assurance to his bearing, some commanding presence in his face and his posture, that brought instant respect and attention. Even Gianni stared. He had never seen Gar like this before.

With a measured pace, Gar told his tale, not hurrying, not lagging. His account was considerably shorter than Gianni's, of course, but it agreed in every particular, save that Gar the mercenary gave more detail of the Stilettos' armament and tactics—and, when he sat down, he left the impression of a terrible and ferocious force about to fall on Pirogia.

Silence held the hall for a few seconds after he sat. Then Carlo Grepotti shook himself and demanded, "What would you have us to do? Arm, and go out to attack them?"

"The best defense is a good offense." Gar stood again. "Yes, there is some sense in what you say. But there's better sense in being sure you can win before you attack, and that's done by massing overwhelming numbers."

"Ah, so we're to employ mercenaries! I might have known you would encourage us to spend more money and more on men of your trade!"

"That would be wise," Gar agreed, "but it would be even more wise to seek allies. I had thought there were a dozen merchant cities on Talipon, not Pirogia alone."

The hall was silent for a few minutes, while all the merchants registered the idea with shock and tried to absorb it. Then Oldo the Maestro gave answer.

CHAPTER 6

Oldo said slowly, "Yes, there are other such cities, though Pirogia is the only one in which the merchants have become the government in name as well as fact—the others still have a doge or a conte and, though the merchants are the real power, they dare not move without their nobleman's agreement. But ally with those with whom we must compete, in order to prosper? Unthinkable!"

"What would happen after the war was done?" Grepotti demanded. "How would we divide the spoils? For surely, in a war of a dozen city-states, all the aristocratic cities would league against us, and the only way to win would be to conquer them!"

"We could *not* win!" Pietro San Duse cried. "A dozen merchant cities, against fifty governed by noblemen? Impossible!"

"But even if we did," Di Silva said, "the war would never end! With such an army and navy, no one city would dare disband them, for fear the others would league against it! We would have to use that compound army to conquer more territory and more, and the drain on our purses would never end! No, even *I* cannot approve such a league."

Gar stood like a statue, his face flint. "It may be your only chance to stay free and independent."

Oldo shook his head. "We shall find another way—there must be another way! Arm, perhaps, but league? No!" He looked around at the councillors all cowed and subdued by the mere notion of allying with their business rivals. "We must consider what we have heard, my brother merchants, and discuss the issue again, when our heads have cleared." He struck the cymbal and announced, "We shall meet tomorrow at the same time! For today, good afternoon to you all!"

They did meet the next day, but Gianni and Gar weren't invited, having already given their testimony—and more of Gar's opinion than the Council had wanted. Papa Braccalese went, but he came home looking exasperated, shaking his head and saying, "They argued three hours, and could decide on nothing!"

"Not even to reject my idea of seeking allies?" Gar asked.

"Oh, *that* they agreed on—agreed on so well that Oldo began the meeting by saying, 'I think we may safely discard this notion of making compacts with our competitors. Yes?' and everyone cried, 'Yes!'

with Grepotti saying, 'Especially Venoga,' and there was no more heard of *that*."

Gar sighed, shaking his head. "It may be good business, but it's very poor strategy."

"What shall we do, then?" Gianni asked, at a loss.

"What *can* we do?" Papa threw his arms wide. "Business as usual! What else? But if it must be business, let us choose customers and sources as safe as can be found! You, Gianni, will take another goods train out—but you will go north to Navorrica this time, through the mountains, where the only bandits are those who grew up there, and the country is too rough for an army!"

Gar went too, of course—Papa Braccalese wasn't about to let his son go without protection when there was a professional soldier available, and one who, moreover, refused to accept pay for his last assignment, maintaining that he had failed to bring the goods train safely home. *At least,* Gianni thought, *he isn't trying to take the blame for letting the Stilettos burn Ludovico's warehouse!*

Gianni was excited at the prospect of the journey, and delighted at the chance to redeem himself. He was also amazed at his father's faith in him, when he had already lost one goods train. He was bound and determined to prove worthy of Papa's trust—so the awakening was all the more rude, even though he had fallen asleep when it came.

Gianni, she called, even before he saw her; then it was almost as though he had turned to look behind him in his dream, and there she was, dancing languorously against darkness, swirling veils hiding her face and hinting at her form. She was desire incarnate, she was beauty, she was grace, she was all a man could want.

Gianni, she said, *I have warned you against the Stilettos. Why did you not heed me?*

I did, maiden. Gianni felt hurt. *The Council wouldn't listen.*

Nor would your father, if he sends you a-venturing! It is not westward alone that you must fear to go, but northward too, and southward! I would tell you eastward also, if there were anything there but the sea!

Gianni was appalled. *Why is there danger in every direction?*

Because the lords are banding together, even as the giant told your merchants to do! They are banding together and bringing the mercenary armies, to take revenge on you insolent commoners who dare defy your natural masters by building and governing your own city! Oh, make no mistake, Gianni—the giant was right, in every respect! But if you cannot persuade your elders to ally with the other merchant cities, at least do not go out to your doom! Her form began to waver as she turned and turned, shrinking, receding. *Do not go, Gianni . . . do not go . . .*

Do not go! he cried, unconsciously echoing her. *Don't go! Stay a while, for I long to come to know you better! Stay, beautiful maiden, stay!*

But she receded still, saying, *Do not go . . . do not go . . . do not go . . .*

Then light burst, and Gianni sat bolt upright in bed to find he was staring at the sunrise. He squeezed his eyes shut and turned away, but could not quell the feeling of doom that the dream had raised.

Still, it *was* just a dream, and with a good breakfast inside him, his cheeks shaved, and clean clothes on his back, Gianni was able to dispel the lingering nightmare and determine to lead the goods train out, as his father had told him.

First, though, they saw Medallia off—she would not stay for more than a few nights. The hostler drew her caravan up by the door, and she turned to tell the Braccalese family, "Thank you for your hospitality. Rarely have I found folk so welcoming."

"Then you should stay with us, poor lamb!" Mamma gave her a hug, and a kiss on the cheek. "But since you won't, come back this way often, and visit!"

Gianni was worried, too—how had she survived so long, a woman alone in this lawless country? But he bade her farewell nonetheless, holding her hands and looking into her eyes as he said it. For a moment, he thought he might kiss her, so wonderfully desirable did she seem—but some air came over her, some aura that said, *Touch me not,* though she still smiled and returned his gaze, so the moment passed, and he could only watch as she mounted the seat of her caravan, took up the reins, and clucked to her donkeys. Then away she went out of the courtyard, with the family waving.

Three days later, it was only Papa and Mamma who stood waving as Gianni and Gar led five drivers and ten mules out through the gate. Gianni felt apprehensive and nervous, and missed old Antonio severely—but Gar's great bulk was very reassuring, the more so as the giant wore a new rapier and dagger, plus a crossbow, and a dozen other weapons that he assured Gianni were there, though they could not be seen.

Out the city gate they went, over the causeway and out through the land gate—and the oppression deepened, hollowing Gianni's stomach, but he forced himself to laugh at a comment Gar made, and hoped the big man had meant it as a joke.

Two days later, they were following a track through a high valley with steep, wooded hillsides on either hand. Gianni drew his cloak close against the morning chill. Gar did likewise. "I thought your land of Talipon was warm!"

"It is, as you've seen," Gianni replied, "but even the warmest country will be chill in the early morning, up high in the mountains—won't it?"

Gar sat a moment, then nodded stiffly. "You're right—it will. At least, that's how it has been in every country I've visited, though I haven't been up in the mountains in each of them. In some, I only know what I've heard from mountaineers I met."

Gianni looked up at him curiously. "How many lands *have* you visited?"

"Only seven," Gar told him. "I'm young yet."

Seven! It made Gianni's head reel, the thought of visiting seven other countries. Himself, he had only seen Talipon, and a little of the city of Boriel, on the mainland. Not for the first time, he wished his father had let him go voyaging more often.

"Mountains are always places that delight the soul," Gar said, "but they should make one wary. The mountaineers have a hobby of robbing goods trains."

Gianni shook his head with assurance. "There's no fear of that. Pirogia pays a toll to the folk who live here, to guarantee safe passage to our merchants."

"Wise," Gar allowed, "as long as you call it a toll, not a bribe. But let us suppose that the Stilettos have learned that, and have decided to beat down the mountaineers and set an ambush here, as a way to begin their chastising of Pirogia's merchants . . ."

"That *was* just a remark heard in passing," Gianni said dubiously.

"Will you let Grepotti persuade you so easily? Trust your own ears, Gianni! You heard it, and so did I!"

More importantly, Gianni thought, he had heard his Dream Dancer say it. He looked about him with sudden apprehension. "If they were to do so, would this not be an excellent place for an ambush?"

"Yes, but the *end* of this valley would be even better." Gar loosened his sword in its sheath. "We're braced for ambush now, but as we near the debouchment of the pass, we'll begin to relax, to lower our guard. *Then* will be the ideal time for them to fall upon us."

"But our men *have* relaxed their guard," Gianni said, "because they trust in the good faith of the mountaineers."

Gar stared at him in alarm, then turned back to the men, opening his mouth to yell, but a shouted cry of *"At the point!"* came out, came out and echoed all about them, and it took Gianni a second to realize that it was not Gar who had called, but men at either hand. He looked about wildly and saw condotierri charging down the slopes from each side—charging on foot, for the angle was too steep for horses to gallop. Gianni's drivers barely had time to realize they were beset, were only beginning to react, when the bandits struck, struck with the clubs they held in their left hands, struck the drivers on the sides of their heads or their crowns. Three went down like felled oxen; the other two dodged, pulling out swords as they did, but the condotierri were behind them and all about them, twisting the swords out of their hands even as they raised them to strike, then bringing them down with a fist in the belly and a club behind the ear. Gianni cried out in agony, seeing their futures as galley slaves—but it was too late to try to ride to their rescue, for the condotierri had surrounded Gar and him, surrounded them with a thicket of steel, swords striking from every angle, clubs whirling. They were on foot, though, and Gianni and Gar were mounted, striking down with greater force and the advantage of thrusting over the soldiers' guards.

Gar bellowed in rage, catching swords on his dagger and plunging his rapier down again and again. Bandits fell, gushing blood, and others leaped back out of his range, then leaped in again to stab, but Gar was quicker than they, catching their blows on his dagger and striking home as other thrusts missed him. Gianni could see only when the fight turned him far enough to one side or the other, but he had a confused impression that most of the swords aimed at

Gar somehow missed, sliding by him to one side or the other. A condotierre seized Gianni's horse's bridle and pulled the beast forward, just far enough for another soldier to step in behind Gar, swinging a halberd in a huge overhand arc. Gianni shouted, trying to turn to stab the man, trying to reach, but he overbalanced, lurched forward into waiting hands, and heard the halberd shaft strike Gar's head with a horrible crack, a crack echoed by the club struck against his own skull, and even as the familiar darkness closed in, he realized that his Dream Dancer had been right.

But it wasn't the woman who banished the darkness, it was the old man with the floating hair and beard, and there was no persuading this time, no arguing or warning, but only the stern command, *Up, Gianni Braccalese! You have ignored sound advice; you have brought this upon yourself! Up, to suffer the fruit of your folly! Up to labor and toil in the poverty you deserve, and will deserve until you start fighting with your brain instead of letting your enemies overwhelm you with arms!*

But I did only as I was bidden, Gianni protested.

Up! the face thundered. *Up to labor and fight, or must I make this one refuge a place of torment instead of healing? Up and away, Gianni Braccalese, for the honor of your name and the salvation of your city! UP!*

The last word catapulted Gianni into consciousness; his eyes flew open and he lurched halfway up, then sank back onto a cold, slimy surface, his head raging with pain, his eyes squeezed to slits against the glare of the sky—and there was no gentle face floating above his this time, nor even Gar's homely, craggy features.

Gar! Where was the man? Dead? Enslaved? For that matter, where was Gianni? He rolled painfully up on one elbow, blinking through pain, out over a landscape of churned mud under a drizzling rain. He shivered, soaked through, and saw nothing about him but . . .

The huge, inert body, lying crumpled on its side, face slanting down, almost in the mud, with the huge bloom of ragged, bloody scalp in the midst of his hair—Gar, stripped of his doublet and hose, of even his boots, left for dead.

Fear gibbered up in Gianni, and he struggled through the mud toward his friend. Pain thundered in his head, almost making him stop, but he went on, forced himself to crawl for what seemed an hour but could not have been, for the distance could only have been a few yards. He shivered with numbing cold, feeling the rain beat against his skin . . .

Skin! He took time for a quick look down and saw that the condotierri had stripped him as they had stripped Gar, nothing left but the linen with which he had girded his loins for the journey. They had left him, too, for dead—but why?

An awful suspicion dawned, and Gianni balanced on one elbow while he raised the other hand to his head, probing delicately at the back . . . Pain screamed where his fingers touched, and he yanked his fingers away, shivering anew at his answer—he was injured almost as badly as the mercenary, brought down by too strong a blow with a club.

Too strong indeed! He struggled toward Gar with renewed vigor, the energy of panic. If the man were dead, and Gianni alone in this savage world . . .

But his fingers touched Gar's throat; he waited for a long, agonizing minute, then felt the throb of blood through the great artery. Gianni went limp with relief—Gar would recover, would waken, and he wouldn't be alone in the rain after all.

But the rain was cold, and surely the giant might die of chill if Gianni couldn't cover him somehow. He looked about him with despair—the condotierri had left nothing, nothing at all, not a shred of cloth . . .

But there was dried grass by the roadside.

Struggling and panting, Gianni squirmed the necessary few feet to the head of hay, then realized it would do no good to return with a single handful. He tried to ignore the pain in his head, the bruises in his ribs, as he pushed himself up to his knees, gathered up an armful of hay, then returned walking on his knees, one hand out to catch himself if he fell, returned to Gar and dumped the load of hay over the big man's shoulders and chest, though the straw seemed so pitifully inadequate against such a huge expanse of muscle. Gianni leaned on Gar's shoulder as he tried to tuck a few wisps down to hide the mercenary . . .

And the eyes fluttered, then opened in a pained squint.

Gianni froze, staring down, almost afraid to believe

Gar was waking. But the big man levered himself up enough to raise a trembling hand to his head, then cried aloud at the pain of the touch on the raw wound. Gianni caught his hand and said soothingly, "Gently, gently! Let it heal! You'll be whole again, but it will take time."

Gar began to shiver.

"Come," Gianni urged, tugging at his arm. Slowly, Gar pushed himself upright, then sat blinking about him.

"They struck you on the head," Gianni said, "and left you for dead. Me, too. They left us both for dead."

"Us?" The giant turned a look of blank incomprehension on him.

A dreadful suspicion began, but Gianni tried to ignore it as he said, "Us. Me—Gianni Braccalese—and you, Gar."

"Brock?" Gar frowned, fastening on the one word. "Wh . . . what Brock?"

Gianni stared at him for a moment, his thoughts racing. Not wanting to believe what he feared, he said, "Not Brock. Gianni." He pointed at himself, then said, "Gar," and tapped the big man's chest.

"Gar." The giant frowned, turning a forefinger to point at himself, bringing it slowly close enough to touch his own massive pectoral. "Gar." Then he looked up, turning that finger around to reach out to Gianni, tap *his* chest. "Who?"

"Gi—" Gianni caught himself just in time, forcing himself to realize what had happened to Gar—that the blow had addled his wits, perhaps knocked them clear out of his head. Hard on that followed the real-ization that the big man could no longer be trusted to keep a secret, and that Gianni might not want any passing Stilettos to know his own name. He finished the word, but finished it as "Giorgio." It was too late to call Gar "Lenni" again, now—the poor half-wit would have trouble enough remembering his real name, let alone sort out a false one from a true. "And you're Gar."

"Gar." The giant frowned with as much concentra-tion as he could muster against headache. He touched his own chest, then touched Gianni's. "Giorgio."

"Yes." Gianni nodded his head, and the stab of pain made him wish that he hadn't. "Right."

Then he reached out, bracing himself against Gar's shoulder, and struggled to his feet. He gasped at the spasm of agony and would have fallen if a huge hand hadn't clamped around his calf and held him upright. When the dizziness passed, Gianni reached down and hauled at Gar's arm, hoping desperately that the at-tempt wouldn't end with them both sliding back into the mud. "Come. We can't stay here. Soldiers might come."

"Soldiers?" Gar struggled to his feet, though he needed Gianni to brace him, gasping, as he lurched, trying to regain his balance. He stabilized, gulped air against nausea, then turned to Gianni. "Sojers?"

Gianni felt his heart sink, but explained. "Bad men. Hurt Gar." *Counfound it,* he thought, *I sound as though I'm talking to a five-year-old!*

But he was—for the time being, Gar had only as much mind as a child. Pray Heaven it wouldn't last!

"Come." Gianni took his arm, turning away, and tugged. Gar followed, as docile as a five-year-old indeed . . .

No. More docile—like a placid ox, who didn't really care where he went, as long as he was fed.

He would have to find food, Gianni realized—but first, he had to get Gar away from this place. It was exposed, the condotierri might come back to ambush another goods train—or the mountaineers might come for the condotierri's leavings. Gianni led Gar away, but found himself wishing the giant would balk, would object, would say anything to indicate he still had a mind.

He didn't.

CHAPTER 7

It was a long, pain-racked afternoon. Every muscle, every nerve, screamed at him to lie down and never get up, but he couldn't; he was possessed by a morbid fear of that horrible patch of churned mud where he had almost given up on life, and his friend had almost been murdered—the friend who now stumbled along, towed by the arm, shambling like some great, half-wakened, befuddled bear. A feeling of doom seized Gianni, and try as he might, he couldn't shake the conviction that he and Gar would die here, in the mountain wilderness, cold and alone. Yes, there was the chance that they might find help— but only a chance, and a slim one at that.

Finally, trembling with exhaustion, Gianni knew he could go no farther. He looked about, feeling panic bubbling up as he tried to find some vestige of shelter—and saw a huge old tree, far larger than was usual so high up, lying on its side. It had been torn up by some winter's storm, and its roots hung out on every side, forming a natural cave. Gianni steered Gar toward it.

As they came in under the rootlet-laden ceiling, Gianni realized it was a better cave than he had thought, for the bottom of the trunk was hollow. He went in as far as he could, far enough so that the two of them were quite hidden from sight, and sank down onto the wooden surface with a groan of relief—even greater relief than he had thought, for the surface under him was covered with the soft crumbling of rotted wood, a virtual bed of it, fallen from the ceiling and the walls. Gianni threw himself out upon it full length, still cold and wet, but mercifully sheltered. There was even water, for a small pool had formed from drips through a hole in the trunk above. Gianni leaned over and drank greedily, then remembered Gar and turned to offer a drink, but the giant had found a pool of his own, and knelt with his face upturned, catching a steady stream of drops on his tongue. His head almost brushed the top of their hiding place. Satisfied as to his health, Gianni turned back to lie, cold and miserable, waiting for death or sleep to take him, and finding that he didn't really care which came first.

Then he smelled smoke.

Smoke! In a wooden cave? Fear lent him energy; he sat bolt upright, staring at the glow in the gloom, the flicker of a small campfire sitting on a broad, flat stone, its light shining upward on Gar's homely features. The wood must have been very dry, for there was very little smoke, and what there was streamed up and to the side past Gar, to the hole through which the water dripped.

Gianni felt the hair prickle all over his scalp. How had the giant done that? Having the presence of mind to bring a stone inside, rather than trying to light a fire on wood, yes, that was common sense—but how had he lit the fire? He had no flint and steel, nor a live coal carried in a terra-cotta box. "How . . . how did you do that, Gar?"

"Do?" The giant blinked up at him, as though the question held no meaning.

"Light the fire," Gianni explained. "How did you do it?"

"Do." Gar stared down at the flames, brow furrowed, seeming to ponder the question. At last he looked up and gave his head a shake. "Don't know."

It sent the eerie prickling over Gianni's back and scalp again—but he assured himself that whatever Gar was, he was Gianni's friend. At least, Gianni *thought* so.

And if not?

Gianni scolded himself for a fool. Who, but minutes ago, had not cared whether or not Death came to claim him? If it did, what matter whether it came at the hands of the cold, or the hands of a madman? And, of course, it might not come at all.

In the meantime, they had warmth—and Gianni could already feel the heat reaching out to him, drying him, comforting him. The thought of food crossed his mind, and he felt his stomach rebel—the ache in his head was still too painful to permit the thought. But the warmth lulled him; he felt his eyelids growing heavy. Still he fought off sleep, for he noticed that Gar was feeding the fire with their shelter's substance—bits of rotten wood, handfuls of rootlets, pieces of root that he had broken off and piled high. What would happen if that blessed, life-giving fire escaped its rock? What would happen if their shelter itself caught and burned? Oh, Gianni might not care about his own life—but a vision of Gar, poor, near-naked, deprived of his wits, floundering and wailing in the midst of flames, sent the pain racking through Gianni's head again. No, he'd have to stay awake, for he couldn't ask the giant to put the fire out—they needed it too much, and a glance at Gar's profile—empty, but still strong—made Gianni think he wouldn't take kindly to having his fire drenched. No, Gianni would have to wake and watch . . . but the fire was so warm now, so lulling, the rotted wood beneath him so soft . . .

You need not stay awake, said the old man with the floating hair and beard.

Gianni stared. *What are you doing here when I'm awake?*

Fairly asked, the old face said. *Turn it about. If you can see me,* can *you be awake?*

Gianni glanced about him, and saw—nothing. The ancient face floated in a void of darkness. With shock, he realized that he really had fallen asleep. A wave of self-contempt flooded him, that he couldn't even stay conscious for a few minutes after having decided to do so. Then came alarm; what was Gar doing while he slept? What was the *fire* doing?

Do not be alarmed, the face said, almost as though it had read his thoughts. *Sleep easily; the giant is awake and watching, though he has scarcely mind enough to do any more than that. He will keep the fire contained.*

But if he should fall asleep . . .

He can't; the fire has lulled him into a reverie, and he roams among his memories while he watches the tongues of flame. His trance will refresh him as much as sleep would, but his body can still act if there is need.

Gianni relaxed—a little. But the other question came to his mind, now that the most immediate was gone. *Why do I see you now? I'm not seeking death again!*

Are you not? The swirling hair drifted away from one eye, leaving it completely unmasked, and the gaze seemed to pierce through the depths of Gianni's soul.

Gianni shuddered but stared back, resolute. *Well, what if I am? I can't allow it, as long as I have a friend depending on me—on what few wits I have. If that's your concern, you may leave me—or let me leave you.*

That is the least of my concerns, at the moment, the face informed him. *It's not enough that you live through the night—you must live after that, too.*

Gianni frowned. *Why should you care?*

That is my affair, the face said curtly. *Suffice it to say that you must play a part in that affair, a part that will be in the interests of yourself and your city while it benefits me, as a boat leaves eddies in its wake.*

What interests are those? Gianni demanded; he was losing awe of the face.

None of your concern at all! Suddenly, the hair drifted away from the face completely, the eyes flashed, and pain lanced through Gianni's head from temple to temple. Agony held him paralyzed for a moment, a long moment, whole seconds that seemed to stretch into hours.

At last the eyes closed, hair swirled across to veil them, and the pain was gone as suddenly as it had come, leaving Gianni stubbornly staring, but quaking inside. *Hear!* the voice commanded. *A troop of Gypsies comes your way! They'll pass near in the morning! Throw yourselves on their mercy, beseech their aid if you must—but join with them, so that you may live, and come to a safe refuge!*

Some well of stubbornness within Gianni suddenly brimmed over. *And if I don't?*

Then you will die, the face said, simply and severely, *at the hands of the condotierri, or from cold and hunger—but be sure, you will die!* It began to dwindle, hair and beard swirling about it wilder and wilder, hiding it completely as the voice, too, faded, still saying, *Be sure . . . be sure . . .*

Wait! Gianni cried in his dream. *Who are you, to command me so?*

But the face dwindled to a tiny dot, still bidding him, *Be sure . . . be sure . . . beware . . .* and winked out.

Gianni cried out in anger and frustration—and saw a small fire, not a swirl of hair, and the giant half-wit staring at him in alarm. Gianni realized that his own shout had waked him, and tried to cover his gaffe by saying, "It's my watch now. Go to sleep, Gar."

"Sleep?" The giant frowned, puzzled.

"Sleep," Gianni confirmed, and rolled up on his knees. Every ache in his body protested, and his head began to throb again—but he hitched himself close to the fire, took up a stick of kindling from Gar's heap, and said, "Sleep. I'll tend the fire."

Gar gazed at him for a moment, then lay down right where he was and closed his eyes. They flew open again, and he demanded, "Giorgio not sleep?"

Half-wit or not, he still had his exaggerated sense of responsibility. "Giorgio not sleep," Gianni confirmed. He doubted that he could, even if he had wanted to—not after *that* dream.

Gar closed his eyes instantly, reassured. Five seconds later, he exhaled in the quick hiss of sleep followed by the long, slow, measured inhalation, and Gianni knew he slept indeed.

So. He was alone with his thoughts—a nightmare reseeing of that daunting face. But for some reason, Medallia's face seemed to merge with it, overlay it, supersede it. For a moment, Gianni wondered why— but only a moment. Then he gave himself over, with vast relief, to contemplating the memory of that beautiful face, feeling himself relax, unwind, grow gradually calm . . .

But not sleepy. He had been right about that.

* * *

Sure enough, the Gypsy train came into sight in midmorning, just as the face had predicted—and Gianni staggered under the sudden realization that the dream was no mere spiderweb spun from the sandman's dust. Somehow, some genuine man of mystic power had thrust his way into Gianni's slumbers—some man, and perhaps some woman, too . . .

The mere thought made his pulse quicken. Could there really be such a dancer as he had dreamed of, real and alive, and in this world? Could he find her, touch her, kiss her? Would she let him?

He wrenched his attention back to the Gypsies and began to wave and call to them. "Hola! Holay! Over here, good people! Aid us! A rescue!" He hobbled forward, leaning on Gar as much as he pulled him—then suddenly stopped, realizing how they must look to the Gypsies. What could the travelers see, but a couple of filthy, unkempt men, naked save for loincloths—one huge, dark, and glowering, but clearly obeying the other . . .

The Gypsies had stopped, though, and were staring at them doubtfully. Gianni realized he must find some way to reassure them, so he came no closer, but called out again, "Help us, good folk! We're travelers like yourselves, waylaid and brought low by condotierri! Bandits have sacked us and beaten us, so badly that they have addled my companion's wits! He is as simple as a child now! Please, we beg you! Help the child!"

A woman with a bright kerchief leaned forward from the little door at the front of the lead caravan and called something to the men who walked beside.

They looked up at her, glanced at one another, then beckoned Gar and Gianni to come closer. Gianni's heart leaped with relief, and he hobbled toward them as quickly as his bruised legs would take him, towing Gar in his wake.

As they came close, though, the Gypsies backed away, eyeing Gar warily. For the first time, Gianni noticed that they were wearing swords, noticed it because they had their hands on their hilts—long straight swords, with daggers thrust through their sashes. Gianni stopped and said, "Don't worry—he's harmless."

"Unless you tell him to be dangerous," the oldest Gypsy said. His gray mustache drooped below his chin, and gray tufts of eyebrows shaded eyes that glared a challenge at Gianni, who was in no shape to launch into a glib explanation that might both pacify and satisfy. He gathered himself to try, though.

Gar chose just that moment to say, "Tell me about the rabbits, Giorgio."

The Gypsies stared, and Gianni could cheerfully have brained the man. Out of the corner of his mouth, he whispered, "Be still, Gar!" He nearly said "Lenni," but remembered that the newly made half-wit didn't know the false name.

The Gypsies seemed intrigued, though. "Rabbits?" the old one said. "Why does he ask about rabbits?"

A memory of their last pretense must have surfaced in Gar's brain, brought on by similar circumstances—either that, or the giant was really pretending, but Gianni doubted that. "Because when he becomes frightened or anxious, I lull him by promising we shall someday have a little farm of our own, with a garden to give us food, and small furry creatures for him to pet and play with."

The Gypsies exchanged a glance of sympathy that said, as clearly as though they had spoken aloud, *A simpleton.* Then the older one turned back. "It's a good dream, that, and a good way to calm him. Does he become upset often?"

"Not so often at all," Gianni improvised, "but we were set upon by a gang of bandits a mile or so back; they beat us harshly and took all that we had, even our clothes, so he is wary of strangers just now."

"The poor lad," said the woman, still looking out of the little door.

The older Gypsy nodded. "We saw churned and muddy earth, and wondered." He stepped toward Gar, and the giant drew back in alarm. The Gypsy stopped. "We won't hurt you, poor lad. Indeed, we're travelers like yourself, and have learned to be wary of the bandits, too—quite wary. Nay, we won't hurt you, but we will bandage your wounds and give you warm food—soup—and clothing. Will you have them?"

Gar seemed to relax a little. The Gypsy held out a hand, and Gar started, but didn't run. Gianni took a chance and Gar's arm, to tug him forward gently. "Come, my friend. They won't hurt you. They'll help us, give us shelter for a little while."

"Shelter, yes." The Gypsy nodded. "Under the caravan, it's true, but it's better than no roof at all."

"Under?" Gar said hopefully, and took a step forward.

Gianni's heart leaped at the sign of memory. He explained to the older man, "We took shelter with a Gypsy woman in that way, not long ago. He remembers."

"A Gypsy woman?" All the Gypsies suddenly looked up, suddenly alert. "Traveling alone?"

"Alone, yes." Gianni remembered that it had seemed odd at the time. "Her name was Medallia."

The Gypsies exchanged a cryptic glance. "Yes, we know of Medallia. Well, if she gave you shelter and was none the worse for it, we will, too. Come join us."

"I thank you with all my heart!" Gianni came forward, pulling Gar with him. The giant came, still cautious, but moving.

As they neared, Gianni looked at the Gypsies more closely. Their hair was hidden by bright-colored kerchiefs, but their beards were of every color—yellow, brown, black, red, and several different shades in between. Their eyes, too, varied—blue, brown, green, hazel, gray . . . Gianni couldn't help but think how much they looked like everyone else he had ever known, at home in Pirogia. Change their clothes and you could never tell the difference.

Those clothes were gaudy, bright greens and blues and reds and yellows, with here and there broad stripes. Shirts and trousers alike were loose, even voluminous, the shirts open at the throats, showing a broad expanse of chest, the trousers tucked into high boots. They wore sashes of contrasting colors, and men and women alike wore earrings and bracelets.

The merchant in Gianni wondered if they were of real gold.

"Women" because, now that the train had stopped, many more Gypsies had emerged to come clustering around the newcomers. It was the women who took Gar and Gianni in hand, coming forward to say, "Come, poor lads, you must be half dead from cold and hunger."

Gar pulled back at first, frightened, and Gianni had to reassure him. "Nice ladies, Gar! See? Nice!" He shook hands with one young woman, then realized how pretty she was and wished he could do more. Inspiration struck, and he held a hand up to her hair— auburn, with no kerchief to hide it. "May I?"

The woman looked startled and drew back a pace, then gave him a coquettish smile and stepped forward again. Gianni caressed her hair, then turned to Gar and said, "Soft. Warm."

The woman stared, startled, and drew back quickly as Gar raised his hand. "He won't hurt you," Gianni promised.

Warily, the woman stepped forward again, saying, "Just one."

Gar's hand lowered; he stroked her hair, then broke into a beatific smile. "Little, warm! Rabbit!"

The whole troop howled with laughter, the "rabbit" foremost among them as she caught Gar's wrist and held his hand.

"Ho, rabbit!" one of the young men called.

Another cried, "Rabbit, may I pet you, too?"

But one of the girls snapped, "Rabbit indeed! Tell him it's mink or nothing, Esmeralda!"

"Aye!" cried an older woman. "And don't let him dare try to hold you!"

So, laughing and chatting, they took a bemused Gar by the elbows and led him to a nearby brook, where they washed him, dried him, and put Gypsy clothes on his back—though, like Medallia, they had to improvise considerably. Gar was near panic the whole time, white showing all around his eyes, darting frantic looks at Gianni—but between Gianni's soothing and the fact that he was so obviously enjoying the same attentions being heaped upon him, Gar managed to stay on the sane side of hysteria. Finally, with bread and soup in their bellies and the worst of their hurts bandaged, they set off beside the caravans, following the Gypsy men and with Gianni, at least, chatting up at the young women, who leaned out the windows of the caravans to trade banter with him. It was a nuisance to have them calling him "Giorgio" instead of "Gianni," but only a nuisance, and if it helped the poor addle-brained giant to stay calm, Gianni decided, Giorgio he would be, until Gar's wits came back to him.

They did indeed sleep under the wagons that night, but this time, they each had a blanket to shield them from the chill. The day's events swirled through Gianni's brain, the laughter and talk, the banter over the meals and the dancing afterward—he regretted deeply that he had been too bruised and weary to join in, for the girls had indeed looked very pretty as they swayed and whirled. Now, though, the caravans were drawn into a circle, and the whole tribe sat up chat-

ting around the fire—but he and Gar, dog-tired, had
crept away to sleep, the more so because the Gypsies
had begun to talk in their own language, which
Gianni couldn't understand. But the sound of the low
voices, the musicality of the women's, lulled him,
and he felt sleep coming even as he closed his eyes,
felt the warm darkness closing around him once
more, though his weary brain found energy for one
last thought, one last burst of curiosity as to what the
Gypsies were saying to one another . . .

Would you really like to know? asked a voice that
he knew all too well, and a hand reached out of the
darkness with a wand, a long slender stick with a
knob on the end, a knob that reached above his view
and touched lightly, must have touched his half-
dreaming head, for Gianni found himself suddenly
able to understand the Gypsies' words.

"Yes, Medallia," one of them was saying. "Surely
coincidence, that! She wouldn't set a spy upon us,
would she?"

"What need, Giles?" a woman retorted. "She already knows all our plans."

"Well, yes, Patty," Giles said, "but she might be
afraid we'd try to arrest her, or even to—"

"Stuff and nonsense!" Patty said. "AEGIS agents
move against one of our own, just because she dis-
agrees with us? Never!"

"Not just disagreeing," another man said darkly.
"There's always the chance that she might try to un-
dermine our efforts."

"No, surely not, Morgan!" an older woman said,
shocked. "She left because she can no longer be

party to our efforts, as she said—not because she intends to fight them!"

"How can we be sure?" Morgan answered. "More to the point, how can *she* be sure that we wouldn't try to stop her from trying to stop us? No, Rosalie, if I were her, I would definitely try to place a spy among us."

"Well, yes," Rosalie said, "but you always *have* been a little paranoid, Morgan. The point is that Medallia isn't."

Gianni wondered what "paranoid" meant.

"Oh, Medallia has her touches of paranoia, too," said a third woman, "or she wouldn't have seen menace in our plans, when we're only trying to help these poor benighted natives."

Poor benighted natives! Gianni felt a surge of indignation and hoped she wasn't talking about himself and his fellow Piroglans. Besides, who were mere Gypsies to call city people "benighted"?

"The Gypsy disguise works well enough for us," Morgan argued. "It allows us to go anywhere we want on Talipon, and we can always split off an agent to assume the costume of any city we want to infiltrate—let him go in to try to change their ways. Why should it be any less effective for Medallia?"

Disguise! They were not real Gypsies, then? Suddenly Gianni realized that he had never heard of Gypsies until he was eleven—only ten years ago. Were there any *real* Gypsies? Or were they all false?

"Medallia only wondered whether we were right at all, to try to lift this whole planet out of the Dark Ages," Patty said stubbornly. "She could understand the benefits of the Renaissance that's beginning here on Talipon, but she had real doubts about trying to bring these people into the modern world, with high technology and secular ideologies."

Esmeralda nodded. "After all, their ancestors came here to escape all that."

"No," Morgan said, "she thought we were wrong to try to persuade the lords to band together—but how else are we ever going to talk them into stopping this constant internecine warfare?"

"That's a worthy goal, yes," Rosalie countered, "but isn't it going to make even more bloodshed, persuading them to believe they have a common enemy?"

"How else can we ever get them to unite?" Morgan argued. "Oh, I know, Llewellyn—you still think we should try to quell them with a religious revival. But aristocrats see religion and life as being separate things, not all one!"

"You see? We can't even agree among ourselves," Rosalie sighed. "I mean, we can, but we keep developing doubts. Is it any surprise Medallia became fed up with the lot of us and just went her own way?"

"Not 'just,' " Patty said darkly. "She thinks we're wrong to try to make the lords see the merchants as their common enemy."

Cold fear ran through Gianni's entrails. Tell the lords that the merchants were their common enemy, so that they would all band together against the mercantile cities? It would be a bloodbath! No wonder they'd hired the Stilettos to "chastise" Pirogia!

"But she said that if we did that, we'd have to

warn the merchants in time for them to disband and hide," Morgan went on. "Or worse yet, to fight back! I tell you, I see her hand in this Pirogian merchant Braccalese, who came up with the idea of trying to persuade the merchant cities to band together!"

Suddenly, Gianni was very glad they knew him only as "Giorgio." But how had they learned of Gar's idea? And how had they come to think of it as Papa Braccalese's inspiration? Worse—what would they do to Papa to stop him! Suddenly, Gianni was very intent on the rest of the conversation.

CHAPTER 8

A merchant's league would undo everything we're trying to accomplish," Llewellyn agreed. "Worse—with the island divided into two power blocs, it might cause civil war!"

Oh, that was very nice. They didn't want a civil war, they just wanted a massacre of merchants. Didn't the fools realize that would be the fruit of their plans?

Apparently not. "We must not forget our goal," Morgan counseled, "to bring peace to this whole strife-ridden planet, where tribal anarchy prevails in the North and warlord anarchy prevails in the South and East. Talipon with its merchant fleet can spread the idea of centralized government and bring the peace of abundance . . ."

"Or the peace of an empire," Giles said darkly.

"Any peace is better than none," Rosalie reminded him.

"True," said Esmeralda. "Peace will allow justice to prevail and education and the arts to flourish."

"But there will never be any peace if we don't establish it on Talipon first," Morgan reminded her. "Malthus's Law will see to that."

"Yes, the fundamental principle of preindustrial economics," a young man sighed, "that population increases geometrically, but food production only increases arithmetically."

"Yes, Jorge, we all know," a middle-aged woman said sourly. "Four people times four people equals sixteen people, but four bushels of grain *plus* four bushels of grain only equals eight bushels. Without industrial techniques, there will always be more people than there is food, until . . ."

"Plague, starvation, or war kills off so many of them that there's enough food for everyone," Rosalie sighed.

Gianni listened in horror, wanting to cry out, to scream, but held bound by sleep.

"Then there'll be peace and plenty for all—until the people outmultiply the food supply, and the whole cycle begins all over again."

"And again, and again, and again," Morgan said darkly. "So any suffering that comes from our plan will be less than there would be without it."

Easy enough for him to say—it was not his people who would die, not his mother and sister who would be raped and sold into slavery, not his house and goods that burned!

"Can backward people like the feudal serfs in the western continent ever accept modern techniques?" Giles wondered.

"They can if they're taught," Rosalie said sternly, "and if they're taught it as a way of getting rich— which doesn't take much, for a serf."

"Yes," Esmeralda said slowly, "and that's the kind of teaching that merchants can do so well. The synergy of the peasant mentality and mercantile greed can produce amazing results."

"So can the groupthink of the tribes in the North," said Giles. "If they all talk long enough and loudly enough at a powwow, they'll forget that greed is wrong, and start farming instead of hunting."

"Then we can sneak in nuclear-powered matter converters, limited so that they won't produce precious metals, until each lord has one," Morgan said.

Even in his half-sleep, Gianni's scalp prickled at the unfamiliar words. Were these false Gypsies really sorcerers?

Morgan's next words confirmed it. "When each lord has a machine that will produce any trade goods that he wants for free, he'll have a distinct advantage over the merchants, and not one single aristocrat will be able to resist the temptation of going into trade."

Resist the temptation! They would ruin the merchants! Heaven knew the noblemen were already taking enough of the merchants' money in the cities in which aristocrats still ruled. The taxes and official monopolies were already punishing, and the lords insisted that the merchants rent their stevedores and drivers from the aristocrats at extortionate rates. If, on top of all that, they began to undersell the merchants with goods they could produce from nothing, they'd annihilate the traders completely! No, they wouldn't do it by underselling, Gianni realized—if the lords became merchants, they wouldn't let anyone compete with them. Trading would be made illegal, for any but the aristocrats' hirelings! They would have monopolies that couldn't be broken!

"But the matter converters really do have to be limited," Esmeralda said anxiously. "If the lords could produce gold and silver just by throwing lumps of lead and stone into a box, then pushing a button . . ."

"Of course not," Morgan said impatiently. "Why do you remind us about this every time we discuss it, Essie? If they could make gold and silver whenever they wanted to, they wouldn't have any reason to go into trade!"

Gold from lead! They *were* sorcerers! Or, at the least, alchemists . . .

"Greed will make the contes and the doges forget their petty feuds and band together to compete with the merchants," Morgan said, with satisfaction. "They only need to see that they actually have a chance of taking over the merchants' trade and getting all the money the merchants are getting now. They won't be able to, of course—the merchants are too skilled, too deep entrenched, and the aristocrats will be far behind them in learning mercantile theory."

"But they *will* learn," Rosalie pointed out. "We really can turn the lords into merchants."

Could they really be so naive? Such was not the lords' way—once banded together, they would send their armies to wipe out the merchants completely, to send the buildings of Pirogia crashing down into the lagoon from which they had risen! Oh, they would leave a few merchants, bound by taxes and loans and dependence on noble patrons, to do the trading for them, and would take all of the profits to themselves—or nineteen parts out of twenty, at least. No, whoever these people were, their plan was disastrous, at least for the merchants—and for the education and culture of which they were so fond, for a great deal of that had come from the patronage of merchants, not aristocrats. Oh yes, the artists would do well under the contes—as long as they only wished to paint portraits of noble faces, and scenes of martial valor. The poets would do well, as long as they wanted to write heroic romances and heap praise on their local conte and contessa, as Ariosto had praised Lucrezia Borgia in his *Orlando Furioso*. Yes, the artists and poets would do well, if they were tame—except that there weren't enough noblemen to support more than a handful of artists. But there were merchants enough to support scores!

"No, our plans must be nurtured," Morgan said complacently.

"Yes," Giles agreed, "and if Medallia really tries to wreck them, we'll have to find a way to stop her."

Even in his dream, Gianni's spirit clamored for him to wrap his fingers around Giles's throat. Harm that beautiful, merciful woman? Never!

The "Gypsies" seemed to think so, too. There was

a horrified silence; then Esmeralda said, "You aren't talking about killing her, surely!"

"No, of course not," Giles said quickly—too quickly. "I only mean to catch her somehow, and keep her from leaving again."

"I don't like the sound of that," Rosalie said darkly.

Morgan said, "Shame on you, for even *thinking* about depriving another sentient being of her freedom!"

"No, no, of course not," Giles said quickly. "But there must be *some* way to make sure she can't do us any harm."

They were silent for a minute or so; then Esmeralda said, "Warn all the people against a renegade Gypsy woman?"

"Oh, no!" Rosalie said. "They might turn into a mob, accuse her of witchcraft or sorcery, and burn her at the stake!"

"Surely these people aren't that barbaric," Esmeralda protested.

Gianni shriveled inside. He knew full well that his people could be very barbaric indeed, when it came to believing in magic. But how could these people be so concerned about charges of witchcraft, when they themselves were sorcerers?

"She was so kind and so gentle," Esmeralda said plaintively. "I can't believe Medallia would actually try to fight us!"

"Not fight, no," Rosalie agreed, but she sounded doubtful. "Perhaps decoying her into some outlying region, where there's a good deal of disease that needs curing . . ."

"She'd see through that," Esmeralda said. "We could send Dell through the villages dressed as a minstrel, to sing about the plight of orphans. In a month, he'd have everyone talking about orphans, and Medallia might set up an orphanage . . ."

"No," Giles said. "Medallia is smart, very smart. She'd see through either of those stratagems. We have to either pen her up, which we won't do, or try to move a step faster and maneuver more cleverly than she."

Morgan's tone indicated agreement. "That shouldn't be hard—we're thirty to her one!"

"We'll just have to play the game fairly, then," Rosalie sighed.

Game? Was that all this was to them, some sort of huge game? But to Gianni and his people, it was life—or death!

"So much for Medallia," said Rosalie, "but what're we going to do with our two waifs and strays?"

Gianni turned cold inside again.

"What *can* we do?" Morgan sighed. "We can't just dump them to starve, not so badly wounded, and with one of them still witless from concussion. That must have been a *very* bad blow to the head!"

Esmeralda shuddered. "Be glad you didn't have a close look at the bruise. The bone wasn't broken, though—at least, not that I could see without an X ray."

"There might be a subdural hematoma," Rosalie

said, frowning. "We'll have to keep a close eye on him!"

"We'll have to take them with us, until we can find some place safe to leave them," Morgan decided. "Prince Raginaldi's castle is only two days away, and we were thinking of stopping there anyway."

"I suppose we'll have to drop them there, then," Rosalie sighed, "though I hate leaving someone in that condition to medieval medicine."

"Not quite as medieval as it might be," Morgan reminded her. "Their doctors still have some advanced techniques and even ways of making antibiotics, that have come down from the original settlers by word of mouth."

But Gianni missed the last sentence or two, numb with shock. Leave Gar and him to the Raginaldi, the aristocrats who were employing the Stilettos? They might not know who *he* was, but the Stilettos would recognize Gar in an instant, and the two of them would be dead in a second—assuming the Raginaldi didn't maim them and send them back to the Pirogia as a warning. No, somehow, as soon as they could, he and Gar would have to escape!

Hard on that thought came another: no time like the present. The Gypsies wouldn't expect them to wander off in the night, so soon after being rescued—but they couldn't be suspicious, either; they'd just take Gar and Gianni for ungracious and ungrateful wretches or, at worst, for a couple of vagabonds who had played a ruse upon them.

Gianni couldn't believe the naivete of these people—especially since they seemed to consider themselves so much wiser than the folk of Talipon, wise enough to meddle in their affairs and to dare to try to chart their destinies! Didn't they know that no lord would willingly have anything to do with trade? Stealing a merchant's money under the name of confiscation or fines for violating a chartered monopoly, yes—but earning the silver themselves? No! Surely they must see that if the lords could ever stop fighting, they would band together to enslave the merchants!

Very true, the face said. White hair swirled about it as though it were the center of a whirlpool.

Gianni realized, with a shock, that he was no longer hearing the Gypsies, and must have fallen completely asleep. *If you know that, you must know how I can keep myself and Gar alive until we come safely back to Pirogia!* he said. *Come to that, you can tell us how to defend Pirogia from the noblemen, and from these soft-hearted bungling meddlers!*

The giant has done that already, the face answered. *He has told your Council they must band together with all the other merchant cities.*

Despair struck. *I shall never convince them of that!*

Take heart, the face advised. *You shall find a way—and perhaps that way will stem from the other course of action you may take.*

Hope sprouted again. *What course is that?*

Protect Medallia, the face said. *Protect her and help her in all that she does, and she may do your persuading for you. In any event, listen to her counsel, for she knows as much as these fake Gypsies, and has clearer sight, with far better judgment.*

This time, Gianni remembered *before* the face started to disappear. *Who are you?*

Call me the Wizard, the face answered, *the Wizard in your mind.* He began to shrink, to recede. *It is time to escape, you know. The Gypsies will not chase you—indeed, they will be relieved to have the burden off their hands—but you must escape now.*

How? In his dream, Gianni called it out, for the face had receded till it was little more than a white oval in the dark.

Walk away, the Wizard answered simply, his voice thin and distant. *Walk away.*

Gianni sat up so hard that he would have cracked his head on the bottom of the caravan if it had been a few inches lower—and that would have been bad, for it would have waked the family who slept inside. He tried to slow his breathing as he looked about him wildly. The campfire was only a faint glow with no one around it. The young men were rolled up in their blankets under the wagons; here and there, someone snored. The older men and their wives were inside the caravans—now that he thought of it, Gianni hadn't seen any children. Before, he had thought they were all inside; now, it made perfect sense that there were no children, if these pretend Gypsies were really wandering troublemakers in disguise. Briefly, he wondered who they were and where they had come from, but before he could consider the matter, a young Gypsy with a sword strolled between him and the glow of the embers, and the necessities of the moment forced the questions out of his mind. A sentry! They had posted a sentry, and probably two, so that if one were attacked, the other might still give the alarm. At least, that was what old Antonio had taught Gianni.

Then he and Gar would have to attack both at once. He rolled over to his knees and crawled over to the darker shape that was Gar. "Gar! Wake up!" he hissed, shaking him by a shoulder—and nearly went rolling again, for the giant flailed out with the arm Gianni was shaking as he came awake with a snort and sat bolt upright. Gianni just barely managed to push his shoulder hard at the last moment, keeping him from banging *his* head on the caravan bottom. Gar brushed the hand away with a growl, and for a second, his eyes glowed with mayhem as he glared up at Gianni, huge hand balled for a blow that must surely have killed anyone it touched . . .

But the eyes calmed as they widened with recognition, and the big man hissed, "Giorgio!"

Well, that settled it—he wasn't shamming. Not if he could remember Gianni's false name when he was freshly waked, and alarmed at that. Gianni pressed a finger over his lips, hissing, "Shhhh!"

"Shhhh." Gar mimicked both the gesture and the tone, then whispered, "Why?"

"Because we have to leave here without the Gypsies knowing."

Gar didn't ask why; he slowly nodded.

"They've posted sentries," Gianni whispered. "We have to sneak up on them, one of us to each of them, and overpower them silently."

"Why?" Gar asked again.

Gianni schooled himself to patience, remembering

that the big man had lost his wits. "Because if we don't, they'll see us going and raise the alarm."

Gar shook his head. "Why? They fall asleep soon."

"Well, perhaps," Gianni allowed, "but only when two others like them take their places."

"No, no." Gar shook his head, then turned to peer out into the darkness. Frowning, Gianni turned to see what he was looking at—and saw a sentry amble up to the fire, yawning, then stand near it, looking about him for a minute or two before he sat down, folding his legs, and staring at the fire. He yawned again as the other sentry came up, also yawning. They seemed not to see each other as the first sentry lay down, pillowing his head on his arm, and began to snore. The second sentry lay down on the other side of the fire. In a minute, he was snoring too.

Gar looked up at Gianni. "Asleep."

"Yes." Gianni realized he was staring, his mouth gaping open. He closed it and said, "Yes, they are." He felt the eldritch prickling up over his back and neck and scalp again. What kind of half-wit was he leading, anyway?

Then he remembered the Wizard in his mind. No doubt he was in Gar's mind, too—but there being less thought in the giant's mind than usual, the Wizard could take up residence there with no trouble. Gianni resolved to be very careful around Gar in the future.

He gave himself a shake and said, "Well, then! Nothing to keep up from leaving if we want to, is there?"

"No," Gar said. He seemed doubtful, but followed

Gianni out from under the wagon, imitated him in pulling on his boots, and trailed after him, off into the darkness.

They trudged a good distance that night, back down the road to hide their tracks among the wagon ruts, then off through the woods, up one slope and down another until they found another trackway. They went south on that trail—or the direction Gianni hoped was south—with some idea of returning to Pirogia again, until Gianni's legs gave out. Gar didn't seem to be in much better shape, but he managed to scoop Gianni up and carry him, protesting, to the shelter of a rocky corner, where they were at least shielded from the wind. There they slept till morning, and mercifully, Gianni saw neither the Wizard's face nor the dancing woman.

They were shocked from sleep by the sound of horse hooves and loud calling. Gianni bolted upright. His bruises immediately protested, but he ignored them. He looked around the huge rock that sheltered them, his heart hammering, and saw a score of soldiers, but not mercenaries—they wore livery, coats of red and yellow, and in their center rode a man in purple velvet doublet and black hose with a coronet about his brow. He was arguing loudly with a grizzle-bearded man in a robe and soft circular hat, with a heavy golden chain about his neck that supported a medallion on his breast. To either side of them strode another dozen soldiers, swatting at the brush with sticks and peering behind every log and into every nook and cranny in the rock faces that flanked the trail.

"Bad?" Gar asked behind him.

Gianni jumped a mile inside, but managed to hold himself down by gripping the rock. "Probably bad—a prince and his chancellor, by the look of them. Best we hide." He turned away, to see Gar already huddling beneath the curve of the boulder, against the side of the cliff. Gianni joined him, but listened as sharply as he could.

"But Highness, they could not have come so far in so short a time!" the chancellor protested. "Even if they had, what harm could they do, two men afoot, and unarmed?"

"You did not think them so harmless when you roused me from my pavilion and set us to hunting them," the prince answered sourly. "If you are right, and they *are* merchants in disguise, we must capture them to punish them, at least."

"They most probably are such merchant spies," the chancellor admitted. "The Gypsies said they had taken in two vagabonds who had asked their help, then fled in the night. I knew at once they were most likely from that group of merchants the Stilettos ambushed two days ago."

Gianni almost erupted in outrage at the false Gypsies right then. The cowards, to sic the aristocrats on them, instead of doing their own dirty work! The hypocrites!

"Yes, and when they brought back their captives, and we found their master's mark on the trade-good bags and tortured the drivers to make them tell who their employer was, what did they say? Gianni Braccalese! The son of that rabble-rousing merchant who is trying to forge an alliance of merchant cities against us!"

Gianni stiffened. Were they hunting *him*?

"Yes, and the Stiletto captain assured us they had left him for dead," the chancellor said heavily, "but what did they find when they went back for the body? Gone! A dead body stood up and walked away! Can there be any doubt that young Braccalese is still alive? Any doubt that he and his bodyguard were the two men who sought refuge with the Gypsies?"

"No doubt at all," the chancellor sighed, "considering that both the Gypsies and the Stilettos described his companion as a giant. But are they really any threat, these two?"

Gianni heard the thwacking and swishing of the searchers growing closer and huddled in on himself, wishing the Gypsies had given him a weapon, even a small dagger. He groped about, knowing the soldiers were bound to find him. His hand closed on a large rock.

"The father is a threat," the prince answered, "and if we hold his son as hostage, he may stop trying to form his league against us."

The chancellor sighed. "Highness Raginaldi, I do not understand why you do not counter his threatened merchants' league with an alliance of aristocrats! Even those Gypsies said as much."

They would, Gianni thought darkly. When this was

done, he would have a score to settle with those false Gypsies.

"I cannot bear the thought of such an alliance," the prince snapped. "The Raginaldi ally with the Vecchio, not to mention the lesser houses? It goes too much against the grain to make common cause with old enemies—but I could almost begin to believe that the merchants may be a bigger threat than any of my fellow aristocrats."

His words chilled Gianni's blood—especially the fact that he had used the word "fellow," not "rival" or "enemy."

But there was no time to brood about that—the thwacking sticks of the searchers were coming closer and closer; Gianni could hear the tread of their boots crunching the underbrush now! He lifted the rock, tensing himself to spring . . .

A shadow fell across him, darkening the niche where they hid—the shadow of a man in helmet and breastplate: a soldier!

CHAPTER 9

Armor rattled, the stick thwacked, and the heavy boots paused at a shout from the other side of the road. "What?" The soldier sounded as though he were right in Gianni's lap—as he would be, in a minute. "What was that?"

"Only a hare," the other soldier's voice came, disgusted. "But for a moment, I hoped."

Hoped! Why? He was as lowborn as Gianni, they were both commoners ... Or *was* that why ... ?

The tramp of boots began again—incredibly, moving away!

"Make sure you search every cranny," a deeper voice commanded.

"I have, Sergeant," the trooper said, his voice growing distant. "No crannies over here."

Gianni sat frozen, unable to believe his ears, unable to believe his luck. Had the man really not noticed? Impossible!

The hare. It had to have been the hare. Saved by a rabbit!

But that was only one soldier, and the first in line on their side of the road. Gianni tightened his grip on his rock once more, gathering himself, tensing to fight all over again. One of them *had* to grow curious about this nook between boulder and wall . . .

But they didn't. One by one they passed by, calling to one another and hurling joking insults, with the sergeant barking them back to work whenever they laughed too loudly. Maybe it was because they didn't want to find the fugitives, maybe it was because they didn't care—or maybe it was some other, eldritch reason; but they passed. One by one, they passed by, the horses' hooves passed by, and the voices of the chancellor and his prince receded with them, off into the distance, gone.

Still Gianni crouched, hand on his rock (though no longer clenched), not quite believing they had escaped.

Finally Gar stirred, crept out on hands and knees, peered around the boulder, then finally stood, staring after the soldiers, his face blank, eyes wide.

"Are they gone?" Gianni began to uncurl.

"Gone." Gar nodded firmly. "All. Gone."

Slowly, Gianni stood to look. Incredibly, it was true—the soldiers had passed them by, had disappeared into the trees that hid the road, and the dust of their passage was settling.

"Go now?" Gar looked down at him.

"Uh—yes!" Gianni snapped back to the here and now. They must not lose this chance! "But not down the road, Gar. Up over the ridge—and the next ridge, and the next, until we stand a fair chance of coming nowhere near Prince Raginaldi or his men!"

They found another road, but it went east and west. Still, the road from Pirogia had led them west into the mountains as well as north, so Gianni led Gar east. At the worst, he supposed, he could follow this road to the seashore, where they could build a raft and float home if they had to.

When darkness came, Gar plucked at Gianni's sleeve, pointing toward the wooded slope to their right, then set off exploring. Gianni followed him, frowning, until Gar pointed to a fallen tree—an evergreen that must have fallen quite recently, for very few of its needles were brown. Gianni saw the point immediately: the trunk had broken below the line of boughs, but not broken completely—it angled downward, giving room enough to sit upright beneath it. He set to work with Gar, breaking off enough of the branches beneath to make room for them to stretch out full-length, and they had a tent. The broken branches would even serve as mattresses.

Then Gar surprised him further by coming up with a handful of roots and some greens, so they didn't go to bed hungry after all—well, still hungry, but not starving. As they ate, a thought sprang in Gianni's mind, and he looked up at Gar, weighing the risk of saying it. Curiosity won out, and he asked, very carefully, "Have your wits begun to return?"

"Wits?" Gar looked up in surprise, then frowned, thinking the question over. Finally he judged, "Yes."

A wave of relief swept through Gianni, but caution came hard behind it. How quickly would *all* those wits return?

And, of course, there was still the possibility that Gar was pretending.

The next morning, they set off down the road again, with Gar stopping every now and then to strip berries from a bush and share them with Gianni, who concluded that the giant had been trained in woodlore from his childhood, and old knowledge surfaced with hunger at the sight of the berries without his actually having to think about it. For himself, city-born and city-bred, Gianni would have been as apt to pick poisonous berries as nourishing ones.

They came out of the pass onto sloping ground, with an entire valley spread out before them. Gianni halted in amazement—he hadn't paid much attention to the view coming up, since his back had been toward it, and he had been too concerned about his drivers and mules and cargo. Now, though, with no goods to protect, he found himself facing the vista, and even though he was cold and stiff, the sight took his breath away.

"Beautiful, yes?" Gar rumbled beside him.

"Yes," Gianni agreed, then looked up sharply. "How much *do* you remember now?"

"More." Gar pressed his hand to his head. "Remember home, remember coming to Talipon, meeting you." He shook himself. "I must make an effort; I *can* talk properly again, if I work at it."

"Do you remember our meeting with the Gypsies?"

"No, but we must have, mustn't we?" Gar looked down at his gaudy clothing. "I . . . *do* remember soldiers looking for us."

Gianni nodded. "The Gypsies told them about us."

"Then we would do better to go naked than in the clothes they gave us." Gar began to pull his shirt out, but Gianni stopped him.

"The mountain air is cold. We can say we stole the clothing while the Gypsies slept."

Gar paused, staring at him. "Steal from *Gypsies*? And you thought *I* was the one with addled wits!"

Suspicion rose. "Were you shamming, then?"

"Pretending?" Gar gazed off over the valley. "Yes and no. I was tremendously confused when I waked and found myself with you in a mire, and I couldn't remember anything—neither my past, nor my name, nor how I came to be there. You seemed to be a friend, though, so I followed you. The rest?" He shook his head. "It comes and goes. I remember sleeping under a wagon, I remember the soldiers going by, I remember everything since I waked this morning." He shrugged. "I'm sure the gaps will fill themselves in, with time. Even just talking with you now, I've begun to recapture the habit of proper speaking."

"Praise Heaven your wits were addled no worse than that," Gianni said with heartfelt relief—but the suspicion remained: Gar could be lying. He tried to dismiss the thought as unworthy, but it wouldn't stay banished.

Gar pointed downslope. "There's the fork in the road, where you told me we could go northeast to the coast or northwest to Navorrica. It would seem that, like Shroedinger's cat, we have gone both ways."

"Shreddinger?" Gianni looked up, frowning. "Who was he?"

"Why, the man who owned the cat." Gar flashed him a grin. "It never knew where it was going to be until it was there, because it was in both places at once until the moment came when it had to decide— somewhat like myself these last few days. Come, let's retrace our steps southward from the fork, and it may be that both parts of me shall pull together again."

He set off down the slope, and Gianni followed, not sure that he hadn't preferred the big man *without* his wits.

As they came to the fork, though, they saw two other people coming down the other road. Both pairs stopped and eyed each other warily. "Good morning," Gar said at last. "Shall we share the road?"

"I have never seen Gypsies without their tribe and caravan," one stranger answered.

"Oh, we aren't Gypsies," Gianni explained. "We only stole some clothing from them."

The man stared. "Stole clothing from *Gypsies*? I thought it was supposed to be the other way around!"

"The Gypsies have always been blamed for a great many thefts they didn't really commit," Gar explained. "It was very easy to put the loss on them, for they were gone down the road, where they could neither deny it nor admit it. In any case, they don't seem to guard their laundry lines any better than anyone else." He offered a hand. "I am Gar."

The other man took it, carefully. "I am Claudio." He nodded to his partner. "He is Benvolio."

"A pleasure," Gar said, and glanced at Gianni. The young man smiled, recognizing a signal, and stepped forward with his hand open. "I am Gianni. We lost our clothes to the Stilettos when we had the bad luck to run into them."

"You, too?" Benvolio stared as he took Gianni's hand. "I thought *we* were the only ones with such bad luck."

"Oh, really!" Gianni looked him up and down. "You fared better than we, at least—they left you your clothes."

"Yes, they did that." Benvolio let go of his hand with a grimace. "Took our cart and donkey and all our goods, yes, but they did leave us our clothes."

"They took our whole goods train, and our drivers to sell to the galleys," Gianni said, his face grim. "They would have taken us, too, if they hadn't thought we were dead."

Claudio nodded, commiserating. "I'm sure we would be slogging toward Venoga and an oar this minute, if we hadn't run as soon as we heard them coming, and if the woods hadn't been so thick that they couldn't ride in to follow us. It seems Stilettos would rather lose their prey than chase it afoot."

"Wise of them," Gar said sourly. "For all they knew, you might have had a small army of mountaineers waiting to fall on them."

Claudio looked up in surprise. "A good thought! Perhaps we should have."

"Only if we had *been* mountaineers," Benvolio said, with a sardonic smile. "Since we are not, they would have taken our cart and donkey before the Stilettos had their chance."

"True, true." Gar nodded. "More true, that they might not be averse to taking us to sell to the Stilettos if they find us. Perhaps we should travel together?"

Claudio and Benvolio took one look at Gar's great size and agreed quickly.

They had only been on the road another hour before they met two more wayfarers—but one of these was leaning on the other and limping badly, so badly that now and again he would hop, his face twisted with pain. Both wore rags, and the one with two good legs was sallow and pinched with hunger. He looked up at Gianni and his party with haunted eyes and seemed about to bolt; probably all that prevented him was his lame friend.

"Good day," Gianni cried, holding up an open hand. "We are poor travelers who have lost all our goods to the Stilettos, but moved too fast to be taken for their slave parties. Who are you?"

"A thief and a beggar," the lame man snapped, "just released from the prison of Prince Raginaldi."

"Released?" Gianni stared. "Fortune favors you, and all the saints too! I thought that once a man vanished into that dark and noisome pit, he vanished forever!"

"So did we." The thief still looked dazed, unable

to understand his good fortune. "But the jailers cast us out, cursing us and spurning us, saying we would have to find our own bread now, for the prince needed his dungeon for more important prisoners than we."

"More important?" Alarms sounded all through Gianni. "What manner of prisoners?"

"They didn't say," said the thief, "only that there would be a great many of them."

"Has he turned you all out, then?" Gar asked.

"Almost all," said the beggar. "There were a murderer or two he kept, but the rest of us are set free to wander. Some went faster than us."

"Almost all went faster than we did," the thief said in a sardonic tone.

The beggar looked up with a frown. "If you feel that I hold you back, Estragon . . ."

"Hold me *back*?" the thief snorted. "You hold me *up*! Can you not see how heavily I lean on you, Vladimir? I'm a thief, not a fighter—and you and I were always last to the bowls of leavings the warders shoved into our pen!"

Gianni had a brief nightmare vision of a dozen men clamoring and fighting over a bowl of garbage. "You must rest," he said, "and eat, as soon as we can find food."

"Food?" The thief looked up, grinning without mirth. "Find it if you can! This night and day since we were set free, we have had nothing but a few handfuls of berries that we found by the wayside, shriveled and bitter, and some stalks of wild grain."

"Can we find them nothing better than that?"

Gianni asked Gar. The big man frowned, but didn't answer. Instead, he picked up a few pebbles and went loping off into the fields beside the road. He was back ten minutes later with a brace of hares. Gianni decided he liked Gar better in his right mind.

While they ate, though, two even more bedraggled specimens came hobbling up to them—a man in worn and grimy motley, who leaned upon the shoulder of another, who wore a black, wide-sleeved gown that was stiff with dirt, almost as stiff as the mortarboard he wore upon his head. Gianni could see at a glance that the sleeves held pockets for ink and paper, and knew the man for a scholar, while his companion was a jester.

"Ho, Vladimir!" the jester said in a hollow voice. "Have you found food, then?"

"Aye, because we have found charitable companions," the beggar answered. He turned to Gianni. "Would you take it amiss if we shared with Vincenzio and Feste?"

"Not at all," Gianni said.

Gar seconded, "If we had known they would join us, I would have brought down more rabbits."

"Oh, do not split hares over us." The jester sat down stiffly, folding his legs beneath him, and raised an open hand in greeting. "I am Feste."

"I am . . . Giorgio." Some innate caution kept Gianni to using his alias. "This is Gar."

The giant inclined his head.

"I am Vincenzio." The scholar, too, held up an open hand.

"Should we not call you 'Doctor'?" Gar asked.

"Oh, no," Vincenzio said, with a rueful laugh. "I am only a poor Bachelor of Arts, not even done with my studies to become a Master. I ran out of money, and needed to wander from town to town, hiring out my knowledge to any who had need of it. The prince's men assumed I was rogue and a thief, and clapped me in irons."

Understandably, Gianni thought. He had heard of many wandering scholars who *were* just such thieves and rogues as Vincenzio mentioned—and he would not have wagered on the man's honesty himself. "No greater cause than that?"

"Well," said Vincenzio, "it might have been the conversation I was having with the village elders, about the ancient Athenians and their notions that all human beings have the seeds of greatness within them, and deserve to be treated with respect—even to have some control over their destinies . . ."

"Which means their government," Gar said, with a sardonic smile. "Yes, I can see why the soldiers clapped you in irons. They gagged you, too, didn't they?"

"And a most foul and noisome cloth it was." Vincenzio made a face. "Indeed, I had thought we would be thrown right back into that dungeon when those Stilettos stopped us half an hour ago."

"Stilettos?" Gianni looked up sharply. "What did they do to you?"

"Only searched us, as though they thought we might have gold hidden in our garments for the steal-ing," Feste said with disgust.

"Did they beat you?" The beggar looked up with wide, frightened eyes.

"No, they seemed too worried for that," said Vincenzio. "They sent us packing, and we blessed our good fortune and fled, thanking all the saints." He frowned at the others. "I'm surprised you didn't run afoul of them, too—they were set up to block the road so that they might search every traveler who came by."

"We saw them from a curve of the road above," Vladimir confessed, "and thought it wiser to risk a slide down the slope than an encounter with mercenaries."

"Nearly broke my ankle," Estragon grumbled, rubbing that joint. "It seems I chose wrongly, as usual."

"Did they say what they were searching for?" Gar asked.

"Nary a word," Feste said, "and we didn't stay to ask."

"No, I'm sure you didn't," Gianni said.

"They were even too worried to beat you for their amusement?" the thief asked, wide-eyed.

"Even that," Vincenzio assured him. "Did I not tell you we blessed all the saints?"

"Let us say a blessing again." Gar took the spit off the fire. "We're about to dine. Does anyone have a knife?"

No one did, so they had to wait for the meat to cool before Gar could break it to portion it out.

The next day, they kept a wary eye on the road ahead, and at the slightest sign of soldiers, they took to the underbrush. In that fashion, they crept warily by two separate roadblocks, closely enough to hear the soldiers muttering and griping about such senseless duty—but there was an undertone of nervousness to their grumbles, almost of apprehension. After the second, they came back onto the road and fell in with a trio of peasants in tunics as filthy as anything the other recent prisoners wore. They looked up, startled, at Gianni's hail, saw Gar's size, and leaped aside—then stared.

"Peace, peace!" Gianni cried. "We are only poor travelers, like yourselves."

"Very like yourselves," said the oldest peasant. "Vincenzio! Feste! Why have you moved so slowly? I can understand why Vladimir and Estragon would, since the one is lame and the other so deeply weakened—but why you?"

"We move more slowly, Giuseppi, because we are wary of the Stilettos," Vincenzio answered.

"Wisely said," Giuseppi said ruefully. "With each set of them, we thought surely this must be the last. Three of them have searched us now, searched so thoroughly that we had thought they were going to turn us inside out. Praise Heaven they let us go our way without beating us!"

"They seemed to be worried," Vincenzio agreed. "By your leave, Giuseppi, I'll continue to go slowly, and step off the road if I see any sign of them."

"I think we'll join you," Giuseppi said. "Who are these?"

"Giorgio and Gar," Vincenzio said, by way of introduction. Both raised palms in greeting.

"We won't starve, so long as they're with us," Estragon explained, "and there's a hare to be found in the woods about."

"A hare would be most welcome indeed!" Giuseppi said fervently, and Gar was off on another hunting expedition. This time he brought back partridges and plover eggs, and by the time they were done eating, they were all on friendly terms.

In midafternoon, they saw a lone man striding wearily ahead. Gar called to him, his tone friendly, but the man looked up, stared, then dashed madly into the wood. Gar frowned and waved their little troop to a halt. "Come out, friend!" he called. "We mean you no harm, no matter how rough we look! But there are condotierri on the road, and we will fare more safely together than alone!"

"How truly you speak!" came the quavering voice; then the traveler appeared again, holding a staff at the ready. "What assurance do I have that you are not yourselves bandits?"

He had good reason to fear them, Gianni saw, for by his clothing, the man was a merchant, and a prosperous one at that.

"Only the assurance that we too fear the Stilettos, for most of us have been searched by them, and all of us have suffered at their hands," Gar answered. He held up an open palm. "I am Gar."

"I am Rubio—and Heaven has preserved me from a beating, at least." The man kept his staff up. "But as to searching, they have surely done that, aye, and kept what they found, too!"

"Found?" Gar was tense as a hunting dog. "What did they steal?"

"My jewels! All my jewels!" The man held out his robe, that they might see where the hems had been slashed. "All the wealth that I was taking from Venoga to Pirogia, that I might begin business anew away from the conte and his kin! But they couldn't suffer to let me go, no, but robbed me blind on the highroad!"

"Poor fellow!" Gianni felt instant commiseration. "Why didn't you take at least one guard?"

"Where could I find one who could be trusted?"

"Here." Gianni gestured toward Gar. "Of course, you hadn't had the good fortune to meet him."

The merchant looked up with a frown. "Is this true? Are you a guard who can be trusted?"

"I am." Gar pressed a hand to his head. "At least . . . so long as my wits stay with me . . ."

The other travelers drew back in alarm, but the merchant said, "What ails you?"

"Too many blows to the head," Gar explained. "They come and go . . . my wits . . ."

Gianni looked up at him anxiously, and the other men drew back farther—but Gar opened his eyes again and blinked about at them, then forced a smile. Gianni heaved a sigh of relief, then turned to the merchant. "So the Stilettos are only about their old game of thieving—but why are they in so much of a hurry?"

Whistling sounded ahead.

They all looked up in surprise, to hear someone sounding so cheerful in a country beset by bandits. "I confess," said Gar, "to a certain curiosity."

"I do, too." Gianni quickened the pace. "Who can

this be, who is so carefree when the times move on to war or worse?" He and Gar paced ahead of the group, around a turn in the road, and saw a tradesman, in smock and cross-gartered leggings, strolling down the road with his head thrown back and his thumbs thrust under the straps of his pack, whistling. From the tools that stuck out of that knapsack, it was clear that he was a craftsman of some sort.

"Good day to you, journeyman!" Gianni called as they came near.

The tradesman looked up, surprised, then grinned and raised an open hand. "Good day to *you*, traveler—and to . . ." His eyes widened at the sight of Gar. "My heavens! There is a lot of you, isn't there?"

"Not so much as there has been," Gar said, smiling. "I haven't been eating well."

"Who has?" the tradesman rejoined. "If I have bread and cheese, I count myself fortunate. I am Bernardino, a poor wandering carpenter and glazier."

"A glazier!" Gianni was impressed. "That's a rare trade indeed. I am Gia—Giorgio, and this is Gar. We are travelers who have fallen afoul of the Stilettos. We had to steal new clothes."

"Took the shirts off your backs, did they?" Bernardino chuckled. "Well, at least they left you your boots! Me, I had the forethought to be paid in food, and they didn't think it worth stealing when they searched me."

"There's some wonder in that alone," Gar said, "though it speaks well for your prudence. Tell me, how do you find work as a glazier?"

"Rarely, which is why I'm also a carpenter—but when I do, it pays well."

"A whole cheese, no doubt," Gar said, grinning.

"Aye, and several loaves." Bernardino beckoned him closer and whispered, "And several silver pennies, hidden where even the Stilettos shall not find them."

"Tradesmen were ever ingenious," Gianni sighed, and forbore to ask in what part of the cheese Bernardino had hidden his wealth. "You have just had work as a glazier, then?"

"Yes, at the castle of Prince Raginaldi, mending the leading where it had worked loose from the glass." Bernardino shook his head in wonder. "It's strange, the faith people have in glass, even when they know there are gaps between it and the leading. Do you know, the prince went right on haggling, even though I was there outside his window on my scaffolding and heard every word he said?"

"Haggling?" Gianni stared. "Isn't that beneath the dignity of a prince?"

"It would seem not," said Bernardino, "though I suppose the man he bargained with was so important that only a prince would do. Though," he added reflectively, "he didn't *look* important—rather dowdy, in fact; he was dressed so somberly, only a long robe and a round hat the color of charcoal—and he spoke with an accent so outrageous (not to say outlandish) that I will swear I had never heard it before, and could scarcely understand him at all! Nor could the prince, from the number of times he had to ask the man to repeat what he'd said, or to judge by the questions he asked."

"What were they discussing?"

Gianni looked up at Gar, surprised by the sudden intensity of his tone. Bernardino was startled too, but answered readily enough. "The buying of orzans."

"Orzans?" Gar turned to Gianni, frowning. "Those rich orange stones? Tell me more of them."

"They can only be found in the depths of limestone caves," Gianni explained, "and you can see new ones growing on the stalagmites and stalactites, I am told—but they won't be true orzans for hundreds of years. The new ones are still cloudy, and very soft. Your true orzan, now, that has lain under huge weights of rock for hundreds of years, I doubt not, is pure and clear as the sun, which it resembles, and hard enough to cut anything but diamond." He frowned up at Gar. "You still don't recognize them?"

"I do," Gar said slowly. "I've seen them for sale in a market far from here, very far—but they gave them a different name."

"Orzans or oranges, what matter?" Bernardino shrugged. "The stone does not care."

"They cannot be dug for," Gianni explained, "because the pick that beaks the rock away is as likely to fracture the jewel as its surroundings. No, the gatherers can only walk around the cave every day, waiting for a new segment of wall to break away—and it may disclose an orzan, or it may not."

"What of limestone quarries?"

"There are a few orzans found there," Bernardino

admitted, "though they are far more likely to be broken than whole. Still, even a scrap of orzan fetches a price worth picking it up."

"And this outlander offered the prince a high price for orzans?" Gar asked.

"A high price indeed, which is strange, because they're not all that rare."

Gianni nodded. "Semiprecious at best."

"But the price the strange somber trader offered for one alone would feed me and house me for a year! Though not a family."

"A high price, surely," Gar said with strange sarcasm.

"Oh, His Highness offered the man a variety of jewels—he laid them out on black velvet, a riot of color that made me faint to think of their value," Bernardino assured them, "but the stranger wanted only orzans."

"I'm sure he did," Gar said softly.

"It has taken long enough for us to catch you," Vincenzio said. Gianni looked up and discovered the rest of his new companions gathering around them on the road—but Gar turned instantly on the merchant and demanded, "The jewels the Stilettos took from you—were there orzans among them?"

"Two or three, yes," Rubio said, startled. "Indeed, they took them first, and their sergeant was about to spurn me away with the rest, and I was about to thank my lucky stars, when he thought again and took the rest of my jewels—the swine!"

"No doubt," Gar said to himself. "Those, I'm sure, were his pay."

Rubio frowned. "What do you mean?"

Gar started to answer, but broke off and whirled to stare ahead.

Giuseppi suddenly looked up, then gave a shout, pointing. They all followed his gaze and saw a cloud of dust boiling out from a curve in the road ahead.

"Soldiers!" Rubio cried. "Hide, one and all!" He turned away to the underbrush as horsemen emerged from the dust cloud. That was all the former prisoners needed; they bolted off the road, with Gianni right behind them . . .

Until he heard the huge, hoarse roar, and turned to see Gar charging down at the horsemen, arms flailing like the sails of a windmill, bellowing in incoherent rage as he attacked a whole party of cavalry, on foot and bare-handed. Gianni's stomach sank as he realized the giant had lost his wits again.

CHAPTER 10

Gar flailed about him with a total lack of skill, but with devastating strength. His fists knocked two Stilettos off their horses; then he caught the leg of another horse and heaved, throwing the animal over and the man on top with it. But as he straightened, a horseman behind him struck down with a club.

Gianni jumped in the way with a feeling of despair, leaping high and catching the club, knowing his own stupidity but also knowing that he couldn't leave Gar to fight alone. He was amazed when the Stiletto tumbled out of his saddle, his club falling free, but not so amazed that he didn't remember to strike the man with his own club as he hit the ground. He didn't get up, but a friend of his was swinging down with another club, and Gianni blocked with his cudgel in both hands, then swung it two-handed at the man's skull—but the soldier blocked, and a blow from behind made the world swirl around Gianni; he felt the cudgel slipping from his fingers, felt himself stumbling back against something warm and hairy, felt huge hands fasten onto his wrists with exclamations of disgust from above. When the world stopped tilting, he saw Gar on his knees with his hands bound behind him, felt rough hands tying his own wrists, and saw his whole company of refugees gathered together in a circle wide-eyed, moaning, and surrounded by horsemen.

"What are we to do with this lot now?" one Stiletto asked with disgust. "The captain said we weren't to waste time gathering men to sell to the galleys until we had searched every traveler and the campaign was over!"

"Yes," said a young man with more elaborate armor and an air of authority, "but he wasn't thinking of people who were so stupid as to fight back. *Those,* I think, we can ship off to the galleys—or at least pen them in Prince Raginaldi's castle until His Highness delivers judgment. Come along, you lot! Sergeant, drive them!"

And off they went to the castle, hustled so fast that they had to run. The Stilettos didn't slacken the pace until a few men had begun to stumble and fall. Then they slowed down, but the captives still had to trot. It was just as well they had no breath to spare, Gianni reflected—he didn't want to hear how they would be cursing Gar and him, for getting them back into the prison from which they had so lately been freed.

As they came to Castello Raginaldi, Gar looked up. Gianni was too miserable with forced marching and prodding spear butts to care much where he was going, but he followed Gar's gaze. The big man was staring up at the towers of the castle—and there was something strange about the tallest one. Squinting, Gianni could barely make out a skeletal contraption, a spidery triple cross mounted on a slender pole. He frowned, trying to remember which saint had a triple cross as his symbol, but could think of none. Why would the prince have such a thing atop his castle?

Perhaps it was some sort of new weapon. Yes, that made sense. Gianni determined to watch closely, to see how it was used. Then a spear butt struck his shoulder blade, and he lurched into faster motion again.

Across the drawbridge they went and, mercifully, the horsemen had to slow because of its narrowness—mercifully, because all the captives were stumbling with weariness. The Stilettos held the slow pace as they came out into a huge courtyard, where soldiers practiced fighting with blunted swords, and cast spears and shot arrows at targets. Iron clanged on iron from the smithy, far away against the castle wall, and the keep towered above everything, throwing its ominous shadow over them all.

They rode deeper into that shadow, but only to the wall of the keep itself, where a huge cage stood, iron bars driven into the hard-packed earth of the courtyard, then bent six feet high to slant upward to the stones of the wall. The roof was thatched over those bars, but the sides were open to wind, rain, and the baking sun. The door stood open, and the Stilettos herded them through it with snarls and curses. The recycled prisoners stumbled in and fell to the ground with groans of relief—at least they didn't have to run from the drubbing of spear butts any more. The door clanged shut behind them, and the sergeant fastened a huge lock through its hasp with a sound like the crack of doom.

Gianni sank down in a patch of sunlight with the rest, looking about him. The place was messy, but not squalid—apparently someone had shoveled it out and heaped fresh straw against the castle wall—but it had clearly housed many, many men before them. Since it wasn't big enough to hold more than a score, Gianni deduced that it must be the holding pen for prospective slaves. It seemed odd to him that there was no separate cage for women, until he remembered that there wasn't much of a market for female slaves except for the young and pretty, who were generally kept safely at home. In fact, there probably would not have been much demand for male slaves either, if it hadn't been for the galleys—peasants were cheaper, since their parents made them free of charge, and were always at a lord's bidding.

It galled Gianni to think of people being used as merchandise, but he knew that was how the lords, and their hired Stilettos, saw the commoners.

A shadow fell across him. Looking up, Gianni saw Gar settling down cross-legged by him. With resentment, Gianni realized that the big man wasn't even breathing hard, scarcely sweating at all—the pace that had so exhausted the other captives had been light work for him! "It's easy enough for *you*," Gianni grumbled. "After all, you're the one who got us into this mess!"

"We won't stay in it long," Gar said softly, his eyes on the courtyard.

Gianni stared, unbelieving. The half-wit who had brought down the wrath of the Stilettos had disappeared again. "Have your wits come back so soon?" he asked. "Or were you shamming?"

"Shamming, this time," Gar told him, his voice still low, "pretending, so that we could get into Castello Raginaldi to see for ourselves what's going on."

"See for *your*self," Gianni said bitterly. "Our companions have seen more than enough already! Oh, you've brought us in here easily enough—but how shall you bring us out?"

"Not quite so easily, but with a great deal more subtlety," Gar told him. "First, though, I want a look at that tower." He nodded at the spidery triple cross.

Gianni stared. "All this—putting us all in danger of the galleys—just so you can look at a tower you might have gazed at from the top of a ridge?"

"I couldn't have seen inside it," Gar said patiently, "and you won't go to the galleys—no, none of you."

"How can you be so sure?"

"Because," said Gar, "the time for fair play has passed." And he would give no more information than that, only turned aside Gianni's questions with short lectures that veered quickly from the point until the young merchant gave up in exasperation.

When night fell, though, Gar became much more communicative. He gathered the prisoners around him and said, low-voiced, "We're going to leave this castle, but before we do, I must see what secret the prince is hiding in his tower."

"What does your curiosity matter to us?" Giuseppi said bitterly.

"A great deal, because I've begun to suspect why the noblemen have paid the Stilettos to steal as they have never stolen before, and why they seek to screw the merchants down as though they were boards to walk upon."

Gianni stared. What did Gar mean? They knew why the lords had united against the merchants— because of the scheming of those fake Gypsies! Though, now that he thought about it, they did seem an awfully ineffective lot, to have so mobilized the lords—in fact, they seemed far more the kind of people who sat around and argued heatedly about what to do rather than the kind who actually did it.

Giuseppi frowned. "What reason do they need, other than greed?"

"They've had that all along," Gar explained, "though I think it's increased hugely this last year. But I have to *know*, you see, or I can't fight them with any hope of winning."

Ambiguous as it was, that seemed to make sense enough to the others; they subsided, grumbling. It didn't make much sense to Gianni, though, and he found himself wondering why they could be so easily convinced.

Then he looked into Gar's glowing eyes, and saw why.

"Come!" The giant rose, stooping slightly because of the roof. "Follow and do as I bid, and you shall be out of this castle before dawn!"

They murmured a little as they followed him, then went quiet as he stood by the gate, reaching out to lift the huge padlock in both hands, staring at it as though by simple force of will he could make it open. Slowly he wrapped his fingers around the curving top of the lock, wrapped the other hand around the keyhole, then began to twist . . .

The lock groaned, gave off a sharp cracking noise, then wrenched open, the curving top curving even more, its tip shredded.

The prisoners stared, speechless.

Carefully and silently, Gar removed the lock from the hasp, laid it on the ground, then opened the gate and crept out into the night. Wordlessly, they followed as Gar turned toward the keep—but Gianni reached up to pull on his shoulder. "You're going the wrong way!" he hissed. "The gatehouse is over there!" He pointed, his arm a bar of urgency.

"But the gatehouse isn't what I came to see," Gar whispered back, his tone gentle. He started toward the keep again. Gianni glared after him a minute, then threw up his hands in exasperation and followed. Everything considered, it was probably safer with Gar than without him, if his wits lasted. *Of course,* Gianni thought inanely, *if his wits were sound, would he have come in here in the first place?*

But there was no good answer to that question, so he followed with the rest of them.

Gar drifted up to the door of the keep like a shadow made gigantic by candlelight—only this shadow clasped a huge left hand around a sentry's mouth and pressed fingers to his neck. The man folded without a sound. Gar handed him to Gianni and stepped across the doorway just as the sentry's partner turned to look. He stared, speechless with surprise—then speechless because Gar's palm covered his mouth, pressing him back against the wall, as the other hand pressed his neck. In minutes, he, too, slumped unconscious. Gar handed him to Giuseppi and whispered, "Tell Claudio and Benvolio to put on their livery."

Claudio chuckled as he dressed the unconscious soldier in his vermin-ridden garb.

"Be sure they stay unconscious," Gar whispered to Vladimir, who nodded and pulled the bodies into the shadows, then sat down beside them with one of their own truncheons in his hand. "Keep the watch," Gar hissed to Claudio and Benvolio, and they nodded, then lifted their halberds slanting outward and stood vigilantly at the door. As an afterthought, Claudio pushed it open for Gar. He beckoned his little company forward, and prowled into Castello Raginaldi.

Stairs wound upward alongside the entry hall, and Gar headed straight toward them. Just as he came to their foot, hard footsteps sounded, and a Stiletto captain came around the turn. He saw Gar, yanked at his sword, and managed a single shout of anger before one big hand clamped down on his mouth and the other swung a borrowed truncheon. The captain's eyes rolled up as he slumped down. Gar handed him to Feste, hissing, "You're promoted. Strip him and dress! Bernardino, Estragon! Bind him and gag him, then hide him."

"With pleasure," Bernardino said, grinning, as Feste stooped to start stripping the captain. He grumbled a little at shedding his motley, but it was very grimy, after all, and the clean livery felt much better.

Gianni was amazed that they were all so eagerly following Gar, so blindly obeying him. But he was no better off himself; his pulse had quickened with excitement at the audacity of it, and at the hope of striking a blow at the noblemen and their tame condotierri. Up the stairs they went with Feste strutting at their head, his hand on his new sword. No one else stopped them until they came to the top, where two more guards stood at either side of a brass-bound oaken door. They snapped to, halberds slanting out at the ready, as Feste came in sight, then relaxed at the sight of his clothing. "Oh, it's *you*, Captain," one said, then looked more closely. "Hold! You're not the captain! And who's that monster behind . . ."

Gar stepped past Feste and cracked their heads together. Their helmets took most of the force of the blow; one of the guards turned jelly-kneed but managed a shout of alarm anyway, before a right cross to the chin felled him. The other was shaking his head and blinking furiously, trying to bring his halberd to bear, when Feste clubbed him on the side of the head with his sword hilt. The man folded.

"Not quite the way the sword was meant to be

used," Gar said, "but it will do. An excellent improvisation, Feste. The rest of you, quickly! Into the chamber! Trade clothes with them and tie them up!"

"How?" Gianni shoved at the door. "It's locked!"

"Yes, but not that strongly." Gar grasped the handle, glared at it, and pushed. The lock groaned; then the door opened. The fugitives stared, then came alive and dragged their captives into the room. Feste turned about, hand on his hilt, the captain of the guard on sentry-go. Gianni shut the door—but as he did, he glanced at the lock. And shivered. The bar had sunk back into the wood, unbroken. Somehow, Gar had opened that lock as surely as though he had held the key!

No time to worry about it now—they were in darkness, except for a swath of moonlight through a small window that served to show them, at least, where a candle sat by a tinderbox. Gar's shadow obscured the window and the candle for a moment; there was the scratch of flint on steel, then a soft glow that grew into a small flame. Gar held it to the wick, and the flame grew brighter. Then he closed the tinderbox, and the light was less, but constant. The candle flame showed them a circular room about twelve feet across with walls of mortared stone, a water stain where the roof needed patching, a table and chair near the window, where the candle stood—

And on that table, a low rounded shape that Gianni first took to be a giant egg. Then he saw that it had a curved handle on top and decided it must be a curling stone, such as the old men used for playing their unending lawn game on the village greens . . .

Until he realized the stone had a long, thin strip of light across its front, a strip with numbers on it.

Beneath that, there were five circles, each a different color, and now that Gianni looked, the handle on the egg had a little wire wrapped around it, a wire that ran up the wall and disappeared into the roof. Gianni saw that Gar had followed its route, too, and asked, "The triple cross?"

Gar nodded. "Yes, and I think it's a triple cross in more ways than one."

"What is this?" asked Vincenzio. "An alchemist's workshop?"

"Something of the sort. Don't let it trouble you. We won't stay here long." Gar sat down and peered at the lighted strip. "Back up my memory, Gianni—it's becoming moth-eaten. 'Eighty-nine-oh-one m.H.' "

" 'Eighty-nine-oh-one em aytch.' " Gianni repeated dutifully. "What does it mean, Gar?"

"It means," said Gar, "that our false-Gypsy friends have competitors they don't know about."

"Orzans!"

Gianni turned to look, and saw Rubio leaning over an open sack with jewels running through his fingers. "Orzans, hundreds of them! And there are four more bags like this one!"

Gar nodded, mouth a grim line. "I had thought as much. No wonder this room is stoutly guarded." He turned back to the curling stone and touched the green circle. Gianni reached out to stop him, his heart in his mouth—then froze as he heard the stone say, in a strange, very thick accent, "Prince Raginaldi, please answer!"

"What is *that*?" Rubio cried, leaping to his feet.

"Shush!" Gar hissed. "It's only a magical memory, nothing more."

The stone spoke again. "Since you do not appear to be near the far-talker now, Your Highness, I will ask you to call Zampar of the Lurgan Company when it is convenient. Thank you." There was a chime, then silence.

The men stared at one another with wide, frightened eyes. "Sorcery!" Rubio hissed.

"No, just great cleverness," Gar assured them. He touched some more colored circles, then said, "Gar to Herkimer. Do you hear me?"

"Yes, Gar." The reply was instantaneous; the voice was well modulated, cultivated, gentle. "I am glad to hear you alive and well."

"Well enough," Gar replied. "Herkimer, please start eavesdropping on—eighty-seven-oh-two, was that, Gianni?"

Gianni felt a chill. So soon? "Eighty-nine-oh-one em aytch, Gar."

"Eighty-nine-oh-one m.H.," Gar repeated. "Not so well as I might be, Herkimer; my brain may need an overhaul after this little jaunt. Check who uses that frequency, please."

"The Lurgan Company, Gar. Since your departure, I have become aware of their activities through their transmissions."

"The Lurgan Company, yes." Gar's lips were thin again. "What is it?"

"A semilegal syndicate who have been known to break laws designed to protect backward planets, Gar."

"How can they be legal at all, then?" Gar growled.

"By setting up their headquarters on planets that do not yet subscribe to the full I.D.E. code," the voice told him. "When a host planet does agree to full enforcement of that code, the Lurgan Company moves to a newer planet."

"Semilegal perhaps, but ethical not at all," Gar growled. "What information do you have about orzans, Herkimer?"

This time there was a pause of several seconds before the voice answered. "They are extremely rare fiery gems that are found only on Petrarch, Gar. They begin as crystals grown from water laden with a rare mineral that dissolves out of impure limestone through seepage in caves; those that have been buried under rock for several centuries acquire the luster and clarity that makes them so prized as ornaments."

Gar glanced at the gems in the big sack and hissed, "Put them back, Rubio." He turned back to the stone. "Current market value?"

"A flawless one-carat specimen would pay the annual power bill for a small city," the voice replied. "Consequently, the only market is on Terra and the older, very wealthy colonies, such as Hal IV and Otranto."

"The playgrounds of the rich," Gar muttered. "I thought they looked familiar."

"Your great-aunt does have one such pendant, Gar, yes."

Gianni felt as though his hair were trying to stand on end. Terra? Hal Four? Otranto? These were names from legend, names of fairy-tale realms!

"It's all as I had thought," Gar said. "Thank you, Herkimer. Please keep monitoring that frequency."

"I shall, Gar. Be careful."

The room was suddenly amazingly silent.

"Who was *that*?" Gianni whispered. "Your tame wizard?"

"Eh?" Gar looked at him, startled. "Well, yes, I suppose you might say that. Not a bad analogy at all, in fact." Then he scowled at the other young merchant. "Leave the bag here, Rubio!"

"It's a fortune, Gar," Rubio protested, "the chance of a lifetime!"

"The chance of a hanging, you mean! Steal that bag, and Prince Raginaldi will never rest until he has found it again, and when he does, he'll have you flayed to make sure you haven't hidden any of them under your skin! Leave them, and he may forget about us. Which reminds me . . ." He turned to touch the colored spots again, muttering, "Eighty-six . . ."

"Eighty-nine-oh-one em aytch," Gianni said quickly.

"Thank Heaven one of us has a memory," Gar growled. He finished punching, then turned toward the door, not even looking as he said, "*All* of them, Rubio!"

"Only as many as were stolen from me, Gar!" the young merchant said stubbornly.

"I suppose that's only just," Gar sighed. "But not

a fragment more, mind! Now outside, everyone, and silently!"

They went out, and Gar closed the door carefully; Gianni was sure he heard the lock turn, but with a tame wizard, why not?

"Not a *tame* wizard," Gar whispered as they started down the stairs, and Gianni jumped; he would have thought the giant had read his thoughts. "More of a friend—well, an associate."

"But still a wizard." Gianni frowned up at him. "Does he appear in your dreams?"

"No," Gar replied, "but he says I appear in his."

Gianni digested that as they went down a few more steps. Then he asked, "What was that object?"

"Magic," Gar answered.

"Of course," Gianni said dryly.

CHAPTER 11

As they were coming down, another pair of guards came out of a side passage and started up the stairs. They saw Gianni's party and stared. "Captain!" said one. "Why are the prisoners . . ."

"That's not the captain, you dolt!" the other snapped, and thrust with his halberd.

Gar reached past Feste and pushed the weapon aside, just as the fake "captain" drew his sword and put the tip to the man's throat. The guard's mouth opened to shout—and froze in silence.

The other guard *did* manage a shout, just before Gianni closed his mouth with an uppercut. He fell back down the stairs and struck his head against the wall, but the helmet protected him enough so that he was only groggy as he tried to climb to his feet, croaking, "Alarm! Prisoners ... escaped ..." until Gianni jumped down beside him, caught up the man's own halberd, and held the point to his throat. "Be still!" The man looked up at the gleaming steel and the hot, angry eyes above it, and held his tongue.

Gar stepped forward and touched his fingertips to the first guard's temples. The man jerked, staring; then his eyes closed, and he slumped. Gar caught him and eased him down. "We still have two men out of uniform. Take his livery." Then he stepped down to touch the other guard's temples. As the man sagged back onto the stone, Gianni asked, "What did you do to them?"

"Put them to sleep."

"I can see that!" Gianni reddened. *"How?"*

"Believe me," Gar told him, "you don't want to know." He went on down the stairs, leaving Gianni to follow, seething—but also wondering. He'd been suspecting for some time that there was much more to Gar than met the eye, and that he didn't like what he wasn't seeing.

As they came out into the courtyard, the only three not wearing Prince Raginaldi's livery were Vladimir, Gar, and Gianni. "Join us," Gar said softly to Bernardino and Vincenzio as he beckoned to Vladimir. "Gianni, hold your arms behind you, like this, as though they were bound. The rest of you, level your halberds at us—that's right. Now, Feste, march us all together to the gatehouse, and tell the porter and the sentries that you've been ordered to take Gianni and me out to hang us from a tree, because the prince has judged us to be rabble-rousers too dangerous to let live."

Feste frowned. "Will they believe that?"

"Why should they not?"

Feste gazed at Gar a moment longer, then shrugged and went forward to lead the way. The other men clustered around Gianni and Gar and moved toward the gatehouse.

"What if the guards recognize us from the Gypsies' descriptions?" Gianni muttered.

"Then they'll be sure the prince knew what he was doing," Gar muttered back. "In fact, we just might come out of this with everyone thinking we're dead."

"Not when they don't see our bodies hanging from a tree near the drawbridge, they won't!"

"True," Gar sighed, "and when they find a half dozen naked guardsmen."

"In fact, they'll be after us even harder!"

"Don't let it bother you," Gar assured him. "They can only hang us once."

Gianni shivered at the casual, offhand way he said it. For a moment, he imagined he could feel the noose tightening about his neck—but he shook off the fantasy and plodded angrily after Gar.

As they came to the gatehouse, Feste barked, "Halt!" The rest did a creditable imitation of a soldier's stamp-to-a-stop. "Drop the bridge!" Feste ordered the real sentries. "The prince has commanded that these two be hanged at once!"

The sentries stared, and one said, "He can't wait till dawn?"

"Who are you to question the prince's orders?" Feste stormed.

"I don't know this captain," the other guard said doubtfully.

" 'You will,' " Gar muttered to Feste.

"You'll know me soon enough, and better than you like, if you don't obey orders!" Feste raged. "The prince wants these two hanged outside as a warning to any who would defy him! Now lower that drawbridge!"

"As you say, Captain," the taller sentry said reluctantly, and turned to call into the gatehouse. Gianni waited with his heart in his throat, hearing the huge windlass grind away, thinking the bridge would never stop falling, thinking crazily that the sentries must see through them, their disguises were so transparent. How could they possibly accept Feste as a new captain when they had never seen him before? He couldn't believe experienced soldiers could actually be persuaded by so obvious a lie!

So when the sentries stepped aside and waved them on, he followed mechanically, amazed—and, as they came out across the moat, he found himself wondering how it could ever be that the soldiers had obeyed. He could only think that Feste was far more persuasive than he seemed.

"No shouting," Gar said, his voice taut, "not a sign of victory till we're half a mile away! Just march us back into the woods over there, and keep marching!"

Silently as a funeral procession, they marched through the moonlight and into the trees, with Gianni expecting any minute to feel a crossbow bolt in his back. But they came into the blessed darkness unscathed and marched on for twenty minutes more until they came to a clearing, where Gar stopped and said, "Now."

The men cut loose with a howling cheer, throwing their borrowed helmets up into the air, then running fast to avoid them as they came down. Gar turned to grin at Gianni and slap him on the shoulder. Gianni felt himself grinning back, all his nervousness sliding away under the triumph and sheer joy of being alive and free.

When they calmed a bit, Gar said, "They'll be searching for us by daybreak, if not before. Drop those soldiers' clothes right here and hide them in the bushes. Keep the belts and boots—you can trade them to peasants for whole suits of clothes."

"What about the halberds?" Rubio asked.

"A dead giveaway," Gar said, "and if you let them give you away, you'll be dead indeed—soldiers take a dim view of peasants beating up other soldiers."

"But that leaves us unarmed," Vincenzio protested.

Gar hesitated a moment, then said, "Break off the handles so you can thrust the heads into your belts as hand axes. That way, you'll each have a walking staff, too. You'll need it."

"We will?" Feste looked up at him alertly. "Why?"

"Because as long as you're on the road, you'll be in danger. You need a refuge, and the one place that's sure to take you in is Pirogia."

"Pirogia!" Rubio cried indignantly. "I, a man of Venoga?"

"There's a lot of country between us and Venoga,"

Vincenzio reminded him, "and most of it's infested with Stilettos."

Feste frowned. "Why should Pirogia admit us?"

"Because I'll vouch for you," Gianni said. "You can join *our* army."

"I didn't know Pirogia *had* an army."

"We don't, but we will," Gianni said grimly, "and very soon, too."

"But each pair of men go by a different route," Gar counseled. "Find different bypaths within this wood, and come out at different points. The more of us there are together, the more the prince's men will be sure we're the fugitives who stole their clothes. At the very least, if you absolutely must go by the same road, let one pair go out of sight before the other starts from this wood. If you can, trade your boots for the clothes of a woodcutter or a poacher. Go now, and meet us at Pirogia!"

He and Gianni set the example by striking off through the woods without any trail.

The rest of the trip home was surprisingly uneventful, but Gianni later decided that was because they had learned how to cope with the roving bands of Stilettos who roamed the countryside—and because Gar kept his wits, though he certainly did a good job of pretending to have lost them when he needed to. A dozen times they heard horsemen coming and managed to hide in the brush, or to lie down in a roadside ditch and cover themselves with grass, before the riders came in sight. They were always Stilettos, of course—they seemed to have driven all other traffic

off the roads, except for the occasional farm cart. Gar
and Gianni hid in one of those, too, and rode it for a
mile before the carter began to wonder why his
beasts were tiring so quickly. Only twice did Stilettos
catch them out on the open road without any cover,
and both times, they played Giorgio and Lenni to
such excellent effect that the soldiers settled for giving them a few kicks, then riding on as the "half-wit"
and his "brother" fell by the wayside.

Finally, one day in the middle of the morning,
Pirogia's steeples rose over the horizon. Gianni ran
ahead a few hundred feet until he could see his whole
city spread out before him and shouted for joy. Grinning, Gar came up behind him, clapped him on the
shoulder, and passed him, striding toward their haven.

As they came up to the land gate, though, four
grubby forms lifted themselves from around a campfire and hailed them. "Ho, Giorgio! Ho, Gar! What
kept you?"

"Only the road, and a few beatings from Stiletto
gangs." Grinning, Gianni clapped the jester on the
shoulder. "Ho, Feste! But why are you camped here
outside the city?"

"Oh, because the guards wouldn't let us in without
your word," Feste told him.

"They were quite rude about it, too," Vincenzio
added.

Glancing at him, Gianni could see why—dressed
in a patched woodcutter's smock and sandals, he
scarcely looked like the man of letters he was.

"They told us they didn't even know a man named

Giorgio who traveled with a giant!" Rubio said in indignation.

"Ah! I'm afraid there's a good reason for that, friends." Gianni felt a rush of guilt. "My name isn't really Giorgio, you see."

"Not Giorgio!" Vincenzio frowned. "But why did you lie to us? And what *is* your name?"

"I lied because the Stilettos were looking for me, and my real name is Gianni Braccalese."

"Gianni Braccalese!" Rubio cried. "Oh, indeed the Stilettos are looking for you! We overheard them talking about the hundred ducats the prince has promised to the man who brings you to his castle!"

Gianni stared at him, feeling a cold chill—until Gar clapped a hand on his shoulder, saying, "Congratulations, my friend. A price on your head is a measure of your success in fighting the lords' tyranny."

Gianni stared up at him, amazed at the thought. Then he grinned. "Thank you, Gar. Not much of a success, though, is it?"

"Just keep being a pest to them," Feste advised. "You'll bring a thousand before long."

Gianni grinned and punched him lightly on the arm, surprised at his own delight in seeing these vagabonds. "Come, then! Let's see if I'm not worth more to you than I am to the prince!" He led them toward the land gate, and as he came in sight of the sentries, he called, "Ho, Alfredo! Why didn't you let my friends in?"

"*Your* friends?" The sentry stared. "How was I to know they were *your* friends, Gianni?"

"Who else travels with a giant named Gar?" Gianni jibed. "You might at least have sent word to my father!"

"Oh, *that* kind of giant!" Alfredo looked up at Gar, looming above him. "I thought he meant a *real* giant—you know, out of the folk tales—twice the size of a house, and thick-headed as a ram."

Gar inclined his head gravely. "I am flattered."

"No, no, I didn't mean *you*!" Alfredo said quickly. "I meant . . . I mean . . ."

"That you *weren't* like that," said the other sentry, "and neither of us could remember your name."

"I quite understand," Gar said gravely. "It *is* rather long, and difficult to pronounce."

The other sentry reddened, but Gianni said, "Don't let him needle you, Giacomo. He only means it in fun."

"Yes, quite enough needling, Gar," Feste said. "I'm sure he gets the point."

Gar gave him a pained look. "I thought you were a professional."

Giacomo gave them a jaundiced eye. "Rather silly lot you've brought, aren't they?"

"They're just giddy with happiness at having come safely home," Gianni said, then amended, "*my* home, at least. Let us all in, Giacomo. They're recruits for the army."

"Army? We only have a city guard!"

"It's going to grow amazingly," Gianni promised. "Oh, and there should be four more men coming—a beggar, a thief, a glazier, and a young merchant of Venoga."

"Venoga! We're to let one of *them* in?"

"You would if he wanted to trade," Gianni reminded him. "Besides, he's rather had his fill of noblemen. I think he may prefer to change allegiance to a city where there are none."

When they came into the courtyard of the Braccalese home, Gianni's father nearly dropped his end of the cask they were manhandling onto a wagon, when Gianni and Gar came in sight. He called for a worker to hold it in place, then ran to embrace his son. His wife heard his cry and was only a minute or two behind him. When they were done with fond exchanges, and Papa held his son at arm's length, Gianni said, "I'm afraid I've lost you another goods train, Papa."

"It's on my head, not his," Gar said, his face somber.

"On his head indeed! They broke his head so badly that he lost his wits for a while! In fact, we're not sure he's found them for good yet!"

"His teachers at school weren't sure, either," Feste put in.

Gar glared daggers at him, and the Braccaleses laughed. "We're delighted to have you back alive, son," Papa said, "for there's not one single goods train has gone out from this city in a fortnight that has *not* been lost! Oh, the lords have us well and truly blockaded by land, you may be sure!"

"But not by sea?" Gianni's eyes glittered.

"Not a bit! Oh, one or two of our galleys had brushes with ships that looked to be pirates—but they were so inept they must have been lordlings' hirelings." Papa grinned. "Our galleys can still defeat with ease the best the lords can send against us!"

Gar nodded. "Free men fighting to save their own will always best driven slaves."

"It seems so indeed." Papa's eyes gleamed with added respect as he looked up at Gar.

"He has brought you something worth a hundred ducats, though," Feste said.

Papa stared at him. "What?"

"His head."

"It's true," Gianni confessed. "My new friends here tell me that the lords have put a hundred ducats on my head."

"And a thousand on your father's," Vincenzio added.

Mama turned pale, and Papa's face turned wooden, but Feste only sighed. "Poor Gianni! Every time you try to make your own way in the world, you find that your father has been there before you!"

The tension broke under laughter, and Papa asked, "Who are these rogues?"

"Our road companions," Gianni said. "They helped us escape from Prince Raginaldi's castle, so I invited them to join Pirogia's army."

"A good thought," Papa said, turning somber again.

But Mama gasped, "Prince Raginaldi! How did you run afoul of *him*?"

"By stealing his hen." Feste looked up at the sudden stares of surprise all about him, and shrugged. "Well, you said he had run a fowl."

They groaned, and Gar said, "If that's what you

were paid for, friend, I can see why you were wandering the roads. Signor Braccalese, this is Feste, who purports to be a professional jester."

" 'Purports,' forsooth!" Feste snorted. "Do you 'purport' to be mad, Gar? What shall I say you 'purport' to do next?"

"Wash, if I may." Gar held up grimy hands. "If you will excuse me, gentlefolk, I have an appointment at the horse trough."

"You shall do no such thing!" Mama scolded. "We have a copper tub, and kettles to heat water! You shall all bathe as gentlefolk do! Come in, come in all, and share our bread while we wait for the water to heat!"

The travelers cheered, and Feste sighed, "I thought they would never ask," but Mama didn't encourage him any further, only shooed them all inside and set about the task of organizing an impromptu celebration.

The next morning, Gianni woke to shouted commands and the sound of tramping. He leaped from his bed, ran to the window, and saw Gar, in the center of his father's wagon yard, barking orders to eight men who were marching in two rows of four—the four vagabonds and four of Papa's drivers. Gianni stared, then pulled on his clothes and dashed out into the courtyard. He came up to Gar, panting, "Why didn't you tell me? I want to learn this, too!"

"Very good, very!" Gar nodded. "Find a pole to put over your shoulder, Gianni, and step into line!"

Gianni ran to fetch a pole, then slowed, frowning. "What's the staff for?"

"To represent a spear or halberd—I'd rather teach them drill without the real weapons, so they don't cut each other's heads off every time they turn about."

"Economical," Gianni said judiciously. "But what's the point of teaching them this marching, Gar?"

"About *face!*" Gar cried, just in time to keep the men from tramping head first into the wall. As they turned back, he said to Gianni, "It teaches them to act together, instantly upon hearing a signal, so that an officer can send them where they're needed in battle, and have them point their spears in the right direction in time to keep the enemy from stabbing them." He flashed Gianni a conspiratorial smile. "It also mightily impresses Council members."

Gianni stared at him, amazed at such duplicity in Gar. Then, slowly, he smiled.

"Master Gianni!"

Gianni turned. A boy came running up, panting. "The sentries at the land gate, Master Gianni! They say there are four men there, four strangers, who claim you will vouch for them, to let them enter the city!"

"I will indeed." Gianni smiled. "Thank you, lad." He pressed a coin into the boy's palm. "I'll go and fetch them right away." He turned to Gar. "I *will* join your marching, Gar—but I'll bring you four more recruits first."

"Give them my compliments," Gar said, grinning, and turned back to bark a command, then swear as the back row had to duck to avoid the tips of the front row's staves. Gianni went back inside, marveling at Gar's high spirits—he enjoyed the strangest things.

Gianni took the time to straighten his clothes and shave, fortunately—fortunately because, as he crossed the Piazza del Sol, he saw a Gypsy caravan drawn up beside the canal. His pulse quickened, and he veered toward it like a compass needle swinging.

There she was, sitting under an awning propped out against the side of the caravan, reading a goodwife's palm. She glanced up and must have recognized Gianni, for her eyes widened, and she stared at him for a brief second. Only a second; then she was staring down at the woman's hand again, and Gianni had to stand and fidget until she finished. He glanced up apprehensively at the line of men and women lounging and chatting with one another as they waited their turns to hear their fortunes—but when the housewife smiled happily, paid Medallia, and rose to leave, Gianni was up to the table like a shot, ignoring the outraged cry behind him. "Godspeed, fair Medallia."

She looked up, perfectly composed now. "Good day, Gianni Braccalese. It is good to see you safely home."

Only "good"? No more than that? Gianni tried to control a massive surge of disappointment, and had to force his smile to stay in place. "It's a joy to see you returned to Pirogia. To what do we owe this treat?"

"Why, to good business," Medallia said easily,

waving at the line of waiting customers. "If you will excuse me, Signor Braccalese, I must tend to my shop."

Signor! "Of course," Gianni said slowly. "But when you're finished . . . may I meet you here in the evening, to chat?"

"Do you wish your fortune told?" She looked up at him with wide, limpid, innocent eyes.

Not unless you're *my fortune*, he thought. Slowly, he said, "Why . . . yes, I suppose I do."

"I shall be here all of today until sunset, and tomorrow too," she said. "You may have to wait your turn, though. Good day, Signor."

"Good day," he muttered and turned away, his face thunderous. It was strange how the sunlight no longer seemed so bright, even stranger how stupid his fellow citizens suddenly appeared, chatting and laughing, completely at ease, while Fate rolled toward them with the thunder of the hooves of an army. Didn't they realize the enemy was nearly at their gates? Didn't they realize their freedom, their prosperity, their very lives might soon be snuffed out at a lord's whim?

No. Of course not. No one had told them.

Gianni resolved that he must make an appointment to speak to the Council again at once, that very day if possible! The fools would see, they *must* see! And blast Medallia for pretending that she meant no more to her than any other customer, anyway!

But what if he didn't?

CHAPTER 12

Gianni tried to shrug off his gloom as he went to greet his companions. He told himself that Medallia was only one pretty woman among many, and one he hadn't even come to know very well—but he was amazed at how little the thought cheered him, and at how much his fancy had fastened upon her. But he forced a smile and waved at the guards at the inner gate, even managing to exchange a few cheerful remarks, and was able to put on a good show by the time he reached the land gate. He saw Vladimir, Estragon, Rubio, and Bernardino, and called, "You lazy layabouts, you idle road walkers! What makes you think you're good enough for Pirogia?"

They leaped to their feet, Rubio the merchant reddening with anger—until they saw Gianni and laughed, coming forward with open arms. He embraced each of them, surprised at how the greetings of these relative strangers cheered him.

"It's intolerable, Giorgio!" Rubio said indignantly. "They tell me they can't trust a man from Venoga!"

"Yes, but if you had come with a goods train behind you, they would have let you in quickly enough," Gianni assured him. "Besides, they're pulling your leg—I argued that out with them yesterday."

Rubio stared; then a slow grin spread over his face. He turned to the two guards, who had rolled up their eyes, watching the sky in innocence. "You scalawags! You've no more hospitality than your friend Giorgio here!"

"And no less, either," Alfredo assured him. "But who is Giorgio? I see only Gianni."

Rubio turned to Gianni in shock, and so did the other three—but Gianni only smiled apology and said, "Forgive me, friends, but the lie was necessary. The prince had set a price on my head."

"A price?" The thief frowned. "I should have heard about this! What's your full name?"

"Gianni Braccalese."

Estragon stared; so did Vladimir. Rubio and Bernardino looked from one to the other, at a loss. Gianni felt a perverse sort of pride.

"Yes," said the thief, "I had heard of you indeed! Oh, if I had known who I was traveling with, I would have walked alone!"

"We were safer together," Gianni assured him, "and will be in the future, too. Come in, come in and accept my mother's hospitality! Then, if you wish,

you can join our new army . . . I mean . . ." He
glanced uneasily at Vladimir, then away, ashamed of
himself.

"Perhaps not a soldier, but from what I know of armies, they can find some use for me," the lame man
assured him. "Take me to your general, Gianni. Let
him decide."

Gianni grinned and clapped him on the back.
"There's no general yet, but only our old friend
Gar—and yes, I think he'll find a place for you.
Come in."

Mama Braccalese welcomed the quartet with full
hospitality, though she was a little put off by the beggar and the thief, and accorded them a hot tub each
as her first gesture of welcome. Gar did indeed assure
the beggar that there would be work enough for him
as a quartermaster, but for the time being, he should
learn the trade of a fletcher, learning the making of
crossbow bolts and the compounding of gunpowder
for the cannons.

As they were finishing a late and rather large
breakfast, Gianni's father came in, his face grim, but
his eye alight. "The Council will hear you tomorrow,
Gianni—and I think they will listen more closely,
now that so many have lost good trains. But who are
these?"

When the introductions had been made and his
welcome extended, Papa took Gianni aside and said,
"Be sure that you practice what you're going to say
to the Council—but first, walk about the city and
sense its mood. I know our people seem their usual
cheerful selves, but there's an undertone of concern

there. Everyone knows that things aren't the way they should be, though no one's sure what's wrong yet."

So that afternoon, Gianni went for a stroll in the market, then along a canal and down some small rivers, crossing bridges and listening to conversations. His father had been right—there was tension there, and rumors were flying. People were doomsaying left and right. A grocer near the Bridge of Smiles was telling a customer, "Truly, the beards on the grain are much longer than usual, and the butcher tells me the goats' hair and the sheep's wool is much thicker than ever he has seen! It will be an early winter, a long and hard winter, mark my words!"

"I'll mark them." His customer tried to look skeptical, but didn't succeed very well.

Along the River Melorin, he heard two housewives gossiping as they walked along with their shopping baskets on their arms. "I feel it in my bones, Antonia! Fever is rising from the water! It will be a plague such as the Bible tells of, or I know nothing of healing!"

"I could believe that your bones know," her neighbor scoffed, "but if there's to be any plague in this city, it's more likely to come from the gutters than the waters."

Her eyes were haunted, though, and Gianni could see she didn't doubt that a plague might be due. The day seemed more chilly suddenly, and he hurried on.

By the waterfront, he heard an old sailor telling some boys, "Aye, a sea serpent, lads! Saw it myself, I did—a long skinny body sticking up from the water, way up, way *way* up, with a small flat head atop."

"It wasn't a very big sea serpent, then," one of the boys said, disappointed.

"Oh, it was huge! The head was only little when you saw it atop so huge a neck! It was half a mile off if it was an inch, and we blessed our luck when it turned and went from us! But they won't be turning away from ships this year, oh no! All kinds of monsters will rise from the sea, aye, and chase after our ships, to drag them down!"

The boys moaned with the delight of safe fear, their eyes huge—but a young sailor passing near overheard the old salt and frowned, then hurried off, his brow furrowed.

Gianni began to feel alarm himself—the people were claiming everything bad about the future except the real danger. If they weren't told the truth soon, if these rumors weren't quashed, the city would shake itself apart.

As the sun was setting, though, he turned his steps back toward the Piazza del Sol, his pulse quickening—but the market stalls had been shuttered, and the caravan was gone. For a wild, crazed moment, he thought of searching the city for the brightly colored wagon, then remembered that he had already been roaming for hours, and that there were so many islands that even those that could be reached by the network of bridges would take him a week and more to search thoroughly. Heavy-hearted, he went home, to be cheered by the presence of his new friends.

After supper, Gar took him aside and asked, "You talk to the Council tomorrow, then?"

"Yes, if I can think of what to say," Gianni answered.

Gar shrugged. "Tell them the plain truth—what you've heard, and what you've seen. If they give you any trouble, introduce me again. I assure you, with what I know now, I can scare them as badly as the worst brimstone-breathing preacher."

Gianni grinned and promised he would.

But that night, the swirling, dancing figure illuminated his dreams again, glowing more brightly than ever she had before. *Gianni Braccalese!* she called. *You must tell them to flee, Gianni!*

Do not flee from me, *I beg you,* he pleaded in his dream.

Silly boy! she flared. *Can you think of nothing but love?* But her voice trembled when she said it. *Think of your fellow citizens instead! You cannot even dream of the might the lords shall bring against Pirogia when they unite all their armies—or of the horrendous engines of death their far-traveling merchant allies will lend them! There is no hope of victory, none! You must persuade all your fellows to flee!*

To leave Pirogia? Gianni cried, aghast. He had a brief, lurid vision of the beautiful bridges burning and falling, the elegant houses tumbling into the bright piazzas as flames burst from them while Stilettos ran from house to house, looting them of gold and plate and crystal and paintings, and smashing what they could not carry. *No, never! We cannot desert our Pirogia!*

If you do not, you shall die, you shall all *die!* The

dancer stilled, her hands upraised, pleading. *You must abandon the city, Gianni, all of you!*

They wouldn't listen to me even if I told them that. Gianni felt a hardening and crystalizing of purpose as he said the words. *Our only hope of protecting our wives and mothers is to arm ourselves and fight!*

You cannot! she wailed.

Don't put too much faith in the princes, Gianni told her. *At sea, they're weaker than any fisherman—and no army can march across the water to Pirogia. No, dry your tears, I beg of you—and let me see your face.*

Never! The veils began to swirl again. *Can you think of nothing but lust, Gianni Braccalese?*

Nothing but love, he corrected, *for I have loved you with a burning passion since first I saw you.*

Have you indeed? she said acidly. *And what of the Gypsy maiden Medallia? Does she interest you not at all?*

That brought Gianni up short, and on the horns of the dilemma, he took refuge in truth. *She too has captured my fancy. Yes, it could be love, if I could come to know her.*

You've not come to know me!

More than Medallia, he corrected, *for I have never been alone with her.*

But long to be, I'm sure! How fickle you are, Gianni Braccalese, how inconstant! How can you love two women at once?

I don't know, Gianni confessed, *but I do.* He had never thought himself to be so base as to betray one love for another, but found that he did. Was he no better than any of the other strutting bucks about town? Were all men so shallow? *I do not understand it, but it's there. Please, O Beauty, let me come to you!* He willed himself to move toward her, and seemed to be beginning to do so when she snapped, *Never!* and whirled her veils high to hide herself as she began to recede, flying from him at an amazing rate, shrinking smaller and smaller until she was gone, leaving him alone in darkness, with his dreams empty.

Gianni waked feeling fuzzy-headed and filled with grit, as though he had drunk far too heavily the night before, when in fact he had tasted only a single glass of wine. "That's what comes of dreaming of women you can't have," he growled at himself, and rose to wash and shave.

With breakfast improving his mood and his best clothes on his back, he entered the Council chamber beside his father, Gar looming behind both of them. They entered a hall filled with consternation.

"Have you heard?" A jowly burgher confronted Papa Braccalese. "Prince Raginaldi marches on the city from the north, with thousands of men!"

Both Braccaleses stared. The first thing Papa could think of to say was, "How do we know?"

"Old Libroni's chief driver brought the word back, along with the tale of how a band of Stilettos had reived him of his whole goods train and left him for dead! Oh, he is in frightful condition—emaciated, with bruises and crusted wounds! None doubt his word."

Papa cast a quick look of vindication at Gianni, then said, "Many thanks, old friend. Come, let's find our seats."

They went on into the hall, hearing voices on every side:

"Conte Vecchio marches from the west with a thousand men!"

"The Doge of Lingretti marches from the south with two thousand!"

"The Stilettos are marching three thousand strong from Tumanola!"

"The Red Company are marching with two thousand!"

"Pirates!" a messenger shrilled, running into the hall and waving a parchment. "Captain Bortaccio says he had to run from a fleet of pirates! He lost them in a low fog by sailing against the wind, but they come in a fleet of thirty!"

The clamor redoubled at this news, and the Maestro began to strike his gong again and again, crying, "Councilors! Masters! Quiet! Order! We must discuss a plan!"

"Plan?" shouted a bull-throated man in velvet. "There can be only one plan—to flee!"

"We can*not* flee!" Old Carlo Grepotti was on his feet, eyes afire, trembling. "By land or by sea, they shall cut us down and take us all for slaves if we flee! We can do nothing but stay and pray!"

"We can *fight*!" shouted a younger merchant, and a roar of approval answered him. The Maestro pounded his gong again and again until they quieted enough for him to hear himself call out, "Sit down!

Sit down, masters and signori! Are we fishmongers, to be brawling over a catch? Sit down, as befits your dignity!"

Many faces reddened, but the merchants quieted and sat down around the great table. The Maestro nodded, appeased. "Braccalese! This meeting is called at your request! Have you any news that will help us make sense of this whole hornet's nest?"

"Not I, but my son," Papa said. "Gianni, tell them!"

Gianni stood up—and almost sat right down again; his legs turned to jelly as he stared around him at the host of grim, challenging faces, the youngest of them twenty years older than he. But Gar muttered a reminder—"You've faced Stilettos"—and it did wonders for Gianni's self-confidence. His fear didn't vanish, but it receded a good deal.

He squared his shoulders and called out, "Masters! Again I took a goods train out, this time northward into the mountains—and again we were beset by Stilettos, and our goods train lost. My guard Gar wandered with me till some Gypsies gave us clothes, food, and a place to sleep—but when they thought we slept, the Gypsies talked among themselves. They were false Gypsies, spies"—he hoped he was right about that—"set to encourage the lords to unite to crush us merchants!"

The hall erupted into uproar again, and Gianni looked about him, leaning on the table, already feeling drained, but quite satisfied at the emotion he had brought forth. The Maestro struck the gong again and again and, when quiet had returned, fixed Gianni with a glittering eye and asked him, "Why should Gypsies care whether we live or die?"

"We couldn't understand that, either, Maestro," Gianni said, "until we encountered a glazier on the road, who told us of a conversation he had overheard—a conversation between Prince Raginaldi and a dour, grim merchant from very far away who could barely speak the tongue of Talipon, but who offered the prince a scandalous price for orzans."

"Scandalous price?" Eyes glittered with avarice. "*How* scandalous?"

What was the cost of power for a small city, anyway? For that matter, what *was* such power? Gianni improvised, "Three months' profit from ordinary trading."

"For each *jewel*?"

Gianni nodded. "For each one."

The hall erupted into pandemonium again. The Maestro rolled up his eyes and left the gong alone until the hubbub had started to die of its own, then struck the gong once and waited for silence. "Do you say these false Gypsies were agents of this foreign merchant?"

"That's the only way it makes sense to me, Maestro," Gianni told him. "But it's not just *one* merchant, it's a whole company—the 'Lurgan Company,' they call themselves."

"A whole company? Why didn't they come to *us*?"

Gianni shrugged, but old Carlo Grepotti cried, "Because they knew we would beat the price even higher! These foolish lords will take whatever they're offered!"

"Aye, and steal every gem they can find to sell!" cried another merchant, and the hubbub was off again. The Maestro aimed a blow at the gong, then thought better of it and sat back to wait. Finally his fellow merchants realized just how contemptuous his gaze was and subsided, muttering. The Maestro turned to Gianni again. "Have you any answers to these questions they raise?"

"Only guesses, Maestro," Gianni said, "But I think I'll let Gar tell you those. He had the idea of having us captured by the Stilettos so that we could break into Castle Raginaldi and look for more information. He should be the one to tell you what we found."

"Break into Castle Raginaldi?" a younger merchant cried. "How did you dare?"

"More to the point, how did you get *out*?" another man demanded.

"All for Gar to tell—it's really his story, and his boast." Gianni turned to his friend. "I yield to the free lance."

"Free no longer, but bound to serve you and all of Pirogia." Gar rose to his full height, shoulders square, and looked somberly about the room. Any objection to his speaking died under that glare. Calmly then, and without hurry, he told them about their raid into Castle Raginaldi—and told it with all the dash and spirit of a practiced storyteller. The merchants hung riveted to his account, all eyes on his face, and the hall was silent except for his voice until he had finished with their escape from the castle. Then he paused, looked all about the room, finally turned to the Maestro, and inclined his head. "That is all we saw, Maestro, and all we heard."

The room erupted into noise again—exclamations of wonder, and not a little scoffing. The Maestro let it run its course, then asked Gar, "What was this strange egg-shaped thing?"

"A magic talisman that allowed the prince to talk with the Lurgan traders, even when they were far from his castle," Gar said. "That way, when he had enough orzans to be worth the trip, they could come to get them, and give him his gold."

"I do not believe in magic," the Maestro said.

"Rightly, too," Gar replied, "but it's easier to say 'magic talisman' than 'an alchemist's device,' and it's beyond understanding in any case. What matter is what it *does*."

"Apparently you've some understanding of it, if you could use it to talk to a friend of your own."

"Yes, my lord. I also understand how to use a cannon, but I would be hard put to tell you how its powder worked, or why."

Gianni noticed that he didn't say it was impossible, just difficult—but the Maestro accepted the answer. "And who is your friend Herkimer?"

"Another mercenary," Gar said readily, "who will come to our aid if I ask it, and take the noblemen from the rear. Think of him as an alchemist with cannon—excellent cannon, for he makes better gunpowder."

"And he can watch this Lurgan Company for you?" The Maestro was looking rather skeptical.

"Well, eavesdrop on them, at any rate," Gar said,

"though what he hears would have to be very dire before he would drop a message for me into your Piazza del Sol, taking the risk of knocking a hole in someone's head."

"Have you no talisman to use for talking with him?"

"No, my lord. It was with the kit that I had when I came to your city, but which the Stilettos stole along with the rest of my gear."

"Will they know it for what it is?" old Carlo asked.

"I doubt it," Gar told him. "It was well disguised." He didn't elaborate, and Carlo Grepotti managed to bite back the question.

"What is your advice?" the Maestro asked.

Gar shrugged. "I'm a mercenary soldier, Maestro. Of course I advise you to fight."

"Forget your profession for a moment." The Maestro waved a hand, as though he could clear Gar's mind of all preconceptions with a gesture. "Try to think as a merchant, not as a soldier. Would you not advise us to flee, to evacuate the city?"

"No," Gar said, instantly and clearly. "It would be almost impossible to move so many people so quickly—many would be likely to die in the trying—and no matter where you went, the Stilettos would sniff you out and kill or enslave you."

"We could divide into many bands, and go in many directions," a merchant offered.

"If you did, you'd only make it easier for the Stilettos to kill you," Gar said, "and give sport for many noblemen and their armies as they hunted you down—sport for them, and employment for all the

Free Companies, not just the Stilettos. No, masters, your only hope is to stay and fight. Yes, many of you may die—but many more will live!"

"But we have no army!" cried another. "How can we fight the lords?"

"By burning your bridge to the mainland," Gar said. "Gianni tells me it was designed for that, and whoever thought it up built wisely. Yes, it will take time and money to rebuild, when we have beaten off the lords—but it's the smallest of the losses you could have. With it gone, no army can come at you without ships—and your navy is unsurpassed; I'm sure they will scuttle any army the lords try to bring against you."

"Some boats might reach us," a merchant said darkly.

"Yes, and for that you *will* need soldiers." Gar nodded. "I can make your young men into an army for you, and free lances will come quickly enough if we spread word that we're hiring. In fact, we've brought back eight men from our travels who are willing to serve with you; I spent yesterday drilling them and taking the first steps toward turning them into an army. Will you come see them? They're waiting outside."

There were a few voices of denial, but the vast majority were more than ready to see a show. They answered with a shout of approval, and the Maestro cried, "Adjourned! We shall meet again outside! Stand around the edge of the piazza, masters!" Then he struck the gong, and the move toward the doors began.

Even as they came out, they saw Gar's eight men drawn up in three rows of four each—three, because a few of the Braccalese drovers had been fired with military zeal when they saw the tabards Mama Braccalese and her friends had made, splendid golden tabards with the eagle of Pirogia painted on them, as some hint of livery. The merchants exclaimed as they came out, seeing the men drawn up in a square with plumed hats and the sun glinting on their halberds (they had fitted new handles to the trophies of their raid on Castle Raginaldi). At Gar's command, they came to attention, and the drummer and trumpeter he had hired began to play. Then, as he barked orders, the twelve marched across the square, turned as one and marched across its breadth, then wheeled and marched across it on the diagonal. Again he called, and they turned to march straight toward the Maestro with old Carlo Grepotti beside him. One more barked command, and they stamped to a halt, front row dropping to a crouch, halberds snapping down to point directly at the spectators.

The merchants burst out cheering, and the few voices of dissent were drowned in an accolade that heralded the founding of Pirogia's army.

CHAPTER 13

The whole city threw itself into a positive fever of preparation for war. Furnaces roared in the foundries day and night, casting cannon for the navy and the city walls; peasants streamed in through the gates with carts full of food, and stayed to enlist in the army if the city found room for their families—for these peasant farmers had no illusions about what happened to the people in the villages when their fields became battlegrounds.

One of those farmers, however, turned out to be a problem. A messenger came knocking at the Braccalese door just as the family was sitting down to breakfast, and the servant appeared in the doorway seconds later. "Master Paolo, there's a messenger from the Council in your study."

"A messenger from the Council? So early?" Mama exclaimed, and her face was full of foreboding.

"It must be urgent if it comes so untimely." Papa rose and went to the door, saying, "Begin without me, family, Gar. It might not be short."

But it was. He came back only minutes later and sat down at table again, tucking the cloth into his neck and saying, "Eat quickly, Gianni, Gar. I think you had better come along."

"What is it?" Suddenly, Gianni's appetite was gone.

"A spy," Papa told them. "Eat, Gianni. You'll need it."

They ate, then went out the river door, stepping into a sculling boat, and went not to the Council chambers but to the magistrate's hall—and it was Oldo Bolgonolo who greeted them, not as Maestro but as a magistrate. He ushered them into the courtroom, where a mild-mannered, bland-faced man stood before the bench in chains. He wore a simple farmer's smock and leggings, and seemed entirely inoffensive.

"What did he do?" Gianni asked.

Oldo waved him to silence and said, "Master, signori! This peasant was seen watching the soldiers drill, and later seen going to the stall of a pigeon seller in the market. There is no crime in that, but the pigeon he bought, he took down to the quay, tied a scrap of parchment to its leg, and sent it winging into the air. The man who followed him shot the pigeon through the wing. It heals, and may be of use to us in sending a message other than this." He held out a scrap of parchment. "Read, and advise us as to his judgment."

Papa took the parchment and scanned it, scowling, but Gar asked, "Who bore witness against him?"

"One of the city spies you advised me to commission, and the stealthy one has already proved the worth of your advice. But he also whispered to one or two other folk that the man was doing something suspicious, and they saw and remembered. He kept them from offering violence to this poor deluded soul . . ."

"Deluded!" the man burst out. "You, who would upset the old ways and take from us the assurance of the noblemen—you dare call *me* deluded?"

"He seems to have had a good lord," Oldo said, with irony, "and doesn't realize how lucky he was, or how rare his master is."

"So he admits his crime?" Gar asked.

"He does," Oldo confirmed. "Four citizens confronted him and bore witness to his deeds."

"But not your spy!" the man said hotly.

"Counterspy," Gar corrected. "It is *you* who are the spy."

"A counter indeed, a counter in your game," the man sneered. "They wouldn't let me see the man himself!"

"Of course not—once a spy's face is known, he can be of little more use," Gar said. "He was wise enough to see you had other accusers. In fact, I would guess he himself made no accusation, only supplied information."

The spy chopped sideways with his hand in a dismissive gesture. "What will it be now? The gallows? Go ahead—I'm ready to die for my lord!"

"Oh, I don't think that will be necessary," Gar said mildly, and to Oldo, "I'd recommend he be a guest of the city, with a room to himself. Not a very luxurious room perhaps, and not a very rich diet—but only a guest with a barred window, until the current unpleasantness is done. It may be his lord will value so loyal a retainer—value him enough to trade us a dozen prisoners of war for him."

"An excellent thought," Oldo said, with a gleam in his eye. The prospect of bargaining appealed to him. "Guards, take the prisoner away and clap him in a cell alone, where he can spread no more of his insidious talk!" As the watchmen hustled the peasant away, Oldo turned to Gar. "I thank you, friend, for the excellence of your advice. I shall appoint more counterspies, and have them watch our new citizens very closely."

"And the old ones, too," Gar reminded him. "Some of them might lack confidence in the navy and our new army, and might try to guarantee their family's safety by selling information to the lords."

Oldo's face darkened. "It goes against the grain to even think of it, but I shall do so. Do you really think it necessary for the counterspies to seek to have other citizens bear witness, though?"

"Very important," said Gar, "for a position like that opens itself to abuse of power very easily and readily. A counterspy could settle an old quarrel or gain long-awaited revenge, just by accusation. No,

Maestro, I strongly recommend you require witnesses and proof."

"Well, so we shall, then," grumbled Oldo. "But I thank you, masters."

As they came out of the courtroom, Gianni said, in a shaken voice, "I had never thought there might be spies among us!"

"Oh, there most definitely are," Gar assured him. "It's a fundamental principle of war."

"But what of the lords' armies? Will we have spies among them?"

"We already do," Gar answered. "Do we not, Signor Braccalese?"

Papa nodded, looking grim, and Gianni suddenly felt very young, and very, very naive. He reflected, though, that he was learning very rapidly.

So was his city. The merchant town that had felt no need of an army was studying war with a vengeance. The shipyard hired every carpenter in town, and half-built houses had to wait while keels were laid and caravels built. Chandlers bought every bale of hemp the farmers could bring, every skein of linen thread, to make cables and sails.

There followed the most frantic two weeks of Gianni's life. Gar taught him how to drill with the others, taught him in a day as much as they learned in two, then left him in charge of training the recruits with the help of the captain of the Pirogia City Guard and a few of the guardsmen. Mama and Papa Braccalese kept track of the young men who enlisted, while Vladimir the beggar took charge of ordering up tabards, plumed hats, and weapons. The workshops of the city threw themselves into turbulent activity; lamps burned all through the night, and the citizens of Pirogia could scarcely sleep for the sounds of the hammers beating at all hours in the forgeries. Old Carlo Grepotti worked side by side with Vladimir, grumbling over every single ducat spent but dutifully doling out the gold to the tradesmen of his city as he did. The Maestro himself took charge of raising money for Carlo to spend, going from merchant to merchant and arguing very reasonably that generous donations would forestall a Council vote on the need for higher taxes.

Gianni was very proud of his fellow citizens—the young men came trooping in, waiting in long, long lines for the scribes to take down their names (and many who were not so young—Gianni was glad he could leave it to his father to explain to old Pietro why a sixty-year-old man with gout and rheumatism should not enlist). He had his hands full overseeing his road companions as they trained the young men in drill, each hopeful soldier with a pole over his shoulder until he could learn how not to hit his mates with it as he turned and wheeled. Vincenzio kept his men in line with all the sternness of a schoolmaster, protesting in an undertone that this was no fit occupation for a man of letters; Estragon the thief reveled in actually giving orders to the law-abiding; and Feste was in his element, posturing and strutting as he led his troops. Gianni was constantly on the run from piazza to piazza, trying to keep up with the drill practice in the mornings and the weapons practice in the afternoons, when his lieutenants became pupils themselves, studying halberd-play and archery and swordsmanship from the Pirogia City Guard.

At the end of the first exhausting day, Gianni threw himself down in his bed, sure he would sleep so deeply that dreams wouldn't dare come near him—but the circle of light appeared and expanded before he could wish it away or dare command it to be gone, expanded to show him the face of the Wizard, hair and beard swirling. Gianni still felt a little fear, but much more exasperation. *What do you want this time?*

The wizard stared in surprise; then his brows drew down in anger, and pain stabbed Gianni from temple to temple as the deep voice thundered around him. *You forget yourself, child! Do not think that because I honor you with a glimpse of me, you are entitled to insolence!*

I . . . I beg your pardon, Gianni stammered.

Better, the voice said, no longer all about him, and the pain ceased as abruptly as it had begun. *I have come to tell you that you have done well, Gianni Braccalese, in persuading your citizens to fight.*

Thank you. But this was one time that Gianni really didn't want the credit. *Gar had more to do with it than I, though. Why don't . . . I mean, would it not be more effective to talk to* him?

He is not born of Pirogia, nor even of Talipon, and has no access to your Council by himself, the Wizard said. *For better or for worse, it must be you through whom I save the world of Petrarch.*

Gianni couldn't answer, he was so astounded, so aghast at the Wizard's colossal arrogance. Who was *he* to speak of saving a whole world? A city, perhaps, but a *world*?

But an army is not enough, the Wizard told him, *nor even the marines that your friend Gar intends to raise.*

Marines? Gianni wondered what that was. Something to do with the sea, yes—but nearly everything in Pirogia had to do with the sea. *What else can we do?*

You can raise all the merchant cities against the aristocracy. The cold eyes seemed to pierce Gianni's brain, transfixing him, depriving him of all powers of resistance. *You can bid them cut off the last vestiges of power that their contes and doges may have, even expel those noblemen completely—after all, their guilds and merchants' councils really rule their cities already. Then they too can raise armies and build navies, and the lords will have to split their forces, and will be unable to combine against Pirogia completely.*

But the other cities may be defeated! They may fall!

Then Pirogia must come to their rescue when you have driven off the Prince and his minions, the Wizard said sternly. *Your city must make alliances, Gianni Braccalese. You must form a league of merchant cities, a true federation, a republic!*

A republic of merchant cities? Gianni's brain reeled under the vision of the seacoast of Talipon all united as one nation, leaving the interior split up into a score of ducal cities. They would fight with viciousness and not the slightest trace of mercy, those aristocrats. Many people of the merchant cities would die . . .

But many of them would die if they didn't fight the lords, too—the false Gypsies and the Lurgan Company had seen to that. *It may be as you say . . . there may be a chance of success . . .*

It is your only *chance of success!* The Wizard's voice was harsh with anxiety, with urgency. *Tell your father, tell your Council! The die is cast, Gianni Braccalese, the wagers are placed! You must ally or die, and all the other merchant cities with you!*

Gianni realized the truth of what the Wizard said. It was do or die, now—and if the lords eliminated Pirogia, they would go on to enslave or crush all other merchants, too. *I shall do as you say,* he promised. *But the Council has already rejected such a notion.*

Before the lords marched on them, yes! Now that they know they must fight, you will find them much more willing! Tell your father! The face began to recede, hair and beard swirling up to hide it. *Remember—tell! Persuade! Or fall and die!*

Then the face was gone, and Gianni woke, shivering with fear—but also with elation. The prospect of a league of merchant cities awed and enthralled him—a league with Pirogia as its leader! With all the navies of the island at its command, all the new armies of the coastland coordinated in their strategy! The day of the nobleman was done!

If the Council could be persuaded.

* * *

The Council was persuaded.

Gianni's father returned home from the meeting, jubilant and brimming over with his triumph. "There wasn't the slightest hint of disagreement! They heard me out, they voted unanimously, and the couriers are already taking fast boats out past the bar!"

Gianni and Mama stared in amazement. "However did you manage it?" she asked.

"I told it to them as though it were an idea new-made, as though I had never told it to them before and they are all intent on war now, for even those who opposed it understand that once it has begun, their only hope of survival is to win! They didn't need persuading—they were ready to embrace the idea, *any* idea, that would give them a greater chance of winning!"

While Gianni was drilling the army, Gar combed the waterfront for stalwart young men, catching them before they could line up to enlist—young merchant sailors and sons of fishermen. He took two hundred of them under his personal tutelage, promoting the quickest learners to corporal at the end of the first day and to sergeant at the end of the second. He marched them about on the quays from dawn till dusk. They were exhausted and cursing him by the end of the first day, but drilling like professionals by the end of the week, with no signs of weariness even as darkness fell. Then he taught them weapons drill, and at the end of the tenth day buttonholed the city's two admirals. The result of their conference was that he marched his fishermen aboard a dozen ships in the morning and sailed out to the horizon, where ship met ship, for all the world looking as though they were fighting one another. They came sailing back at noon with the soldiers dragging their pikes, but the captains and admirals glowing—and the two hundred were dubbed "marines," and marched on board to row out to the bar, waiting.

They didn't have to wait long for a small, swift courier boat to come running back with the news that a pirate fleet was approaching.

The admirals sent the courier on with word for the Maestro and the Council before they set sail to meet the pirates. That word ran through the town, and when Gianni realized that his soldiers were virtually the only ones who weren't down by the docks waiting with bated breath, he called for fifty volunteers to guard the bridge to the mainland and sent everyone else off to wait and hope and pray with the rest of Pirogia. The hours dragged by, and people began to curse beneath their breath—but there wasn't a single echo of cannon fire, nor a trace of gunsmoke in the sky, for the navy had done its job well and attacked the pirate fleet far from the city.

Dusk fell, and people began to go home, dispirited and worried—but sausage sellers appeared, hawking their wares in the midst of the crowd, and a few enterprising wine merchants realized the chance to rid themselves of some of their worst vintages, so most of the crowd stayed, sipping near-vinegar and bolstered with meat that was best not studied too closely, waiting and hoping but growing more and more fearful by the hour, then by the minute.

Finally, hours after darkness had fallen, a shout went up from those who waited out by the headland, a shout that traveled inward to the watchers on the quays. "Ships! Sails!"

But whose? Impossible to tell, when all they could see was moonlight glinting on canvas in the distance—and the gunners stood by their cannon in the harbor forts while Gianni barked commands, and his brand-new soldiers marched forward to stand at the edge of the quay, hearts thumping so loudly that the crowd could almost hear them, halberds slanting out, waiting for sign of an enemy. The civilians gave way, letting themselves be elbowed back, more than glad to yield place to the soldiers in case the ships were pirates.

Then a shout of joy went up from the headland and traveled inward. As it reached the quays, three ships rounded the headland, their standards clear in the torchlight from the forts, the emblem on the one intact sail huge enough for all to see—the eagle of Pirogia! Then the citizens recognized the ships of their own building, and a shout of joy went up and turned into mad cheering that seemed as though it would never stop. The soldiers waved their pikes aloft, shouting in jubilation too.

More ships followed them, and more. The first of them glided up to the quays, and weary but triumphant sailors leaped over the side, elbowing their way through soldiers who laughed with joy and clapped them on their shoulders, cheering them on as they plowed into the crowd in search of sweethearts, wives, parents, and children.

Last from the last ship came the rear admiral, leaning heavily on Gar's arm. A reddened bandage wound up across his chest to his shoulder, but he was smiling bravely, and the light of victory was in his eyes.

"A surgeon, a surgeon!" Gar cried. His uniform was blackened with gunpowder, rent with sword cuts in a dozen places; he had a bandage around his left arm and another about his head—but he seemed clear-minded and able.

The surgeons took the admiral away, and Gianni ran up to clap Gar on the back and wring his hand, crying, "Congratulations! All hail the hero! A victory, Gar, a fabulous victory!"

"My men's, not mine." But Gar was smiling, his eyes alight. "But it was a fabulous battle, Gianni! I wish men could turn away from war—but if there have to be wars, they should be like this!"

"Tell me how it was!"

"We left the harbor with the morning breeze to waft us out to sea. A mile out, the fore admiral, Giovanni Pontelli, led half of our forces further out, past the horizon, while the rear admiral, Mosca Cacholli, led the rest of us on southward, following the coast, to meet the pirates as far from Pirogia as we could. With the wind at our backs, we made good time, and the breeze was beginning to turn toward shore when we met the pirates off Cape Leone. Admiral Cacholli hove to and gave the command to begin the bombardment. You know how I insisted the cannon be placed, Gianni—all on the deck, covered by canvas in case of storm, but none belowdecks, or the crew would be truly deafened by the sound, roasted by the heat, and suffocated by the smoke. Well, it wasn't much better on the decks, but all my gunners can still hear their orders and none died of smoke—though I think the sun's heat may have been just as bad as any on a gun deck. Still, my cannoneers pulled the canvas off their guns, loaded, and fired. The whole ship swayed with the recoil, but I had also insisted the ships not be too high, so they didn't capsize, and my crews proved the worth of their drill, because no one was crushed by the guns as they rolled back. Cacholli staggered the fire, so that as one ship fired, another was reloading and a third was taking aim, and we loosed a round every minute or so.

"Well, the pirates just weren't expecting anything like it. It was a horrendous noise, even over two hundred yards of water, and they had never faced such a rolling bombardment. We sank a dozen of their ships, for they turned broadside to fire at us, and their long galleys gave us excellent targets, while our little caravels, with so much space between them, gave them very little to aim at and less to hit. We couldn't hear their cannon because of the din of our own, but we saw their shot splash into the water in front of us—in front, between our ships, behind us, and every place except on our ships themselves. Simply put, their gunners couldn't even hit us!"

"Not a single one?" Gianni asked, eyes wide.

"Well, one of our caravels lost its mast and three deck hands; I could swear the shot hit by accident! But no matter how good our bombardment, it wasn't enough to decide the battle by itself, because there were three of them to every one of us, and the rest pressed on through the bombardment to grapple us. We turned and ran, and the pirate galleys fell farther and farther behind with every minute. The sea heaved beneath us, our little ships bucked and seesawed like horses, and the waves broke over our bow and drenched us with salt spray—but we were sailing against the wind, tacking, and the pirates had no idea how to do that. Oh, they furled their sails, but the wind still blew against them, and their oarsmen had to strain to make any way at all. Those oarsmen must have been new slaves pressed to learn to row in a week! Try as they might, they fell farther and farther behind us, and when we had distance enough, Admiral Cacholli turned us for another broadside and another, chewing their fleet to bits. Finally the pirates gained some modicum of sense and sent a wing to row up on our flank while we bombarded, so when we turned to run again, they came down from seaward with the wind behind them, and grappled us."

Gar's eyes glittered. "Then was the test of my marines, and they surpassed those poor farm boys forced to masquerade as pirates as thoroughly as a warhorse surpasses a child's pony! The 'pirates' came over the side with their scimitars waving, but my marines met them with a line of halberds. They ran the first wave through, then chopped the second wave in chest and hip. As they tired, they fell back and left the third wave of pirates to the second rank of marines, who stabbed and chopped as well as the first. But the pirates' officers drove them on with lash and blade, and they came over both rails in such numbers that my marines had to drop their spears and lug out their swords. Then it was man to man and blood and steel, each on his own. Three farm boys came at me all at once, yowling like demons and chopping as though their swords were axes. My blood sang high, for it was kill or be killed, so I tried to forget that they were forced to it and lunged, running the first through and ducking so that his body slammed into my shoulder. I straightened and threw him off as I parried his mate's slash, then stepped aside to let the third stumble past me—but I put out my foot and let him fall, even as I parried the second's slash again, then beat down his blade and ran him through.

"Then, incredibly, there were none more at me. I looked about and saw two of my marines back to back, beleaguered by a dozen plowboys—poor fools, they didn't realize that only six at a time could do any good, and they were getting in each other's way. I caught one by the shoulder, yanked him back, and stabbed him through the other shoulder, then turned to catch another by the arm and send him after the first. He tripped and went down, and another marine stabbed as he fell. I caught another and another, wounding each as he turned—but by the time I'd uncovered my two marines, they had slain all six of the men within reach. We turned and went looking for new quarry.

"That was the way of it. My marines went through the sea robbers' ranks reaping death until the 'pirates' began to throw down their arms and cry for mercy. Then my captains managed to rein in their sailors as

I called back my marines, and ordered them to lock the pirates in the holds of their own ships."

"But that was only the flank," Gianni said, his eyes wide.

"Only the flank, but they delayed us long enough for the main body to catch up with us." Gar nodded, his face turning somber. "There were half a dozen ships in the center of their line who were the real pirates, and they grappled and boarded. Then my boys died—one of each five, as we learned when the battle was done—but each took half a dozen pirates with him, and those who lived took ten and more. One huge brute came at me, all mustaches and leering grin. I parried his slash, but he kicked at me; I blocked the kick with my shin and thrust at him, but he was quick enough to catch his balance and slap my sword aside with his blade. I leaped back, but not quite quickly enough, and his cleaver took a slice off my arm—there . . ." He nodded at his wound. "I bellowed in anger and thrust before he could recover, ran him through like the pig he was, and turned just in time to see another like him chopping one of my lads through and yowling with delight as he did. The whole view darkened with redness then, and I leaped in to catch him by the hair and shave him gratis. I would have bandaged the cuts I made, but there was no point, since he'd lost his head." Gar shook his head in self-disgust. "But I let my heart carry me away there, and turned from his execution to see three of his smaller mates coming for me with swords waving, howling like the north wind. I ducked and stabbed upward, running one through just under the breastbone as I caught up the butcher's scimitar from the dead man. I cut with it at the man on my left, and he skidded to a halt to block with his own as I parried the blow from my right, then swung my rapier about and ran the man through. Then I turned to my left and caught the fool's next slash, scimitar against scimitar, and ran him through with my rapier.

"So it went. We paid a high price in blood and life, but we cleared all the real pirates from our decks, then boarded their ships and slew the few who were left, throwing their bodies to the sharks. They'll be in blood frenzy all along this coast for weeks, so bid everyone to forgo swimming."

Gianni shuddered. "But the rest of the fleet?"

Gar's eyes glinted again. "While the false pirates were struggling to reach us, Admiral Pontelli had been sailing past them on the other side of the horizon. Now when they grappled, he swooped down on them with the wind at his back, hove to, and fired point blank at their rear. It was a fearful carnage, they tell me, and the foolish false pirates had jammed themselves too closely for no more than a few of them to beat their way clear with their oars. Indeed, they did more damage to one another than the admiral did, ramming into their own ships and breaking each other's oars—and oarsmen," he added darkly. "When they'd sorted themselves out, our ships grappled them one by one, and my marines made me proud of their training again. They lost only a dozen and were disgusted with the work they had to do, for they were fighting untrained plowboys again, who surrendered quickly enough, though, and we locked them in their holds as we had before. Then we set prize crews to each ship—they should be sailing into the harbor before dawn. They have to go slowly, for they've no oarsmen and only skeleton crews, but we've doubled the size of our fleet!"

"A fabulous victory!" Gianni cried. "But how can you be so sure that the false pirates were peasants forced into service?"

Gar grinned from ear to ear. "Why, because when our admiral struck the sword from the hand of *their* admiral and bade my marines seize the man, he cried, Unhand me, lowborn scum! Know that I am the Conte Plasio, and worth more than all your ragtag horde put together!"

Gianni stared in disbelief, then broke out laughing, slapping Gar on the back. But his mirth slackened and died when he heard the wailing from the back of the quay.

"I said we lost men," Gar said, his face darkening, "marines, but sailors, too. It was a great victory, and cheaply bought, when you see how many we sank and how many we won—but we did pay a price, and there'll be many who mourn this night."

Gianni stared toward the sounds of grief, suddenly realizing how real the war was—that it was more than some gigantic contest, some game lords played to relieve their boredom. Their playing pieces were living human beings, and their play ended in tragedy.

"The philosopher told us that eternal vigilance is the price of freedom," Gar said softly beside him, "but he forgot that vigilance must all too frequently end in war, and those who say it's better to die free than to live a slave must think long and truly before they say it."

Gianni heard, felt the question sink deep within him—but heard the ring and the hardening of instant certainty, too. "I hope I won't have to pay that price, Gar," he said, "but I will if I must."

"Yes." Gar nodded. "After all, you've come near to paying it twice, and that without even having a chance to fight to stay free, haven't you? At the last, the question is not whether or not you'll die, but how."

The day after the battle, the courier boats came back—three that first day, two the next, and five more on the third. All the other merchant cities, after furious debates in guildhalls and councils, had finally seen that they must fight or be ground under the noblemen's boots. With the three cities that wavered, news of the navy's victory against the lords' thinly disguised fleet turned the tide, and they, too, cast their lot with Pirogia. Their ambassadors met in the Council Hall, and with ponderous ceremony signed a Charter of Merchant Cities, agreeing to fight together under a strategy devised by Pirogia. That was all they would promise, and only for the duration of the war; peacetime details would be thrashed out when (and if!) peace came. But it was enough to make the Pirogians jubilant again—and to bring Gianni the most splendid dream of his life.

The circle of light appeared amidst the darkness of sleep, and Gianni braced himself for another encounter with the cantankerous old Wizard, but the expanding circle of light showed not floating hair but swirling veils, and it was the Mystery Woman who undulated before him, not the grim old face—and her gyrations were more pronounced than before, slower, more rhythmical, more enticing. There was an aura about her, an aura of desire—not his, but hers.

Bravely done, Gianni Braccalese! Her voice was warm all about him; he could have sworn he felt breath in his ear. *You have done well and wisely to persuade your father, and the merchant cities have listened to your reasoning! The league is formed, and it is your doing, O my brave one, all yours!*

Gianni bathed in every word of her praise—indeed, he felt it as caressing all over his skin—but honesty made him protest, *It was Gar's idea first, and my father who brought it to the Council!*

But the arguments your father used were yours, and it was you who pressed him into making the demands again! Oh, you are brave and worthy and valiant, and all that a woman could want! She swam closer, closer, and her face remained shadowed, even though the veils stilled and dropped, and the glory of her figure shone in a wondrous rose-hued light. Gianni gasped and felt his whole body quicken, aching for her—and discovered that he *had* a body in this dream, a body far more muscular and unblemished than his real one, naked and fairly glowing with his desire for her.

And she was there beside him, taking his hand and laying it upon her breast, then moving it gently to caress. Mechanically, he continued the action when her hand stopped, staring in fascination and awe at the glorious curves of breast and thigh and hip. Some lingering scruple screamed at him that this was wrong because they weren't married, but she must have heard and breathed, *No. Nothing is wrong, in a dream—for you have no control over your dreams, and therefore can have no guilt; they do with you as they please.* And she did indeed seem to be doing with him as she pleased, caressing his body too, wherever she wished—and more clearly, wherever *he* wished . . . *Oh, be very sure that you have no control over* this *dream,* she assured, *for I do, every instant. Come, do as I wish, for you can do nothing else— your only choice is to fight your desires while you do as I please, or to fulfill those desires, as is only right, very right, perfectly right—in a dream. Dream with me, Gianni, for there can be no guilt and no sin here, and the only wrongness is to refuse the gift of pleasure thus given.*

It was true, her words rang true within him, and Gianni threw away all scruple and inhibition, giving himself over fully to her and her wondrous dreambody, and the pleasure vouchsafed him. He who had never lain with a woman but always dreamed of it, dreamed now in earnest, and learned the ways of lovemaking to their fullest in the depths of his sleep.

CHAPTER 14

There was one aspect of war, at least, that Gar had not had to teach the people of Pirogia. The merchants, and especially the Council, had always had a very healthy interest in the events that happened in and around the other cities—who was buying what, who was selling what, who was in league with whom, who was marching against whom—so the fishermen and the peasants had all known, for many years, that the Council of Pirogia, and some individual merchants, would pay well for information of all sorts. Gar had not had to point out to the Council that intelligence about enemy troop movements was worth even more than general news, and much more hazardous to obtain; the Council had doubled, then tripled, the price of its own accord, and several peasant families who had been burned out by soldiers recovered the whole worth of their farm and livestock just by telling their tale to the officers of the Council. Indeed, that was how the news had come that had panicked the merchants into authorizing the gathering of the army.

Even so, Gianni found it hard to believe that even the peasants whom Gar had persuaded into going out and seeking information again and again, and who brought back hair-raising tales and became amazingly adept at gathering information, could have brought back as much as the giant knew, or brought it as fast as he learned it. He also noticed the new medallion Gar wore pinned over his heart, but assumed it was just a sort of last-ditch armor.

Nonetheless, Gar did tell his officers and the Council that the other merchant cities had already fortified their walls and were training their own armies. That surprised no one, but how could he have learned it so quickly? How could he have discovered that many of the lords had taken their men back to their home cities to punish these insolent upstarts? Above all, how could he have known it a day or two before spies came back to confirm it? Nonetheless, it was apparently true—and when the number of peasants fleeing into Pirogia suddenly increased fivefold, Gar told them the aristocrats' army was near. The next afternoon, when that army appeared on the ridges across from the city, Gar assured them it was only two-thirds the size it had been.

Whatever its size or condition, Prince Raginaldi knew his one chance when he saw it, and sent a troop of cavalry charging down the slopes and across the seaside plain to catch up with and pass the last of the fleeing peasants, to capture the land bridge and causeway.

But Gar knew the importance of that chance, too, and had sent his soldiers out that morning to hurry the laggards and warn then that the city wouldn't wait for them. Even the most stubborn had finally abandoned their carts and their goods and fled to the city, riding pillion behind Pirogian cavalrymen—and the last of them cleared the land gate a good quarter-mile ahead of the prince's army. Two swift-footed volunteers followed the refugees back along the causeway, lighting fuses as they went—and as they ran through the inner gate, the first explosions shook the island. Turning about, they watched spellbound as a huge geyser rose up from the lagoon, scattering bits of the causeway in all directions. Then another section blew, and another, waterspouts marching across the strait toward the inner gate, each shaking the ground beneath it, each with a shorter and shorter fuse.

"Back! Away!" Gar called, and the army took up the cry with him, herding people away from the gate. Protesting, they withdrew, truculent but disturbed by the soldiers' concern—and discovered the reason, when bits and shards of stone and wood showered the piazza, striking down the gateway itself.

Finally, the last of the explosions died, the last of the deadly rain of shards and scrap fell and ceased—and the whole city watched in deathly quiet as the waves roiled where the causeway had been, and the horsemen a half-mile distant shook their fists and shouted in frustration. Everyone stared; everyone realized how completely cut off from the mainland they were—and everyone realized that the siege of Pirogia had begun.

It was indeed a siege, and could only be a siege, for the inland lords had no idea how to manage a navy. They conscripted every fishing boat they could get; they brought down riverboats while the city men sat and watched—and laughed. Finally, the lords loaded a hundred picked soldiers onto the craft and pushed out from shore.

They were halfway to Pirogia, and the soldiers were cocking their crossbows and nervously readying their halberds, when six of the Pirogia's caravels came sailing out from behind each side of the island, sailing against the seaward breeze.

The lords' conscripted fishermen saw, and began to paddle frantically, trying to speed boats that already moved as fast as they could with the wind filling their sails. But the captains shouted, and the caravels shifted tack and glided down onto the ragtag fleet like falcons upon a flock of pigeons. A few of the lords' soldiers shouted defiance, raising cumbersome muskets to rest against the gunwale, then firing with a huge flash of powder and thunder of noise— but the horses took fright, as did the fishermen, and the musketeers hadn't realized what recoil would do in a boat. Over they went in a flailing of horse legs and soldiery arms—and troopers cried out in panic, unable to swim. The fishermen, at least, had the sense to swim back and cling to their overturned boat, but the Pirogian sailors, laughing hugely, tossed ropes down next to the soldiers, who caught them and let themselves be fished out like so many bedraggled, wet dogs.

Some other ships, with quick-witted fishermen for captains, furled their sails and tried to dodge the caravels by running oars—but the soldiers, unused to such gyrations, teetered and shouted and lost their balance, knocking one another overboard. In one boat, the fishermen saw their chance and turned on the few remaining soldiers with their oars, tipping them over, knocking them out, then rolling them over the gunwales and rowing for all they were worth toward Pirogia and freedom. The others, slower-witted, more merciful, or more loyal to those who paid them, turned their boats back to haul the soldiers aboard—and were themselves hauled up short by the caravels' grappling hooks. Marines dropped down into the smaller boats, and the fight between dripping soldier and seawise marine was brief. Even so, a few marines died, but each caravel took its score of soldiers prisoner. Then they turned back to Pirogia, leaving a scattering of wreckage behind them—but most of the boats, intact, drifted behind the caravels, lashed to lines as prizes. A few soldiers' bodies washed up on the beach that evening, but by that time, ninety-six of their surviving comrades were grumbling around fires in the cellar of the Council house, which was hastily fitted out with bars as an improvised but very effective prison.

But Gar looked out over the scene of their triumph and shook his head. "The prince is saying, 'Never mind—they must feed a hundred more, and Heaven only knows how many peasants fled to them in the last few days. Their food cannot last long.' "

"He doesn't know that the refugees are swelling the ranks of your army," Gianni said.

"But their wives and children and elders are not," Gar reminded him, "and even our soldiers must eat. Is the prince right, Gianni? Will our supplies disappear like a morning's frost?"

"I saw frost when we wandered in the mountains," Gianni said thoughtfully, "but I had seen a rain of plenty before that, and all my life." He pointed toward the bar. "There comes your answer, Gar."

The giant looked up and saw a caravel tacking in against the offshore breeze.

"Wine from the southlands, grain from the northern shore of the Central Sea," Gianni said, musing. "Pork from the western shores, beeves from the eastern ... No, Gar, we won't starve. Far from it—and that ship bears wool, too, or others will, and every goodwife who has fled to us can card and spin and weave. That ship will take our stout Pirogian cloth back to trade for more food, and will also bear dishes and glassware from the clay and sands of our islands. No, we won't starve ..."

An explosion echoed from the mainland, and they saw a ball flying through the air, straight toward the ship. They held their breaths in an agony of suspense, but the ball splashed into the sea, raising a geyser and rocking the ship, but not harming it. Gianni breathed a sigh of relief. "I didn't know the lords had a cannon that could shoot even that closely."

"Neither did I," Gar replied. "Did any of the lords buy a gun from your armories?"

Gianni frowned. "Not that I know of—and surely no one would have been foolish enough to sell one of the cannon made with the secrets of your new ideas!"

Gar grimaced. "I don't like the idea of keeping knowledge to ourselves, Gianni—but for once, I must admit secrecy is wise, at least until we have won this . . ."

The cannon thundered again, and another ball climbed into the sky. Again they held their breath, but as the shot rose to its peak, Gar relaxed. "Too high."

Sure enough, the ball passed right over the ship and splashed up a spout on its far side. They could hear the sailors' cheers, though faintly at this distance.

"They're safe." Gianni relaxed as well. "No cannoneer could hit a ship at such a distance—but for a minute, I thought he could."

"He can, and he will," Gar said grimly. "He has their range now, and the next ball will strike home. Can you signal to the men on the ship?"

Gianni stared up at him in alarm—but before he could turn and run to the signal flags, another shot rang out. He and Gar both watched, holding their breath, as the cannonball arced upward, speeding toward the ship, and sailors struggled to spread some more canvas, hoping against hope that they could outrun the shot . . .

It smashed into their side just above the waterline; the ship rocked, water poured in, and the caravel began to list toward starboard. They could faintly hear the captain shout, and the crew ran for the longboat. The ship shuddered, swinging over so the deck stood at a sharp angle; sailors skidded and fell overboard.

"That one boat can't hold them all," Gar snapped, but Gianni was already sprinting away to send out boats from shore.

Even so, he came too late—a dozen small craft were already springing out into the bay. He watched as they grappled the struggling men from the water—and as the distant cannon boomed, its ball arcing high toward the small craft . . .

Gianni called out, but other men were shouting aboard the boats, and they all pulled away from the wreck quickly. The ball splashed down, showering them with spray and capsizing two. Their neighbors quickly rowed over, hauled out the men, and righted the boats—but two dead bodies floated in the water. Another boat, arriving late, hauled them aboard; then all the small craft dashed for shore as the cannon boomed again. Another ball splashed down, far from the boats near the wreck.

Gianni turned, face flaming with anger, to see Gar coming up. "They didn't have to do that, Gar! Shooting down the ship I can understand—it's war, after all. But to fire on rescue boats is foul!"

"But just the sort of thing the lords might think of," Gar pointed out. "They mean to punish you, after all—and they also mean to make sure you won't try to save the cargo. I think you might say they've made that clear."

"Very clear—and that ends our confidence about

not starving." Gianni gazed out at the sinking ship, feeling his heart sink with it. "What can we do about it, Gar?"

"Where there is one gun, there could be more," the giant said slowly, "but if they had more, they would have used them—and if more than one gunner has the knack of firing so accurately, the others would be firing, too."

Gianni looked up with a gleam of hope in his eye. "Are you saying that if we can destroy that one gun, we can stop worrying?"

"If we also capture that one gunner," Gar confirmed. "It's not a sure thing, mind you, but it's a good chance."

"Then it's certainly worth taking! But why capture? Killing him is easier and less chancy—and after that shot at the boats, I don't see anything wrong with it! We'd rather capture him if we can, I suppose, but—"

Gar interrupted. "I want to talk to him, Gianni. I want to discover where he learned to shoot so well."

"But to capture him, we'll have to go ashore!"

"Exactly," Gar agreed. "How else did you think we could destroy that one cannon?"

Gianni would never have thought of painting his face black. Wearing all black clothes, yes, and a black head scarf, so he and his men would blend into the shadows—but face paint, never. It didn't help that Gar made it by mixing soot with a little bacon grease. Gianni decided that secret raiding was not a job of good aroma.

They skimmed ashore in three light boats with muffled oars, one man to an oar for speed. Gar leaped out as they grounded and pulled the first boat up on the beach, lifting the prow high to make less noise. The coxswains of the other boats followed his example. His men stepped out onto the sand in silence, their steps muted by the soft leather slippers with thick padded soles; cobblers had worked all day at Gar's direction, laboring into the night to make enough of them.

Gar waved his raiders forward. Knives in their teeth, they padded into the tree-shaded blackness of a moonless night.

A sentry seemed to materialize out of the darkness on their right, turning about to look, bored and weary—but the boredom vanished from his face when he saw the raiders, not two feet away from him. His pike came up, and his mouth opened to shout the alarm—but Gianni, galvanized by fear, seized him by the throat, choking off the sound. The man thrashed about, dropping his pike to struggle against Gianni's grip, but another Pirogian slipped around behind him and struck his head with the sand-filled leather bag Gar had invented. The sentry's eyes rolled up; he folded, and Gianni let go of his neck to catch him by the tunic and lower him to the ground. He looked up at Volio with a nod of thanks, then turned to follow Gar, who gave them a nod of approval, then led them off into the darkness again.

They had landed as close to the gun as possible, but the lords had been so inconsiderate as to place it well back from the shore. Gar led them along a winding route between groups of one-man tents, staying as far as possible from both canvas and watch-fire embers. They prowled silently through the darkness—until a sudden grunt made them all freeze. Gianni flicked a glance at the sound and saw a grizzled, red-eyed soldier pushing himself up from the ground, reeking of stale beer and growling, "Who 'n hell is goin' aroun' . . ." Then his eyes widened in alarm as his mouth widened to cry out—and the sandbag hit him alongside the head. His eyes closed as he fell back. Gianni stifled a chuckle; the man was likely to remember them all as a drunken nightmare, and nothing more. He looked up at a hiss from the front; Gar waved them on.

They padded after him through the darkness, keeping a wary eye now for sleepers underfoot—until, suddenly, the cannon loomed before them, darkness out of darkness.

Gar held up a hand, and they froze, for there were sentries, one on each side of the gun. Gianni couldn't help staring—it was far bigger than any cannon he had seen, its platform holding it at eye level. But Gar was gesturing in the hand language he had worked out before they left, and his raiders cat-footed around the huge barrel, just out of range of the watch fire near the sentry.

What it was that gave them away, Gianni never knew—perhaps someone stepped too heavily, or perhaps another stepped too close to the fire, and its light reflected off his eyes. Whatever the clue, the sentry on the far side shouted, "Enemy!" and swung his halberd. A raider cried out in pain, a cry quickly choked off but loud enough to wake the gun crew; then both sentries were howling as they struck about them with their halberds.

Gianni ducked under a swing and came up to strike with his sandbag. The halberd dropped from nerveless fingers, and Gianni caught it up, turning to meet a stumbling attack from muzzy-headed soldiers. His blade sliced flesh; the man shouted in pain, and his companions dropped back, suddenly afraid of the black-clothed demons who had appeared out of the night. The half-minute's respite was enough for the other raiders to strike down the gun crew. Gianni handed his halberd to Volio and turned to face a gunner who was dressed more elaborately than the others and was shouting for help as he held off the raiders with sword and dagger. Gianni drew his own sword, though it was considerably shorter than the gunner's rapier, and leaped in, thrusting and parrying. All about him, soldiers went crazy, yelling and attacking as the raiders fought them off desperately, and Gar shoved a canister into the barrel of the gun. Vincenzio slipped up behind the gunner as he fenced desperately with Gianni, still yammering for aid. Vincenzio swung with his sandbag and the man stiffened, eyes wide; then he crumpled, and Gianni stepped in to catch him across a shoulder.

Then Gar was beside him, flame flaring in his hands, and Gianni saw a long string of some sort vanishing into the cannon's touchhole. The big man caught up Boraccio, slinging him over a shoulder as he snapped, "Carry the wounded and leave the dead! Flee as though the devil were at your heels!" He turned and charged into the midst of the soldiers facing him, bellowing like a bull. The raiders shouted and charged after him, carrying three wounded men between them—but leaving four others already dead.

The sentries recovered and shouted, chopping at the raiders—but their blows fell short as they pulled back, frightened by the wild men from the darkness.

Then a huge explosion blasted the night. The shock wave bowled men over, raider and soldier alike. "Cover your heads!" Gar shouted, but the raiders had run far enough; the rain of iron fragments fell short of them. Soldiers cried out in pain and shock, but before they could recover, the raiders were up and running again.

Gar led them off into the darkness, circling around to the beach again. All pretense at stealth gone, they struck down any soldier who rose to bar their way, then finally leaped back aboard their boats and shoved off—but only two boats out of three.

A hundred yards out to sea, Gar called a rest. The men leaned on their oars, gasping for breath and staring back at the fire on shore, amazed.

"So much for the cannon," Gar said. He looked down at the unconscious form at his feet. "Now for the gunner."

Gianni was sitting on a dock post, watching dawn over the sea, when Gar came up and joined him. "You fought well this night, Gianni."

"Thank you," Gianni said, gratified at the praise. "What of the gunner? Did he answer your questions?"

"Yes, and without the slightest hesitation," Gar

said. "It's almost as though he thinks his answers will frighten us as badly as his gun did."

Gianni frowned. "Did they?"

"Not a bit; they're just as I thought they would be. He's a young knight who's very progressive. He does admit that they have only one such gun, and only he knew how to aim it, being the only gentleman who was willing to learn his gunnery from the dour and dowdy foreign traders—the Lurgans, of course. They not only taught him to shoot, but also taught his armorers how to make a cannon that could fire so accurately but it took their smiths three months to make it, and two were killed testing earlier models, so I don't think we need to worry about the lords making more."

"Not considering how quickly we destroyed it," Gianni agreed, "though I doubt we could do it again."

"*You* may doubt it, but the lords don't. Still, our raid may discourage them from making more. If they do, though, they'll guard them better."

Gianni glanced at him out of the corners of his eyes. "And you'll be thinking up better ways to overcome their guards?"

Gar answered with the ghost of a smile. "Of course."

Gianni relaxed, letting himself feel confident again. He turned to see another ship come sailing in, and was delighted not to hear a cannon boom. "So it seems we won't starve, after all."

"No," Gar agreed, "we won't starve—but the lords may."

They didn't, of course—each lord was supplied by the crops and livestock his soldiers stole from the peasants nearby, most of whom were safe in Pirogia. But they had to ranger farther and farther afield each day, and the idle soldiers who stayed in camp began to quarrel among themselves. The prince set them to making ships, but his shipwrights knew only the crafting of riverboats, and the new vessels were scarcely launched before Pirogia's caravels swooped down to scuttle them, or to bear them away with all their troops. Still the prince forced his soldiers to build, but more and more, they saw the uselessness of their work, and grumbled more and more loudly. Soon they were being flogged daily, and the grumbling lessened—but became all the more bitter for it.

In fact, morale in the besiegers' camp was lessening so nicely, and any attempt at invading seemed so far away, that the defenders began to relax. In vain did Gar warn them that the old moon was dying, that the dark of the moon would soon be upon them, and that they must be extraordinarily vigilant when the nights were so dark—in vain, because the sentries knew that if they could not see to spy out the enemy, neither could invaders see to attack. So, though they tried to stay alert, that little edge was gone, the edge that makes a man start at shadows and hear menace in every night bird's call—but that also makes him look more closely at every extra pool of darkness in the night. They relaxed just a little, until the night that the cry went up from the walls, and the alarm sounded.

Gar and Gianni bolted from their beds—it was a

lieutenant's watch—and shouted for lights as they caught up swords and bucklers and ran for the docks. Black-clad men were pouring in from the sea; even the heads of their spears and halberds were painted black, even their faces. By the time Gianni and his men reached them, they were streaming into the plaza, and there was no sign of the Pirogian sentries.

They had served their city well by crying out before they died. Gianni shouted, "Revenge! Revenge for our sentries!" and threw himself into the middle of the advancing mob, sword slashing and thrusting. Finally the attackers shouted in alarm and anger; pole-arms swept down, but Gianni was too close for any blade to strike him, leaping in and out, shouting in rage, thrusting with his sword as Gar had taught him. Behind him, his men blared their battle cry and struck the invaders, alternating between stabbing and striking with the butts of their spears, quarterstaff style—again, as Gar had taught them. Men screamed and died on both sides, but still the attackers came on.

There seemed no end to them; the black-clad men kept coming and coming, and Gianni's arms grew heavy with thrusting and parrying. But there was no end to the Pirogian soldiers, either, and they were fighting for their homes and their loved ones, not just for pay or fear of an officer.

Light flared with a muffled explosion; the fighters froze for a moment, all eyes turned to the source— and saw flames billowing high into the night.

"The caravel!" Gianni screamed. "Anselmo's *Kestrel*, that was tied up at harbor! They have burned our food, they would starve us! Have at them! Hurl them into their own fire!"

His men answered with a shout of rage and surged forward. Gianni sailed before them, borne on their tide, thrusting and slashing with renewed vigor, pressing the attackers back, back, out of the plaza and onto the docks, then back even farther, off the wood and into the water.

The lords' soldiers cried out in fear and turned to flee into the harbor. Gianni froze, scarcely able to believe his eyes. The invaders were standing out there on the water, helping those who swam to climb to their feet! More amazing still, they seemed to be going without moving their legs, drifting away . . .

Drifting! Now Gianni knew what to look for—and sure enough, the light of the burning ship showed him the balks of timber beneath the soldiers' feet. They had come on rafts, simple rafts but huge ones, painted black. They had hidden against the darkness of the water itself, and guided themselves by the city's blotting out of the stars until they could see the lights of the watch fires!

"Archers!" Gianni shouted. "Stand ready! If they seek to come back, let fly!"

But the archers didn't wait—they sent flight after flight against the men on the rafts, who fell to the wood with shouts of fear or cries of pain. Some knelt on each raft and began to paddle furiously. Slowly, the cumbersome craft moved away from the docks.

Gar came panting up, blood running from cuts on his cheeks and brow and staining the fabric of sleeves and tights. "Where have *you* been?" Gianni snapped, then saw the man's wounds and was instantly sorry. "Your pardon . . ."

"Given," Gar panted, "and gladly. It was not only here that they came ashore, but at every dock and water stair all around the island. I suspected it the instant I heard the alarm and ordered troops to every such site. Then I led my marines from one outbreak of clamor to another. We have run long, Gianni, but we have pushed the lords' men back into the sea."

"It was well done," Gianni said, eyes wide. "You are wounded, Gar!"

"Nothing but cuts," the giant told him, "and you have a few yourself."

"Do I really?" Gianni touched his cheek and was amazed to see the hand come away bloodied.

Gar looked him up and down quickly. "Again, nothing of any danger, but we shall have to see the physician to be sure. I fear many of our men came off much worse—and many more of the enemy."

"Yes . . ." Gianni's gaze strayed to a black-clothed heap near them. "The poor slaves . . . How did they ever think of a ruse so simple, yet so subtle?"

"They didn't," Gar said, lips pressed thin. "This is not the sort of thing that would occur to a Taliponese nobleman raised on tales of chivalry and battle glamour. Test that man's tunic, Gianni. Try to tear it."

Puzzled, Gianni knelt by the corpse and yanked at the fabric. It gave not at all. "Silk?" he asked, amazed. "For thousands of warriors?"

"Not silk." Gar handed down his dagger. "Cut it."

Gianni tried. He tried hard, even sawed at it. Finally, he looked up at Gar in amazement. "What *is* this stuff?"

"The mark of the Lurgan traders," Gar told him, "and if you tested that black face paint he wears, you would find it to be no simple lampblack and tallow, but something far more exotic. The Lurgans told the lords how to plan this raid, Gianni, and gave them the materials to make it work."

Gianni stared up, appalled. "Are they war advisers now?"

"Apparently so," Gar said darkly. "We knew they recognized Pirogia as a threat, didn't we?"

And yourself, Gianni thought, staring up at the grim, craggy face—but he most definitely didn't say it.

From that time on, the sentries stayed alert again, staring twice at every shadow—but needlessly, as it turned out. There were no more night raids, for Pirogian caravels patrolled the channel between the city and the mainland. The grumbling in the lords' camp grew ever worse, and morale ever lower, according to the reports from the spies there. The Pirogians welcomed each new caravel that brought them food, and toasted its sailors with the wine from its casks. Gar, of course, grew more and more tense, more and more hollow-eyed, stalking the battlements muttering to himself. Finally, Gianni asked him why, and Gar answered, "Things are going too well."

Very well, indeed, for the people of Pirogia. Even better, courier boats brought word from other cities, and caravels took arms to them—but they were all port cities, and none lacked for food. They were having more difficulty defending their walls, since only Pirogia had a natural moat to protect it—but none of the inland lords had so very big an army by himself, and all his allies were sitting and fuming outside the walls of their own merchant towns, or with the prince at Pirogia. Gar sent cannons and crossbows and advice, and watched the stew boiling in the prince's camp with a grin.

They also seemed to lack knowledge of sanitation, these inland soldiers who had never lived in groups of more than a hundred with no less than a mile between villages. It wasn't long before the offshore wind bore their stench to Pirogia, and the soldiers the Pirogians captured in their endless sinking of new vessels told tales of dysentery and cholera stalking the camp.

"They're weakening nicely," Gar told Gianni, "but the noblemen only have to learn better siege tactics, and I'm sure they won't lack for advisers."

Gianni thought of the fake Gypsies and the dour Lurgan traders, and nodded. "Do they really know so much of war?"

"No," Gar admitted, "but they have no shortage of books to tell them of it."

Gianni stared—he certainly hadn't thought there would be much room for books in the caravans—but he didn't doubt Gar.

The Wizard appeared in Gianni's dream that night, and told you, *You do well, you and your giant barbarian. You hold the lords at bay, here and all around the coastline—but that is not enough.*

What then? Gianni asked, amazed.

You must give them reason to leave, and more importantly, an honorable *reason to leave—of a sort.*

Gianni frowned. *What sort of reason could there be, for giving up ignominiously and going home?*

A diversion, said the Wizard, and explained.

Gar thought it was a capital idea when Gianni repeated the explanation to him. "Wonderful!" he cried, slapping his knee. "How do you think of these things, Gianni?"

"I really haven't the faintest idea." For his part, Gianni was just glad it had been Gar's knee and not his own.

That night, when the docks were dark and deserted except for the sentries Gar kept posted, a hundred marines with fifteen gunners, ten horses, and five cannon boarded two long, lean, dark-colored ships— captured galleys outfitted with proper sails. Off they went into the night, and as far as Pirogia was concerned, they ceased to exist for a week. Gar and Gianni were both with them, leaving the captain of the guard in command with Vincenzio as his second. The scholar had shown an amazing talent for commanding men; Gianni thought it came from his years of cajoling and maneuvering people into giving him money and helping him go from town to town, saving to return to the university.

By dusk, they were well past the prince's lines, and far enough to the north that a single night's march should take them to Tumanola, the Raginaldis' city. The galleys rowed into a little bay as far as they could and anchored; then longboats began the tedious process of ferrying men and equipment ashore. When they were all gathered, the galley weighed anchor but rowed only as far away as the shadows of the high bluffs that warded the little port. The marines hoisted their packs and began to march, the gunners right behind them with their horses.

It was a long march, and all the men gazed down with relief when they came to the top of the slope that led down to Tumanola. Gar wouldn't let them rest, though, until they had all moved silently into the positions he assigned them, and camouflaged themselves. Then he posted sentries and let his marines collapse gratefully behind their blinds. Gianni collapsed, too, and took what sleep he could, until Gar waked him to take the second watch. Gianni spent the next four hours moving as silently as he could from sentry post to sentry post, but always found his men awake, if not terribly alert. He glowed with pride, and was quite unsure that he would be able to keep the vigil as well as they, with so little sleep—but he did.

Gar woke them all at dawn. They breakfasted as they had supped—on clear water, cold journey bread, and jerky. Then, as the sun warmed the earth, Gar gave the signal for the bombardment to begin.

Cannon boomed to the east and west of the city, slamming boulders into the walls. Alarms rattled inside the city, and the home guard came running to the ramparts. They couldn't know that the booming from east and west came from cannon with no ammunition to throw, that now belched only blank charges; they could only assume the gunners were very poor shots.

But the three cannon before the central gate had boulders and iron balls and fired at five-minute intervals, each shot striking the city gates.

How could they hold? It was amazing they lasted the hour. But when they began to crack worse and worse with each shot, the home guard gathered around, crossbows and pikes at the ready—so as the final shots crashed through the wood, splintering the huge panels, they didn't hear the shouts of alarm from the few sentries left along the wall as scaling ladders slammed into place and grapnels bit into the top of the wall. Those sentries ran to push the ladders away, shouting for all they were worth, but they were too few, and the marines swarming up the wall to their grapnels were far greater in number than those on the ladders. In five minutes, Gar's marines held the ramparts, and Gar himself was leading the assault on the gate from the west while Gianni led from the east. The defenders finally heard them coming, in lulls between purposeless cannon fire; they turned just in time for bolts and spears to bring them down. A few of them did manage to shoot a bolt or hurl a spear, and a few marines died, but the rest of it was slaughter until the soldiers threw up their arms, shouting for mercy.

"Hold!" Gar shouted, and his men froze in midstride. "Sergeants, send men to secure the prisoners!" he snapped. "Soldiers of Tumanola! You have fought well, but you have been outflanked! Lay down your arms and mercy will be yours!"

Warily, the soldiers laid down their pikes and

crossbows, and marines stepped up to lash their arms behind them. Then, with the soldiers lined up against the wall and sitting, bound with a score of marines to guard them, the rest advanced on the castle.

"It looks formidable indeed." Gianni shuddered, remembering.

"It looks so, yes," Gar agreed, "but we know better, don't we, Gianni? After all, we've been inside—and there can't be more than a few score soldiers left to guard it, since most of them are with the prince at Pirogia."

Gianni looked up in surprise, but when he saw Gar's grin, he began to smile, too.

The only difficult part of the siege of the castle was bringing the cannon up the slope into firing position opposite the drawbridge. The defenders started a hail of bolts even before the gunners and their horses came in range—which gave the marines a convenient supply of ammunition as they moved up the slope ahead of the cannon, keeping up such a continuous fire that the defenders could scarcely lift their heads above the wall. The drawbridge fell as cannonballs broke its chains, and struck the shore with a boom almost equaling that of the artillery. Then the gunners sent buckets of nails over the parapets to keep the defenders down while Gar led his marines charging across the bridge, ramming spears through the arrow slits in the gatehouse and firing in staggered ranks, the back row finishing reloading and running to the front as the first rank retired.

The continuous fire kept most of the defenders

prudently down; the few bold ones died with bolts in their chests. A few marines died, too, but their mates came up behind the defenders and grappled hand to hand, knocking them out. Then, in parties of a dozen, they went through the castle from top to bottom, until they were satisfied that it was completely secure.

"A whole city and its castle taken with only a hundred men!" Gianni was dizzy at the thought.

"Yes, but there were only three hundred defending it," Gar reminded him. "We did lose twenty-three men, too." At the thought, his face turned somber.

"My husband shall be revenged upon you!" the princess raged. "You lowborn upstarts shall learn the meaning of royal wrath! You shall be hanged, but cut down before you are dead, then have your entrails drawn forth before your still-living eyes! The end shall come only when your bodies are cut in four pieces and hung up as warnings throughout the city!"

"Perhaps, Highness," Gar said with grave courtesy, "but until your royal husband comes, you shall keep to your apartments with all your ladies. Guards, escort them!" Still, it was he himself who stalked behind the princess, and one look at the determination in his eyes left her no doubt that he would pick her up and carry her bodily if he had to. She shuddered and turned away, lifting her chin and marching proudly to her chambers.

With her shut in and well guarded, and all the castle's servants and defenders locked in the dungeons,

Gianni finally asked, "How long before the prince learns his castle is taken?"

"He knows already." Gar nodded toward the highest tower. "Remember the stone egg? I'm sure the princess used it before she came down to rebuke us. In fact, let's go and listen."

Puzzled, Gianni followed Gar up to the high tower. Sure enough, they found the egg already talking to itself, the heavily accented Lurgan voice alternating with the prince's. "Leave at least a partial force to keep the Pirogians in," the Lurgan voice pleaded.

"Why?" snapped the prince in his cultured (but infuriated) tone. "They come and go as they please in their confounded caravels! Take Pirogia yourselves, if you need it! I and all my allies go to take back my ancestral city and house!"

Gianni cheered, and so did the marines who heard with him. The cheering ran down the stairs and through the garrison, but Gar only stood watching the stone with glowing eyes.

He was up in that room now and then for the next few days, as they waited for the prince and his men. The marine couriers moved more quickly on the converted galleys, and the army of Pirogia moved just as quickly in more of the same ships. They came marching through the gates of Tumanola a full day before the prince and his troops came in sight. They drew up their lines that night, and thousands of campfires blossomed outside the city walls. Gar walked the parapets, reassuring his men; Gianni took his message to the rest of the defenders. "Be warned. Tomorrow, huge metal fish may drop from the skies and fire lightning bolts. Don't be frightened, for a golden wheel will strike them out of the air."

He didn't believe a word of either promise himself, but he did ask Gar about it later. "Where could these metal fish come from, and how could they fly?"

"By magic," Gar said, with a brittle smile, and Gianni could only sigh for patience. "As to where, they shall come from the Lurgan Company—and the golden wheel will be Herkimer."

Gianni frowned. "You mean *from* this wizard Herkimer, don't you?"

"No," Gar said, and wouldn't explain it any further.

The barrage began at dawn, but most of the shot fell short—the prince's cannon were nowhere nearly as good as those of Pirogia, whose foundries had worked according to Gar's advice. Gar's gunners managed to shoot down their opponents methodically, one by one, and the prince, in exasperation, ordered his army to charge.

It was suicidal even at a hundred yards, for Gar's gunners had all the buckets in the city now, and all the nails. The prince's men died as they ran—but between cannon shots, the remnant came closer and closer. They faltered, though, as they realized they were being driven to certain death—and it was then that the metal fish came swooping from the skies.

"Away from the guns!" Gar shouted, and his gunners leaped back and kept running, just before lightning stabbed down from the bloated, gray metal fish shapes. Two guns disappeared in a gout of flame and a thunderclap. The Pirogian soldiers moaned with fear and scrambled to duck down behind crenels or shields—but on the plain below, the prince's army gave a shout of triumph and charged forward.

Then the huge golden wheel came plunging after the fish.

CHAPTER 15

Beams of light stabbed down from the golden ship, striking one end of each of the metal fish. They plummeted, spinning crazily. Only a hundred feet above the earth, flame roared from the bottom of each fish, slowing its plunge—but only slowing; one struck the earth outside the city walls and one inside. The prince's soldiers shouted with fear as they saw it coming and ran, any way as long as it was away from the bulbous, plunging gray shape. The fish struck, and was still.

Later, Gianni learned that the other fish had struck squarely in the courtyard of Castle Raginaldi, breaking its back and splitting its skin. Gar had barked commands, and a dozen marines came running to ring the object with spears—if they had any fear, they didn't show it. When four people in dark gray came staggering from its bowels, the marines clapped them into irons and hurried them into a tower room, where they mounted guard over the prisoners until their commander was ready to deal with them.

On the wall, Gianni wrenched his eyes away from the wrecked fish in the middle of the prince's army, recovering both himself and the initiative. "Fire!" he shouted, and his crossbowmen came to themselves with a start and loosed a flight of bolts at the enemy soldiers. Some went down, screaming; most ran, or hobbled with bolts in their flesh, away from the walls.

"Cannon, fire!" Gianni shouted, and three cannon fired buckets of nails. The cannoneers had aimed high, and the nails came down in a lethal rain. The prince's soldiers shouted in panic; demoralized by seeing a sky monster plunging at them afire, by bolts and raining nails, but most of all by the huge golden disk that still swelled above them with its promise of lightning bolts, they ran. This was no retreat, but a rout—and the troops Gar had hidden in the woods atop the ridge recognized their signal for action. They stormed downward, loosing arrows and bolts, catching the prince's men between two fires and shouting, "Surrender!"

Thoroughly demoralized, soldiers threw down their weapons and held up their hands, crying, "I yield me!"

It spread; in minutes, all the prince's men were surrendering, and Gar came up before Gianni, shouting, "Sally forth! Take surrenders, bind prisoners!" The gates opened, and the army of Pirogia charged out with a shout.

But across the valley, fifty picked men didn't stop to take prisoners—they bored on, and finally came to a knot of soldiers who still fought: men-at-arms and knights, the prince's bodyguard. The fifty Pirogians called for reinforcements, and other soldiers left off taking surrenders to help. In minutes, the knot of men had swelled to hundreds, and the fight was bloody, but brief.

"Keep the command, Gianni!" Gar shouted, and ran to take horse. He leaped astride and went galloping out the gate and across the valley.

Gianni wasn't about to be left behind at such a moment. "Vincenzio! Command!" he cried, then ran to mount up and ride after Gar.

He caught up just as Gar was dismounting and walking slowly toward the circle of spears that held the prince and a handful of noblemen at bay—immobilized, but sneering. Gar walked up to them, erect as a staff, hand on his sword. The circle of spears parted just enough for him to enter. "Surrender, my lords," he called. "You cannot escape."

"And dare you kill us?" the prince spat. "Be sure, lowborn churl, that if you do, every nobleman in Talipon—nay, in the whole of the world—will not rest until he has seen you flayed alive!"

"I dare," Gar told him, "because I am the son of a high lord and great-nephew of another."

Gianni's mouth dropped open. Never would he have dreamt of this!

The prince stared, taken aback. Then his brows

drew down, and he demanded, "What is your house and lineage?"

"I am a d'Armand of Maxima, of the cadet branch," Gar told him. "My home is far from here, very far indeed, Your Highness—perhaps even as far as the world of your Lurgan Company. But even they will not deny that Maxima exists, or that it is home to many noble families."

"I would deny that if I could." The prince's eyes smoldered. "But your bearing and your manner show it forth; blood will tell, and breeding is ever there to be seen, if it is not deliberately hidden." Then outrage blazed forth. "But you *did* deliberately hide it! Why in all the world would the son of a nobleman soil his hands with trade, or defend the baseborn tradesmen and merchants of Pirogia?"

Gar's manner softened, became almost sorrowful. "Because, Your Highness, my lords, all of life draws its sustenance from the ebb and flow of money and the goods and food it represents. You who draw your wealth from land alone are doomed to poverty and ignominy if you do not learn the ways of trade, for the merchants bring the wealth of a whole world to your doorstep—aye, and the wealth of many worlds, as your Lurgan accomplices have shown you. It is not to be gained by stealth or theft, but only by nourishing and caring for the ebb and flow I speak of. Trade is like the grain of your fields, that must be tended and cared for if you would see its harvest. This world has ripened into trade now, and will grow by trade and gain greater wealth for all by trade—unless that ripening is ended by burning the field before the harvest. If you blast Talipon back into serfdom, it will be centuries before Petrarch flowers again, and when it does, it will be the noblemen of another land who reap the wealth—wealth ten times your current fortunes, fifty times, a hundred. But if you nurture and encourage that growth, Talipon will lead the world of Petrarch, and if you come to understand the ways of trade, you shall lead Talipon, and reap the enormous first fruits." He smiled sadly. "Noblesse oblige, my lords, Your Highness—nobility imposes obligations, and your obligation in this new era is to learn the ways of trade, that you may guide its swelling and its flowering. Trade may be only the concern of the commoner now, but it must become the concern of every aristocrat, or you will fail in the calling of your birth."

He stood silent, looking directly into the prince's eyes, and the gaze of every one of the lesser noblemen was fixed upon him.

At last, the prince himself reversed his sword and held it out to the giant. "I yield me to a man of noble blood—but when the ransom is paid and my home restored to me, Signor d'Armand, you must explain this chivalry of trade to me, that I may determine for myself if it is as much the duty of the aristocracy as you say."

Gravely, Gar took the sword and bowed. Then he turned to the other noblemen and, one by one, collected their swords, too. They never even noticed when the great golden disk above them receded, and was gone.

* * *

Looking back on it, Gianni was amazed that they stayed in Tumanola only two weeks, and the time went very quickly—but it seemed far longer, for each day was packed with what seemed thirty hours' worth of events. The prince's army had to be disbanded and the soldiers seen to depart for their homes, then watched carefully to make sure they didn't try to rally. The city had to be searched for weapons, and anything that might be used to wage war brought to a central piazza, loaded onto wagons bound for the coast, and shipped home to Pirogia. The whole matter had to be explained to the prince's subjects, and the Pirogian army carefully policed to make sure the soldiers didn't take advantage of the prince's subjects—Gar was very insistent that there be no looting or pillaging, and especially no rape. It did make the matter difficult for Gianni when several of his troopers fell in love with local women—but he was able to ascertain in every case that not only had there been no rape, but also that the lovers hadn't even been able to be alone together. There were some cases where he was clearly able to determine that the women in question were prostitutes, but he punished his soldiers anyway, even though there were no charges of rape. When the sergeants came to him to demand if he expected them to behave like alabaster statues of saints, he simply answered, "Yes," then explained why they had to behave as examples to the prince's subjects.

There were also tedious meetings with the few merchants of Tumanola, as Gianni explained that their responsibilities and activities were about to undergo a vast and sudden change, then worked out the ways in which their relationship to the prince would be transformed.

All the while, Gar was closeted with the prince and his vassals. The guards at the door reported hearing voices raised frequently and angrily, though Gar's was never one of them. Ostensibly, they were working out the terms of the treaty, but Gar had to explain the need for those terms, of course, and when the guards told Gianni what they had been overhearing, he came to eavesdrop himself. Sure enough, the raised voices were protesting the simple facts of trade, and in a tone of iron patience Gar was explaining why those principles were something that no man could impose or cancel—that it was the nature of trade that was forcing them down the noblemen's throats, not the merchants of Pirogia.

They may have kept the door shut, but the weather was warm, so they left the windows open. Whenever Gianni could spare a moment, he loitered beneath, and heard Gar explaining how government could encourage trade or kill it, and how the noblemen could reap fortunes by regulating trade and taxing it mildly. He also told them how to kill trade, by overregulation and overtaxing. The noblemen argued ferociously, but Gar held firm—it wasn't merely his opinion, but that of centuries of scholars who studied such matters. Where had he come from, Gianni wondered, that merchants had been so active for a thousand years and more?

Finally, he overheard Gar giving the aristocrats inspirational talks about their role in the increasing prosperity of Talipon and, through its traders, of all the world. By the time he was done, Gianni was imbued with an almost religious fervor, a sense of mission, of his obligations as a merchant to improve the lot of all humankind everywhere. If he felt so inspired just from the scraps of talk he managed to find time to listen to, what must the noblemen be feeling?

Finally, with full ceremony, they signed the treaty in the prince's courtyard, where large numbers of citizens and soldiers could witness. Then the Lurgan merchants were brought forth, laden with chains, for their trial. The prince himself presided as judge; Gar presented the case against the Lurgans, and one of their number presented something of a defense. It was weak indeed, partly because he could scarcely be understood due to his accent, partly because he tried to justify the actions of his companions and himself by spouting streams of numbers. The prince ruled that he and his fellow merchants were to be held in the dungeon until the far traveling men Gar had summoned came to take them away. At that, the Lurgans turned pale and spouted incoherent pleas for mercy—all except one, who fixed Gar with a very cold glare and said, "We will remember this, d'Armand. Be sure." But Gar only nodded to him courteously, and watched as he was taken away.

There was no mention of the false Gypsies. Gianni wondered about that.

Finally, the Pirogian army marched out of Tumanola with the citizens cheering them—or their departure, it was hard to tell which—and the soldiers cheering their reluctant hosts—or being rid of the inland city with its humidity and mosquitoes, it was hard to tell which. Everyone seemed to take the cheering as protestations of friendship between the two cities, though. The prince was left with his castle and city again—but with no cannon or army other than his personal guard of a hundred men, and a night watch.

The Pirogians came home to a triumphant welcome from their fellow citizens. The returning army marched down the boulevard on flower petals, and came to the Piazza del Sol to find the Maestro and the Council drawn up to award medals to Gar, Gianni, and their captains. Then they were given time to rest and celebrate.

The next day, though, Gar and Gianni were summoned to the Council to meet the ambassadors from the other merchant cities, all of whom had survived the war, though some had suffered, and all of whom needed urgent guidance on what sort of relations to establish with their returning contes and doges. The deliberations turned into debate about the form and processes that would be involved in the new League of Merchant Cities. All that was really in debate was the specific terms and, as it turned out, ways of limiting Pirogia's power within the League—but all the cities were sure they wanted the League to continue.

There was no question but that Pirogia would lead.

All this time, Gianni slept without dreams, to his relief and disappointment—relief that he had not seen the Wizard again, disappointment that he had not seen his Dream Woman. He earnestly hoped that he was rid of the one and would rediscover the other.

Perhaps it was only that he was working too hard, and sleeping too soundly—or so he hoped.

Finally, the day came when the treaty was signed and the ambassadors took their leave, each with a copy of the Articles of Alliance to discuss with their Councils and ratify or modify. They left with great ceremony and protestations of eternal friendship.

Gianni wondered whether the good feeling would last past the next trading season. Somehow, though, he was sure the League would endure, no matter how intense the rivalries within it became. They were all too vividly aware of their common enemy: the aristocrats.

The next day, Gar thanked his hosts, the Braccaleses, for their hospitality, but explained that he must leave them. Mama and Papa protested loudly, but Gianni had somehow known this was coming. When the lamentation slackened, he said, "He's a wanderer, Papa. We can't expect him to tie his destiny to ours forever."

"But who will lead the army he has built?" Papa wailed.

"Gianni is more than capable of that little chore," Gar assured him. "He has become quite the general in these last few weeks, and has an excellent cadre of officers to help him."

Papa stared at Gianni in surprise; then Gianni saw the rapid calculations going on behind his father's eyes, of the gain in status for his family and the resulting increase in their influence within the city. Slowly, he nodded. "If you say it, Gar, I must accept it."

"Someday," Mama told Gar, "you'll find a woman who will make you cease your wandering, and wish nothing so much as to stay and care for her—aye, and the children she shall give you."

For a moment, there was pain in Gar's eyes—but only a moment; it was quickly masked with a wistful smile. "I dearly hope so, Donna Braccalese—but she isn't here."

Gianni nodded. "He must go."

Not without ceremony, though. That evening saw a hastily prepared but elaborate farewell banquet, in which the councillors pressed rich gifts on their rescuing general, hiding their relief at his leaving—and Gar surprised them all by presenting rich gifts in return, foremost among them a small library which, he said, contained everything he had taught the aristocrats about trade and regulation. Everyone wondered where he had obtained the books, but everyone was too polite to ask.

Then home—but before they went to bed, Gar presented some gifts to his hosts: rich jewelry for Mama, and for Papa, a little machine that calculated overhead, profit, and all manner of other business sums. They pressed a huge necklace of orzans and gold upon him, and everyone retired in wonderfully sentimental melancholy.

Gianni Braccalese!

Gianni sat bolt upright—at least, in his dream—and found himself staring into the eyes of the Wizard. *The giant goes, Gianni Braccalese. If you wish to see him off, you must rise at once!*

How like Gar not even to wait till the household was awake! Cursing, Gianni began to struggle toward wakefulness, but the Wizard said only, *You shall see me no more. Farewell!* And with that, he was gone, and Gianni waked in the act of sitting up and reaching for his clothing.

He was dressed and down to the main portal in minutes, just in time to see Gar softly lifting the bar and pushing the door open. "Wait!" Gianni cried. "If you must go without ceremony, at least let me go a little way with you!"

Gar looked back, smiling—but not surprised. "Well, then, if you must force yourself up at such an unreasonable hour, come along."

They went out into the chill darkness of very late night—or very early morning. Gianni glanced at the east but didn't even see a glow on the horizon. "How far are you going?"

"Into the hills," Gar answered.

Gianni wondered what he intended to do once he arrived. "Horses, then. Why walk?"

Gar nodded. "With you along to take them home, yes."

They went into the stable, saddled two horses, and rode out through the silent streets of the city—so silent that neither of them spoke. The sentries at the inner gate needed no convincing, not when it was Gianni Braccalese and General Gar who told them to open the portal—briefly. They rode out over the pontoon bridge that temporarily replaced the causeway. The sound of the water beating against the hulls beneath them broke the spell of silence. Gianni asked, "Why?"

Gar shrugged. "Why not?"

"Because you could have lost your life," Gianni answered. "Because you went through a great deal of suffering and misery that you didn't have to undergo. Because it wasn't your fight."

Gar said slowly, "Would you believe me if I said I needed the money?"

"With a wizard-friend who travels in a great golden wheel? Besides, if you needed money, you wouldn't be going. Why, Gar?"

The giant sighed. "A man must do something with his life, Gianni Braccalese. He must have some purpose, some reason for living—and for me, the mere pursuit of pleasure is nowhere nearly enough."

They rode in silence a few minutes more; then Gianni said, "But why us? Why make our problems yours?"

"Because you had need of it," Gar said. "Because I couldn't very well make things worse. Because my inborn sense of justice was outraged years ago, so I look for people unjustly treated, to satisfy my craving for revenge that should have been sated long before I met you."

That, at least, made sense. Gianni lapsed into silence again, and it lasted until they had passed the charred stumps of the land gate. Then curiosity drove him again. "Just how far away *do* you come from?"

Gar sighed and tilted his head back. "Look upward, Gianni Braccalese—look at the stars. Each of them is a sun, and most are far brighter than the one that shines on this world. Some of them even have worlds of their own, swinging about them as a sling whirls around the fist of a hunting peasant—and here and there, one of those worlds is warm enough and gentle enough for people to live on it."

Gianni stared upward, trying to grasp the enormity of the concept—then trying to grapple with its implications. "And you—you come from one of those worlds?"

"Yes. Very far away, and its sun is so small that you can't see it from here—but I was born on a planet named Gramarye, and my father was born on a tiny world named Maxima."

"The world in which you are a nobleman," Gianni whispered.

"No—the world in which my great-uncle is a conte. My father is a high lord on the world of Gramarye now, and I am his heir."

Gianni let that sink in for a while, then asked, "Why did you leave home?"

"Because being my father's son wasn't enough for me."

Well, Gianni could understand that. "How did you come here?"

"In Herkimer," Gar answered, "in the great golden wheel. It's really a ship the size of a village, Gianni. My great-uncle, the Count d'Armand, gave it to me. He didn't say it was a reward for leaving, but that's what it came to."

The intense loneliness of the man suddenly penetrated Gianni, and he shuddered. Trying to throw it off, he asked, "And the false Gypsies? Were they, too, from another star?"

Gar nodded. "They're members of a league that calls itself AEGIS—which stands for the Association for the Elevation of Governmental Institutions and Systems."

"Did they *really* believe persuading the lords to crush us merchants would bring peace and happiness, not a blood-bath?"

"Oh, yes," Gar said softly. "I don't doubt their good intentions for a minute. They're very intelligent, very idealistic, and very knowledgeable people, Gianni, who are also incredibly naive, and have a lack of judgment that borders on the phenomenal. Yes, I really do believe that they thought the lords' actions against the merchants would be only commercial competition."

"Incredibly naive indeed," Gianni said, numbed by the enormity of it.

Gar shrugged. "They're determined to believe only the best about humanity, no matter how much evidence they see to the contrary."

"But you didn't tell the prince about them," Gianni pointed out. "You didn't have them arrested and put on trial."

"No. They saw for themselves the folly of their ideas, and the war the noblemen's alliance caused— but they also saw that the merchants' league prevented the worst of it. They've learned humility, Gianni, and guilt alone will make them work for the good of every individual here, not just the princes. Besides," he added as an afterthought, "they're stuck with the results of what we've done here, you and I. They can't very well undo it without causing a war that even *they* can't help but see coming. No, I think you can trust them, in their way. They'll do Talipon a great deal of good, and very little harm now."

"But ... Medallia?" Gianni felt his heart wrench as he asked it. "Was she really one of them?"

"Yes, but she transcended her naivete and was able to believe the evidence of her eyes. She overcame the bias of her idealism and realized that the AEGIS plan wouldn't work here, so she left them to try to form a merchants' league, hoping your commercial leverage could forestall the war."

"But she would have failed, if you hadn't come meddling." Gianni looked up keenly. "How did you do it all, Gar? How did you win our war for us?"

"Herkimer gathered a great deal of information for me," Gar said. "I pretended to be an ignorant barbarian, asking questions so obvious that even an idiot would know the answers, until I had learned the rest of what I needed to know."

Gianni looked up sharply. "It was all a pretense, then—your being a half-wit?"

"We both pretended, at first," Gar reminded him. "But after that blow on the head, when we both waked naked and shivering in the rain? No. That was real—the effect of concussion—but when I came to my senses and realized how useful the pose could be, I pretended. It let me attack the Stilettos without being killed outright, and make them bring us all into the Castello Raginaldi."

"Where you knew what you would find."

Gar nodded. "Yes, but I had to prove it."

"But how did you persuade the other wanderers to do as you said?" Gianni burst out. "I have to command men now, so I need to know! How did you keep the guards from seeing us? How did you convince the porter to lower the drawbridge? No one could have believed Feste's posturings!"

"Ah." Gar rode in silence for a minute, then said, "I don't mean to sound conceited, Gianni, but it's nothing you can do."

"Why not?"

"Because of my father's rank," Gar said quietly. "Because of the gifts I inherited from him."

"*What* gifts? What rank?"

Gar still hesitated.

"You're leaving now, Gar," Gianni pressed. "There's no reason for me to tell your secret—and no harm if I do! What can your father's rank have to do with it?"

"Because," Gar said, "he's the Lord High Warlock of Gramarye."

"Warlock?" Gianni stared a moment, not understanding. Then the implication hit him. "The Wizard! He never haunted my dreams till I met you! Now you're leaving, and he told me only an hour ago that I would never see him again!"

Gar nodded slowly.

"Then it was you who put the Wizard in my mind!"

"More than that," Gar said softly. "I *am* the Wizard."

CHAPTER 16

Gianni stared. Then skepticism rose, and he smiled, amused. "Very good, Gar. You almost had me believing it."

"I assure you, it's true," Gar said, unperturbed.

"Oh, come now!" Gianni scoffed. "If you really are the Wizard, put your thoughts in my mind right now." He closed his eyes. "Go ahead—put a picture into the darkness behind my eyelids!"

"As you wish," said Gar, and suddenly the Wizard was there in Gianni's mind, saying, Now *do you believe me*?

Gianni stiffened, eyes flying open, and the Wizard disappeared. He stared at Gar incredulously, but the big man only nodded gravely, and he wasn't smiling now.

Realizations exploded in Gianni's mind like the

chain of explosions as the causeway blew up. "But if you could put that picture of the Wizard in my mind—then you can *read* minds! *That's* how you knew when the Stilettos were coming! That's why the soldiers didn't see us when they were searching for us! Why the Gypsies fell asleep, why the sentries in the castle slept!" He paused to draw breath. "Was that why we had no more trouble traveling between Castello Raginaldi and Pirogia, too?"

Gar nodded gravely.

"But—dear Lord, the power that gives you!" Gianni turned ashen, remembering his secret thoughts.

Gar frowned. "I don't read other people's minds without a very good reason, Gianni. I do have some standards of right and wrong. But when the other side has an overwhelming advantage, well . . . that's when I don't feel any hesitation about using my own."

"So that's what you meant when you said the time for fair play was over!"

"Oh, yes indeed," Gar said softly.

"And how you lit the fire!"

Gar looked at him in surprise. "I don't remember doing that."

"That's right, you were really an idiot then, recovering from the blow on the head." Gianni frowned. "But I saw the Wizard that night."

"Did you really?" Gar stared. "I remember planning that, before the fight. My mind must have done it straight from memory!"

"But the locks? You didn't really tear them open by brute force, did you?"

"No, I didn't." Gar closed his eyes. "They were simple locks, Gianni. I could have opened them with even a simple mind."

A horrible thought struck. "How did the Gypsies learn about your plan for a league of merchants? And how did they come to blame it on my father?"

"Not from me," Gar assured him. "They had a spy inside Pirogia—I'm fairly sure they had such a spy in each of the merchant cities, and some of the inland ones. No, I didn't put the ideas in their minds."

"And your gifts to my parents?"

"I'm not *that* much of a wizard! No, Herkimer printed out those books—magically, unless you want to spend a year learning the explanation—and dropped them gently in your father's yard in the middle of the night."

"How do you drop something gently? No, don't tell me, I know! 'Magic'!"

"No, science," Gar replied.

"Magic by any other name!" Gianni said with disgust. "And that's how you knew what the lords were thinking, wasn't it? That's why you only needed to *prove* to us that they were dealing with the Lurgan Company!"

Gar nodded. "That's why I had to have us all caught and taken to Castello Raginaldi. Yes."

"But—when the cannonballs sped true, when the spear thrusts turned aside! Was that your doing, too?"

"Very good, Signor Braccalese." The note in Gar's voice went beyond approval. "Yes. I can move things with my mind, too."

"But—the other presence in my mind!" The dreadfulness of the thought hit Gianni, and he turned beet-red. "The Dream Dancer, the woman! Did you . . . ?" He broke off, unable to finish the thought.

"No." Gar turned to him, amused. "I found only echoes of her in your mind—but that was enough to tell me I wasn't the only mind reader on this planet."

"Not the only . . . ?" Gianni stared, astounded. "How many of you *are* there, then?"

"Only one other," Gar said, "and she's one of the very rare ones who crop up naturally, when neither parent could read minds before. She thinks she's the only one there is, for I've been careful not to let her know I know. That's why she understood so much more about your people than the rest of her band— and that's why she left them, to encourage you and your fellow citizens in fighting the lords."

"Her?" Fortunately, Gianni was already staring; he only had to keep on. "No! It couldn't . . . not her . . ."

"Why do you think you're in love with two women at the same time?" Gar asked. Then, before Gianni could answer, while he was still letting the idea sink in, Gar said, "You are rare among your kind too, Gianni. You're a bit of a mind reader yourself. I could have put the Wizard into anyone's mind, but very few could have seen him so clearly as you—and very few could have spoken with him as you did."

"Me? Rare?" Then the next realization hit. "But if you could put the Wizard in my mind more clearly— then Medallia . . ."

"Yes." Gar nodded. "Perhaps that's the real reason she's interested in you, Gianni Braccalese—interested in you as a man, not just as a pawn in her game."

"Interested in me? You don't mean . . . she couldn't be in *love* . . ."

"Oh, yes, she could," Gar countered. "I don't listen to such things in people's minds, Gianni, but when a man or woman is really in love, it shouts so loudly that I can't help but hear. Go to her—now, before she leaves the city."

"I will! Thank you, Gar! Oh, thank you!" Gianni reached out to clasp the big man in a hug, almost tipping them both from their saddles, then turned back toward Pirogia, kicking his horse into a gallop.

Gar watched him go, a sad smile playing over his lips. Suddenly Gianni reined in, turned about, and waved. Gar let his smile broaden, waving back, then watched as Gianni turned and dashed madly for the land gate. When he had ridden across the causeway and disappeared into the city, Gar turned away, rode up to the top of the hill, then dismounted and turned the horse loose, speeding it on its way home with a slap on the rump. That done, he lifted the medallion to his lips and said, "Now, Herkimer." He let the medallion fall and stood, watching the sky as the first rays of sunlight pierced the false dawn, lighting the great golden ship as it fell out of the sky.

Gianni rode hell-bent for leather through the streets that were just coming awake with laborers on their way to work. He drew rein in the Piazza del Sol, and sure enough, the caravan was there, even though she had hidden it someplace else last night. He left his poor lathered horse to cool by itself as he ran to the caravan and up the steps to hammer on the door.

"Medallia! Open! You must not go! Open your door, please!"

The door opened and Medallia stood there, huge-eyed and staring in wonder. Even as Gar had warned, she was dressed for traveling. "Gianni Braccalese! What emergency can bring you in such a panic?"

"Knowing that you are my Dream Woman," Gianni breathed.

She turned ashen. "Who told you such a thing?"

"The Wizard in my mind," Gianni answered.

Medallia went from ashen to magenta. "That confounded playboy!" she stormed. "How dare he . . ." But she broke off, and her staring eyes widened even more.

It was true, Gianni realized—his love for her must have been fairly shouting from his mind, for she stood trembling as he stepped into the caravan, took her in his arms, and kissed her. She was stiff with surprise—then began to melt. Gianni broke the kiss just long enough to close the caravan door and make sure the latch had fallen, then to whisper, "Mystery Lady, I love you." Then he kissed her again, closing his eyes to see the Dancer of his Dreams, her face finally clear and lighted by the radiance of love. It was Medallia's face, and her kiss deepened with each touch and caress, with a splendor that far outshone his dream.

On his hilltop, Gar watched the great golden ship descend. The gangway came down, and Gar climbed up.

"So your trip is successfully concluded, Magnus," said the mellow voice of the ship.

"Yes, but it was a close thing for a while." Gar stripped off his medieval clothing and stepped into a sonic shower. "Lift off, Herkimer. Did you call the Dominion Police?"

"Yes, Magnus, and transmitted all my surveillance recordings to them. They were delighted and sounded quite eager, mentioning something about 'getting the goods' on the Lurgan Company at last."

"That's good to hear." Magnus closed his eyes, savoring the feeling of glowing skin as most of the dirt flaked away. "The people of Petrarch should have a clean start now. I wish them luck."

Herkimer said, "I dectect overtones of sadness in your voice, Magnus. What is the cause?"

"Only that I can't stay and enjoy the happiness that is about to be theirs," Magnus said, "my friend Gianni, I mean, and his Mystery Woman, Medallia." He followed the sonic shower with a thirty-second spray of soapy water, then more sonic scrubbing, and another thirty-second spray of clear water.

As the drier started caressing Gar's body with warm air, Herkimer said, "If you cannot remain, how can Medallia? She is from off-planet too, is she not?"

"Yes," Magnus said, "but she has a good reason— she's going to marry a native." He smiled sardonically. "Medallia will never forgive me for telling Gianni what she is, even though it was her own overmodulation that let the dream leak into my mind, and no mental eavesdropping of my own." He stepped out of the shower and slipped into a modern robe of sybaritically soft and fluffy fabric.

"But the mental suggestions with which you held the vagabonds' loyalty and obedience *were* your doing," Herkimer pointed out.

"Yes, and so was the fervor and courage with which I imbued my troops—not completely by the power of my rhetoric alone," Magnus confessed. He took a tall cold drink from the dispenser and sat down in an overstuffed chair for the first time in months.

"You *could* stay if you wanted, Magnus."

But Magnus shook his head. "Not without a reason such as Medallia has found, Herkimer. I have not yet discovered my home."

"Where shall we look next, then?" the computer asked.

"Show me your list of forgotten colonies with oppressive governments," Magnus said.

The list appeared on the wall screen. Magnus sat back as he looked it over, considering which world should be his next chance to find love and a home—or sudden, blessed death.

THE BEST OF SF FROM TOR

THE BEST OF SF FROM TOR

☐ 53022-5 *THE STARS ARE ALSO FIRE* $5.99
Poul Anderson $6.99 Canada

☐ 51024-0 *FIREDANCE* $5.99
Steven Barnes $6.99 Canada

☐ 53078-0 *ASH OCK* $5.99
Christopher Hinz $6.99 Canada

☐ 53420-4 *CALDÉ OF THE LONG SUN* $6.99
Gene Wolfe $7.99 Canada

☐ 54822-1 *OF TANGIBLE GHOSTS* $5.99
L.E. Modesitt, Jr. $6.99 Canada

☐ 53016-0 *THE SHATTERED SPHERE* $5.99
Roger MacBride Allen $6.99 Canada

☐ 51704-0 *THE PRICE OF THE STARS* $4.50
Debra Doyle/James D. Macdonald $5.50 Canada
